PANZERS

Push for Victory
Book I

Tom Zola

BATTLE OF KURSK

Published by EK-2 Publishing GmbH
Friedensstraße 12
47228 Duisburg
Germany
Registry court: Duisburg, Germany
Registry court ID: HRB 30321
Chief Executive Officer: Felix Julius Raasch

E-Mail: info@ek2-publishing.com
Website: www.ek2-publishing.com

Cover art: Pete Ashford
Author: Tom Zola
Translated from German by Johanna Ellsworth, M.A.
English translation edited by Mary Jo Rabe
Final editing: Jill Marc Münstermann
Proofreading: Felix Julius Raasch, Peter Brendt
Cover Design: Jan Niklas Meier
German Editor: Lanz Martell
Innerbook: Jan Niklas Meier

Paperback ISBN: 978-3-96403-025-2
Kindle ISBN: 978-3-96403-026-9
1st Edition, October 2018

Tom Zola, a former sergeant in the German Army, is a military fiction writer, famous for his intense battle descriptions and realistic action scenes. In 2014 the first book of his PANZERS series was released in German language, setting up an alternate history scenario in which a different German Reich tries to turn around the fortunes of war at the pinnacle of the Second World War. Zola doesn't beat around the bush; his stories involve brutal fighting, inhuman ideologies and a military machine that overruns Europe and the whole world without mercy. He has developed a breathtaking yet shocking alternate timeline that has finally been translated into English.

Zola, born in 1988, is married and lives with his wife and two kids in Duisburg, Germany.

Prolog

Autumn ruled Europe with all its might, and cool breezes swept across Lower Austria when a sturdy man with a receding hairline stepped up to the front door of a noble estate. The night had the new section of Vienna in its grip. The man, wearing a dark coat, lifted his right hand to knock on the door but then he froze. Jumpy, he glanced around but the streets were empty.

The man's left hand tightened its grip around the handles of his tote bag, and finally he knocked on the door – quietly as if he was afraid that someone outside the house might hear him. He heard steps inside the house moving towards the door.

Seconds turned into eternities. Again the man glanced all around; far away, a dog was barking. Instinctively he pulled his coat shut as if it could protect him from assailants or even just unwanted confidants. No doubt about it, Erhard Milch had put himself in mortal danger.

Finally the door opened and a man in his early fifties with angular features stuck out his head. He scrutinized the visitor briefly, blinked and let him inside.

"Moin*, Erwin," Milch whispered in his typical Northern German dialect, reaching out to shake his host's hand. The latter clicked his heels, and only after having saluted raggedly did he shake Milch's hand. Then Field Marshal Erwin Rommel's face, which usually was so serious, actually broke into a smile.

---

* For information about the meaning of German words, a map of the salient of Kursk, Wehrmacht ranks, and more check out the appendix

He quickly ushered his visitor into the living room where yet another man was already waiting for them. Rommel introduced him as Erwin von Witzleben, a fellow field marshal. They shook hands; then the three of them sat down at the dining table, a massive piece of wood with elaborately carved legs.

Von Witzleben, whose thinning hair was barely able to cover his scalp, went right medias res. "Show us what you've got."

With a nod Milch opened his tote bag and took out a large envelope that was stuffed so full it looked as if it was about to burst. He put it down on the table top and pushed it towards Rommel and von Witzleben. The latter opened the envelope and took out a thick stack of documents and photos. Rommel immediately picked up the document on top titled "Lager Dachau". At the same time von Witzleben examined the photos and his eyes grew bigger.

"The Luftwaffe uses the camp for test purposes but since the SS has also been there, horrible things have started to happen in the camp," Milch commented, though the photos more than spoke for themselves. The pictures bitterly confirmed the awful premonitions of several German officers: The Nazis had started to murder whole groups of the population.

"The GröFaz and his gang have finally gone too far. This ... this has nothing to do with war anymore," von Witzleben whispered in a trembling voice. Rommel, who would never say anything negative about his supervisors – not even about him – nodded, his lips pressed together, which for him was a telling gesture. The three men stared at each other. In that moment they were united by one and the same idea.

Berlin, German Reich, November 4th, 1942

It was already after three a.m.; yet in the window of a small apartment in Berlin-Lichterfelde a light was still burning. The last time the city was bombed had been nearly a year ago, and therefore the residents had started to become less cautious again.

The lit-up room inside the apartment was a spartan furnished bedroom with a narrow bed pushed against one wall – this home had lacked a woman's touch for much too long.

An old man in his pajamas sat on the edge of the bed; his forehead was covered with drops of sweat, and he was rubbing his eyes. The retired lieutenant colonel Ludwig Beck was a thin man with a wrinkled face, whose last third of his life was visibly wearing him out. But his physical ailments were not the only thing that kept him from resting. The thoughts spinning around in his head refused to let him fall back asleep. Of course there was also this nebulous fear in him because what he had been doing for years was a dangerous game.

Finally Beck got up to get a towel from the bathroom so he could dry his sweaty armpits. The cool breeze that flowed in from outside made him shiver.

He walked past his bedroom window and took in the empty street and the townhouses across the street with one quick glance. Of course Beck also noticed the black Mercedes with the spare tire above the right fender.

This car had become his around-the-clock companion, and sometimes he wondered if his shadows from the Gestapo still thought they were acting under cover or if it was perhaps part of their perfidious method of intimidation to constantly present themselves openly and brazenly.

Beck returned to his bedroom with his sweat-soaked towel. The dark rings around his eyes gave his face a sagging appearance. His back stooped – he was suffering from arthritis – he stopped at his bedroom window and peered out at the street and the row houses that had been built between 1871 and 1918. Suddenly Beck froze. He blinked; his heart started to hammer into his throat, threatening to strangle him. He swallowed hard and tugged at his Adam's apple while fresh beads of sweat appeared on his brow. The scenario he glimpsed in the street confirmed that his mixed activities would definitely come to an end now: The interior of the Mercedes was empty, but now two dark figures were marching straight up the street towards Beck's house.

Look at those black leather coats and hats, the old colonel general thought, sniffling audibly. *They call it plain clothes. But nobody runs around dressed like that.*

Beck quickly put his fear and terror behind him and had his body functions under control again. He was still able to breathe and could still stand up – that's all he needed in this situation. He straightened his suffering lower back and felt that it had had to carry his body for much too long. Then he wandered over to the closet and pulled a shirt and a pair of pants out of his neat stacks of clothes. The least he could do was to face his judge in dignified clothes – and he wanted to face whatever was coming with his head held high and his back straight. Beck knew death was awaiting him – self-determined if he was lucky – but he was willing to pay the price to

9

preserve his principles. He had done this in full knowledge of the consequences. He would not bend or break his principles just to please this pack of criminals the way so many of his comrades had done. While dressing, he was overcome by a rage that agitated his humanistic heart. Oh yes, he was ready! The doorbell rang. A few moments later Beck opened the front door and looked at the rather glum faces of two Gestapo men; one of them was still young, while the other one was in his late forties. The old colonel general had not expected such a sight. Both men lowered their eyes, and it seemed as if their world view was shaken.

So where had the arrogance of these people gone?

"Herr General, we have to ask you to come with us," the older man said in a low voice without looking Beck in the eye. The colonel general nodded soberly and followed them out of his apartment.

*

Ludwig Beck entered through a heavy wooden door and found himself again inside the office of Colonel General Friedrich Fromm, commander of the Reserve Army and Head of Armament and War Production. Fromm's office reflected his exuberant lifestyle unworthy of a German officer. Oil paintings as tall as a man – still-lives depicting open landscapes – hung on the walls, and red curtains covered the windows while the floor was decorated with a large Persian rug. The walls themselves were paneled with blonde wood, pleasantly reflecting the light shimmering through the shades of small lamps that stood on chests and dressers in all four corners. But Beck was not alone – a dozen high-ranking officers were standing in the room, and now that Beck was finally here, their eyes were fixed exclusively on him. The old colonel general froze for a moment and looked into the eyes of his old comrades in their medal-covered uniforms whose faces mirrored the tension that filled the room. Beck knew most of them, at least fleetingly, and it surprised him to even discover some individuals among the officers who had for all intents and purposes been removed from service. Among them were von Brauchitsch and von Blomberg as well as von Witzleben, Canaris, Milch, Rommel, von Bock, von Leeb. It was as if all of the fronts were silent tonight so that the field marshals of the Reich could meet for a class reunion. If even Rommel was here despite the current situation in Africa, then something really big had to be wrong.

After a few seconds of reverent silence, von Witzleben stepped out of the group and approached Beck. He stood at attention, raised to attention and saluted respectfully. Beck seconded his salute; then they quickly shook hands.

"We're glad you're here," von Witzleben started without a hint of irony in his voice.

Beck again mustered the grave faces of the other officers and noticed that they agreed.

"What happened?" He wanted to know right away what was going on – and von Witzleben came straight to the point. "Yesterday morning the Führer's plane crashed somewhere over Hungary."

Beck's eyes moved from one tense face to another. Pressing his lips together, a fleeting – very fleeting – smile trembled across his face.

"Gentlemen, I must admit I really didn't think you would muster the courage in the end to finish the matter off. I am impressed." Beck nodded. Though he had not been let in on their secret, that didn't matter now. Suddenly he could see better times for Germany in the future.

"No," von Witzleben's voice put a sudden stop to Beck's contemplations. "You don't understand. The Führer had an accident."

Beck's confusion did not go unnoticed by the others. "As you know, the officer corps started to work out a plan for a coup," Milch interjected. "But that takes time. However, we didn't expect to take control before the middle of next year."

Beck's eyes widened in surprise. "That means ..." he started without having to finish the sentence.

"Correct," von Witzleben nodded. The field marshal began to wring his hands. "It really was an accident. And now we're here – confronted with a *fait accompli* without being in control of the situation. There are no plans concerning his successor. The whole country – everything is aligned so much towards the person of the Führer that we have to tread very carefully now."

An important thought suddenly crossed Beck's mind. "What about the others?" he asked sharply.

Now Fromm weighed in on the conversation as the huge officer took a step forward. "Don't worry; they've been taken out. The 'Reichsheini' figured he could exploit the situation and seize power here in Berlin. My men put an end to his pitiful attempted coup last night and detained him. And the fat pig ... well, he's now collecting his jail medal here in Berlin." Some of those present grinned briefly. "Clubfoot is under house arrest in his apartment."

Beck drew a grimace. *At least that's a start*, he thought and then said, "But that's not the whole gang yet."

"That's what we need you for, Herr General." An almost beseeching undertone was audible in von Witzleben's voice. Beck noticed that Rommel gave a slow nod. Von Witzleben continued, "If we don't act fast, chaos will break out throughout the country. All of the opportunists will come crawling out of the woodwork to get their piece of the pie, and that's why we have to form a stable government today. Otherwise we can forget it."

Beck nodded and recognized where they were heading toward.

"But a stable government can only succeed if we present the public with a personality who is widely popular. And that's where you come in."

Beck and von Witzleben looked each other in the eye.

"General, we need you! And that's why we want to offer you the position of president of the new government of the Reich."

Beck's heart pounded wildly in his chest. In just one moment everything had changed – suddenly there was hope again.

"Gentlemen," he replied. "I'm at your service." As soon as these words were spoken, part of the tension in the room evaporated noticeably. Beck took off his coat and hung it up on the coat rack by the door because he wanted to get started immediately.

"There are two things that have priority over everything else," he began, straightening his back as if to intimidate the other officers. "First of all we initiate cease-fire negotiations with all of our enemies immediately. Second..."

The officers looked at each other until Rommel interrupted the increasingly enthusiastic Beck. "Herr General, at this point I must step in. We want you as the president of our Reich, not as the chancellor. Field Marshal von Witzleben will manage the future of our nation as chancellor. We want you to personally ensure the necessary political stability and cover the new government's back. Nothing more, nothing less than that."

All of a sudden Beck was isolated again. He faced a front of warmongers but then Rommel explained the intentions of the officer corps to him: "You see, Herr General, the situation certainly isn't easy but we have to put the straight facts on the table." Now Rommel stepped up to Beck, looking right at him. The old officer's straight posture and his sharply angular features made him appear incredibly commanding – even for the older Beck who was very experienced with people. Rommel was one of a kind, a man whose charisma you could only escape with difficulty.

"Look at who our enemies are," Rommel's Swabian dialect echoed from the walls. "With Stalin in the East and Churchill in the West, we can't expect anything from peace negotiations. On the day the English declared war, Churchill himself said that his goal was to wipe out Germany. That's what he continues to say.

And we can forget about Stalin. So please don't close your eyes to reality."

"In addition there is the Great War," Field Marshal Fedor von Bock interjected from the second row. Beck's eyes narrowed while he continued to focus on Rommel.

"Von Bock is right. In the eyes of the world we're the ones who started the Great War ... and now ..." Rommel paused for a moment, staring at Beck with a stern look. "...And now *that* ..." He didn't finish, yet everyone knew what he was trying to say.

"So you want to keep fighting?" Beck summed it up, crossing his arms. "You want to finish what *he* started – or how am I supposed to understand this?"

"No!" Rommel said decisively. "A fortunate end to the war hangs in the balance in the next weeks, and our opponents are getting stronger every day. Let's act now and continue the war so as to at least achieve a military stalemate. Then we'll be in a good starting position for peace negotiations. Right now the Allies won't accept anything other than our unconditional surrender."

"But then millions of Germans will die," Beck objected.

"That's correct. But our *Vaterland* will survive. We'll be saving our people from being torn apart by the Allies and turned into farmers who will be forced to slave away for the welfare of the English or Russians."

Damn, Beck thought, *old chap Rommel has really managed to make me think long and hard about this. Can you believe that?* Beck started to contemplate the issue. After seconds that dragged on like hours he nodded very slowly. "All right ... but only under the following conditions..."

"Go on, Herr General." Von Witzleben wrung his hands even more vigorously.

"First, take away all power from that Bohemian Private's entire gang – even those in the officer corps. Second, dissolve the Waffen SS, the SA and other Nazi-organizations immediately because the monopoly on arms has to return to the Wehrmacht. Third..."

"There is no need to worry," Rommel interrupted him. "No need to worry. That point's at the top of our agenda. The associations of the SS will be dissolved and their soldiers will be scattered throughout the whole Wehrmacht, with the goal of completely destroying these structures. As you determined so correctly, the Wehrmacht, as the rightful military institution of the Reich, must have the monopoly of arms."

"Third, war crimes. Any government, I am to be part of can not tolerate any longer war crimes. Not in Russia and not in these ominous camps. Anyone who is guilty of these matters will be ... must be ... excluded from the circle of German soldiers. Any government I am to be part of has to commit itself to humanism."

"You don't have to worry about that. The SS will finally be dissolved; the soldiers from the camp divisions won't even be integrated. And the Wehrmacht has stayed clean anyway," Canaris, Head of Abwehr – the German Military Intelligence Service –, chimed in. Beck's eyes narrowed and fixated on Canaris like a predator about to jump. "We can talk about anything," he countered sharply, "but don't think for a minute you can play me for a fool. This war is a dirty war, and none of the sides have covered themselves with glory – including ours."

Some of the officers nodded; others appeared to be of a different opinion. But that wasn't important right now. The only thing that mattered was that the foundation of a new military government was laid during this conversation.

Beck clapped his hands dramatically. "That's it, gentlemen." He looked his old – new – comrades in the eyes.

Rommel nodded, satisfied.

"I sincerely hope, though, that none of you is insane enough to want to hold elections soon?" Beck's eyes traveled from face to face, and now everyone was grinning.

*

One hour later the high-ranking officers had departed again. The majority of them wanted to get some sleep so they could arrange for all the necessary steps to be taken early the next morning. Von Witzleben and Canaris, who had been holding on to a file the whole time, were the only ones who lingered in the wood-paneled corridor for a few moments.

"Please, Sir," the Head of the Secret Service said, "even though it's late. This can't wait. It's bad enough that Fellgiebel didn't want to pass it on to the Führer last summer."

The new chancellor of the German Reich, Erwin von Witzleben, took the file from him and read the title: "Report on the Roundup of the Network of Soviet Secret Service Agents in Warsaw."

My dearest Elly,

I've finally found the time to write to you again and I want to tell you right away that I miss you with all my heart. I bet you're already going crazy with worrying because lately there has been a lot of movement here on the Eastern Front, but please let me tell you that you don't need to worry about me at all.

Ever since Stalingrad I've been convinced that our army is accompanied by a whole division of guardian angels. When I think about what would've happened to our 6th Army if Paulus and von Manstein hadn't gotten us out of the city in the last minute! Since then I've been praying to God every night. Don't laugh at me, please! Fortunately we're currently back in the rear, doing nothing but training and relaxing. But I don't want to burden you with all kinds of military matters; I just want to let you know that some things have improved here since last winter! Paulus is a capable man and probably won't throw us away. But now let me proceed to the most important things: How's our little one doing? Is she listening to her mommy like a good girl? Can you already sleep through the night or is the little brat still crying and complaining every hour? It's already been another four months since we've last seen each other, and my next leave won't be any time in the near future. I guess I'll have to enjoy the summer in Russia until then. The thought that I'm missing out on half of Gudrun's life is painful, but when all this is over, we'll make up for lost time! Please give my love to my mother and my old man. He needs to stop stuffing himself with all that cake! Also

*give my regards to your parents and your sister. I'm thinking
of all of you. All the time. Every day.*
Your Sepp.

On the outskirts of Mezhove, Soviet Union,
April 13th, 1943

After the near-catastrophe in and around Stalingrad and
the following violent battles between Stalin's city and
the Azov Sea in the winter, Tank Regiment 2 had suffered severe casualties. The Russians had swarmed the
lines of Army Groups A and B with an unbelievable
amount of soldiers and equipment and in the end
pushed the front back to Maykop and Rostov, where the
offensive by the enemy finally ended, granting the ema-
ciated German military a break from the action. The 16th
Panzer Division was reduced to 45 percent of its required numbers and therefore had to be taken out of the
combat zone urgently, something which finally had
taken place four weeks before. Panzer Regiment 2
hadn't suffered quite as many casualties – yet the R&R
in the rear was desperately needed. There, off the front,
the regiment was resupplied with men and vehicles.

Leaning against a stern of a beech, Lieutenant Josef
Engelmann sat on the ground in the shade of a cluster of
trees that broke through the open fields of his unit's operational area. In Engelmann's opinion the area was anything but optimal: too much open space, too little vegetation to protect the equipment from prying eyes in the
air, but the commander's protest, sent to the high command leaders, had been in vain.

Wild sunflowers with distinctly smaller and more ruffled petals than the sunflowers the lieutenant knew from the fields at home raised their heads everywhere in the lowlands of the Ukraine while the grass in the meadows presented itself in a rich green. Spring had arrived, accompanied by an unforgiving sun that grilled the weeds and pastures of the country mercilessly. Everything was quiet; you could only hear a man's laughter echo loudly across the fields once in a while. That was Staff Sergeant Kreisel; everybody in the regiment knew him and could identify him by his distinct laughter.

Engelmann, definitely happy with his letter, tucked a pen and some paper into his chest pocket and decided to mail it off today. The tall, slim officer rolled up the left sleeve of his black field jacket, and a Swiss watch became visible on his sweaty arm.

11:38 am German time, he noted, nodding with satisfaction. Now he unbuttoned his other chest pocket and pulled out a red tin can. Taking off the lid, he took out a triangular piece of chocolate and pushed it between his teeth.

Whether it's twenty-five degrees Celsius or not – I have to have my Scho-Ka-Kola, he thought while chewing and stood up. Fine pearls of sweat had formed under his brown hair, which was curly, thick and unruly – so unruly that no pomade of this world could tame it. For that reason Engelmann tried to keep it as short as possible, because as a German officer he simply couldn't look like *Struwwelpeter*.

The lieutenant strolled along the grove of trees and stepped into the open field, where he was greeted by the sun. The black uniforms of the Panzer troop were anything but a blessing in this kind of weather but Engelmann nevertheless had to walk over three hundred yards south through the open plain because that was where the tanks of the 1st Platoon of the 9th Company were located,– the tanks of his platoon. The sun was beating down mercilessly, so Engelmann walked faster.

Sweat was pouring down his body in rivulets and even penetrated the outer parts of his uniform. At least his field cap offered some protection from the sun. It was not until now that the lieutenant realized the luxury problems he was privileged to face here in Ukraine. Just two months ago he had had to fight for his life, was hit by shrapnel, had frozen fingertips and at times an ear blast injury from the noises of war.

And now? Now I'm a little too warm and there are days when I'm bored to tears. What a life! Engelmann certainly didn't want to go back to the front and was happy for each day he was able to enjoy in the rear echelon.

Rear echelon. He savored the words and felt uneasy as he remembered that the good times would soon be over again. The German Army had been trying for a while to eliminate the expression "rear echelon" in order to strengthen the team spirit in the troops but general army slang worked slowly and sometimes not in the desired direction.

Engelmann shook off these thoughts and tried to enjoy the peace of the moment instead. Here in Mezhove the soldiers of the Panzer Regiment 2 even had the option of driving to Stalino to visit the opera house or a movie theater. It was almost like peacetime here even though

Engelmann still wore a loaded pistol, his "pocket flak", on his belt.

After the lieutenant had crossed half the field, he could clearly see his men, who were busy with his platoon's five Panzer IV Ausführung F2, in a small wooded patch. Recently fifty-eight recruits who were supposed to get their special training as quickly as possible had been assigned to the regiment.

As of last week, Engelmann's 1st Platoon was assigned the task of having the newbies familiarize themselves with the Panzer IV, with a focus on maintenance, technical service and tactical conduct – at least in instruction the boys had already learned how to move the vehicle and how to conduct themselves inside it – in theory, anyway. This morning until lunch as well as in the afternoon, camouflage was on the schedule, and the lieutenant liked what he could see from over a hundred yards' distance. But now he wanted to take a closer look at the course of training even though he could fully trust his radio operator and the staff sergeant, Oberfeldwebel Nitz, in such matters.

The lieutenant had finally reached his platoon. Here, at the edge of the small wooded area, the five tanks were parked so deep into the woods that the tree tops provided sufficient protection from the eyes of enemy aircraft pilots though you didn't really have to worry about them almost one hundred and twenty miles behind the front line. Nitz and some of the other men from Engelmann's platoon were supervising the recruits, who crawled all over the tanks like black ants in order to camouflage them with branches and leaves. Other recruits brought huge armfuls of twigs and branches from the trees nearby which they then cut down to size with crosscut saws and pocket knives. When camouflaging an object, the most important thing was to blur the contours, and Engelmann was very satisfied with what he saw.

The Panzer IV in the F variant looked a bit like angular, three-tier pyramids with a rectangular base: A rectangular, smaller cabinet rose out of the wide tank, and the muzzle of a MG 34 protruded from the right side of the front of that cabinet. A basically rectangular turret sat on top, equipped with a 7.5-centimeters or 2.95 inches canon that – in the F2 variant – extended past the tank. All in all, the Panzer IV with its impressive angular design stood out due to its sharp contours that you wouldn't find in nature. For that reason it was so important to focus on the contours when camouflaging the tank so as to turn it into as much of a green lump as possible – a lump that could be mistaken for a row of bushes by distant onlookers.

Of course Staff Sergeant Nitz, a good man, knew that you don't salute in the field; therefore when he saw Lieutenant Engelmann, he only walked over to him to inform him about the status of the training.

"Sir, the training's going as well as we discussed," the staff sergeant reported, tugging on his thin mustache. Nitz was several years older than Engelmann and conducted himself like a strictly correct soldier, always and everywhere. Behind his back, his subordinates often called him "Papa Nitz" because he would always listen to their problems and worries and only rarely acted like a slave driver. He also owed his distinct dialect to the fact that he came from the area around Leipzig.

"All right. It looks like you'll be through by lunchtime, right?"

"Jawohl, Herr Leutnant, we can do it. And as I said, after the lunch break we'll continue with the camouflage nets."

From the basic to the complex. That's how it has to be, Engelmann thought, cheering silently.

"And how's your back?" Here, behind the front line, the soldiers were slowly able to heal from the little ailments they had collected in the past months: impetigo, joint aches and lice were not uncommon during the Russian winter and usually couldn't be treated right away at the front line. Here in the rear echelon, however, the men's health clearly improved – but now the number of those infected with sexual diseases had increased rapidly, though the army was issuing condoms in massive amounts. Nitz, on the other hand, had been complaining about back pain for months, at times fierce and at times bearable, which no military physician had yet found a cure for.

"Bearable, Sir. It has to be," he answered, pressing his lips together.

"Then proceed."

The staff sergeant turned back to the recruits. "Oh no! No, no, no!" Nitz suddenly groaned when he saw what th recruits were doing to the platton leader's tank, marked with white letters spelling "Elfriede" painted on her barrel. "Men, you can't stuff thick branches between the wheels!"

While his words were still reverberating, Nitz already reached the tank and started to pull thick branches out of the chains whereas three recruits in black Panzer uniforms stood next to him, showing remorse. Then Nitz began to explain to the young men why that wasn't a good idea and what they could do instead to camouflage the chains. He talked to them the way one would read a book to a child.

Engelmann couldn't help but grin. He liked people like Nitz – people who used their heads and language instead of just bullying the soldiers with physical exercises and drills. He kept watching the scene for another moment. Then he turned away; after all, he still had to send out a letter. A low and constant roar began to close in from a distance. Looking up, Engelmann noticed a propeller aircraft that was fast approaching from the Northeast. Unimpressed, he turned his head and left the area his platoon's back area. He had to walk more than a mile to get to the command post of the company where the mobile post office had also put up its tents. Above his head, the aircraft roared past. The rumbling of the propeller engine – in the meantime a rare item in the sky – got Engelmann thinking again; though this time he was forced to think about the entire situation. He saw the future with mixed feelings. It was true: A lot of things had improved since last winter but they were all "internal". He considered the situation on the front lines to be very critical. The war on two fronts that Hitler allegedly always had tried to avoid had long since become reality because of the bombing in the West, and the threat of an invasion on the western front hung in the air like a bad persistant smell. Engelmann was glad that von Witzleben had at least ended that madness in North Africa; that he had allowed the Afrika Korps to retreat.

This had saved hundreds of thousands of German soldiers from allied captivity, it had also prevented tons of materials, guns and tanks from being captured by the enemy.

Overall von Witzleben's move had released battle-hardened troops for other theaters of war. But it was not only the overall situation on the global map that worried Engelmann; he also felt as if he was confronted in a subtle fashion every day with all the shortcomings that might cost the German Reich the victory in the end – and these started with such trivial matters as airplanes in the sky.

At the beginning of the war in the East, the whole firmament had been covered by the aircraft of the Luftwaffe, the German Air Force, and when one needed air support in combat, the Stukas – the dive bombers – had been there in a flash. Last year there had already been considerably fewer planes in the sky to support the combat soldiers, and this winter it seemed to Engelmann that for the first time he had noticed more enemy military aircraft than German ones.

This was an observation that applied to all sections of the Wehrmacht. And casualties could hardly be compensated for anymore. When had Engelmann last encountered a unit that had its full manpower? He honestly didn't know.

He also didn't know how much longer the German army would be able to fight this war if it didn't experience a breakthrough somewhere soon. While the Germans had still launched long-range attacks over 1 500 miles in 1941, in 1942 their power had only been strong enough for an offensive against the southern half of the front line. *And this year?* The thoughts rattled around in Engelmann's head while the aircraft's propeller thumped behind his back.

The constant training plans of the past weeks that focused on tactical maneuvers and attack movements indicated that something was brewing. Engelmann didn't believe though that the Wehrmacht would be able to tackle an offensive over half of the Eastern front line again.

He was sure that the attack this year would only cover a small section.

If it continues like that, then next year our war objective will be to take the XY field. Thoughts like these made Engelmann uneasy so he quickly shook them off. After all, nothing was lost yet, and with von Witzleben at the top as well as von Manstein and Paulus here in the East, he could at least rely on capable men.

The lieutenant ran his fingers over the eagle on his chest, the state symbol of the German Reich, and the swastika underneath that was stitched up so much that it was no longer recognizable.

Yes, a lot of things have changed since winter.

Lieutenant Engelmann could hear the aircraft behind his back getting louder and louder; that meant it was coming closer. Turning around, he observed that the propeller engine turned and returned to his platoon's operational area.

Suddenly his eyes widened: There was a red star on the aircraft! Before he could react, the beast prepared itself for a nosedive. Aircraft cannons barked. Leaping on the ground, Engelmann covered his head with both hands. Instinctively he opened his mouth so that his lungs wouldn't burst if there was an explosion nearby. But the projectiles weren't meant for him. They hit the wooded area in front of him, the area where his tanks were – and his men! There was nothing Engelmann could do but watch helplessly while a fast Our Father roared through his mind. The Russian dive bomber stopped its hellfire when it was perilously close to the ground; then it turned around and zoomed away. Mere seconds later it had already disappeared from sight. The roaring of the propeller faded away but now a piercing scream sounded. Nitz ran out of the woods.

"We need a paramedic – here, right now!"

North of Oryol, Soviet Union, April 14th, 1943

It was a quiet evening on the outskirts of Oryol. Though the city that served as the logistics center of the German army was only a few miles away from the front, one could hear neither artillery fire nor any other combat sounds. Everything had been quiet on the front line for weeks, but for the Germans it was becoming obvious that something was in the air. By now, trains loaded with tanks arrived in the city almost every day while large formations of troops were gathering in the surrounding area. A week ago when he had gone to see the physician at the logistics center, Sergeant Berning, a lean, almost bony young man about twenty-three-years old, had even spotted several of these Tiger tanks everybody was talking about. They were large, angular monsters, even bigger than the Panzer IV. Yet now he focused his attention on something else. Berning tugged on his long bangs, which he had combed back while the rest of his black hair was short, sticking out from under his field cap. In the meantime he listened to the voices that filled the air – loud, aggressive words. No doubt about it, an argument was in progress.

The sergeant and his 3rd Squad had moved into an abandoned barn and settled down between hay bales and wooden planks; the narrow light cones of two flashlights cut through the darkness. Of course the soldiers had to make sure that the light never seeped out the building; after all, they did not want to become the targets of dive bombers. Here and there glowing dots danced through the air precisely wherever a soldier was smoking a cigarette. The complete Schnelle Abteilung 253 – the "Fast Battalion", a formation consisting of two reconnaissance squadrons and two tank-hunter companies – had positioned itself here – north of Oryol – in an abandoned kolkhoz and was currently engaged in intensive combat against well-organized groups of partisans, their number estimated in the several thousand. Some of them were quite well-trained fighters. Just today, two units of the section, together with mechanized forces of the Panzergrenadier Regiment 63, attacked campsites of the enemy and were able to celebrate an entirely successful operation. Berning's squad hadn't participated in the action.

In general one could say that since the beginning of the new year the Wehrmacht had the problems in this region noticeably under control – particularly due to less repressive policies for the civil population, combined with specific operations against armed forces. Today's operation was also the subject of the argument that one could probably hear as far as the end of the village: The staff of the battalion commander, who was expressing his rage in deafening screams, was located in the adjacent building. Though Berning assumed that all commanding officers of the companies were present, apart from the commander, he could only hear one other voice: First Lieutenant Haus, the leader of the "black company", who was also screaming and snarling as if the two of them were trying to compete for the most decibels. Though their voices were muffled, the soldiers could make out every word:

"I won't tolerate it any longer, shit like that happening in *my* battalion! You and your men are nothing but a pack of killers and highwaymen, and it's a disgrace, nothing but a disgrace for you to wear our uniforms!" the commander bellowed.

Of course Berning and his men knew what this was about because today's events already spread as rumors via the grapevine, claiming, the black company had shot several women in an hidden partisan ammunition storehouse – unarmed women who had been found dead later.

"With all due respect, wake up, man!" Haus countered loudly. "This is war, not a summer camp. If we don't make short work of these people, you'll have more than just a few partisans here soon!"

"Don't talk such shit! Times have changed and we can't afford to mistreat the civilians!"

"Please, Colonel ... "

"SIR! Dammit, you are to call me 'Sir'! I should never have you kept as a unit when you were assigned to my command! I should have ripped apart your company and split your men over my other units as so many other commanders did!"

"Even though you are my superior officer, I refuse to tolerate your talking about my men like that! My men are soldiers and they have always done their duty..."

"... their duty...?"

"Jawohl, their duty! And I can recall more than one situation when you boys from the Wehrmacht were damn glad we came. The way we're suddenly being treated in this army is outrageous!"

"Do you really believe what you're saying? Well, anyway – what you did today will have consequences!"

„Fine, Herr Oberst. I proudly stand behind my actions and can defend them anytime at any court-martial. All I did was serve my country."

"What you did will have consequences, Haus! I'll dissolve your company no later than tonight and split the soldiers up among the other units. But you – as well as the platoon leader, Raumann, are released from all duties, effective ·from right now. Both of you can take a chair, sit down in the next room, and wait for better weather because you won't be involved in any more operations for the time being. I'll report the incident to the high command, and then we'll just have to see what they will decide about you."

"Then I officially inform you as of now that I'll enter an official complaint about your conduct towards me and my men!"

"Go ahead. You're entitled to do that. And now get out of my sight!"

The evening was suddenly quiet again and the soldiers turned their attention to other matters. Yet Berning was haunted by his own thoughts. He hadn't been there this noon – and he was glad about that for several reasons.

*

Two hours passed. Berning couldn't fall asleep because he was tormented by visions of the future. The events of the past weeks indicated that something major was coming up. Besides fighting partisans, Berning's unit had mainly concentrated on one thing: training. Getting past wire blockades, never-ending sand table exercises, always with the same relief models of the terrain, and hand-to-hand combat in position. Nobody could say yet what it was, but it was all over town that the German army would start this year's offensive soon.

That was what worried Berning because he didn't need a war or an offensive. He would have preferred to just stay any number of miles behind the front line until the *Endsieg*, the final victory. He was about to doze off when a figure with wide shoulders entered the barn, looked around searching.

"Sergeant Berning?" a rough voice resounded through the room.

"Here." Even this one word betrayed the sergeant's Austrian dialect. Sitting up halfway, Berning groped for his flashlight with one hand because it was pitch-black in the barn. The figure stepped up to him and stood at attention.

"Obergefreiter Steffen Kolter reporting for duty!" he announced. Berning, who was already half asleep, turned on the flashlight and pointed it directly at

Kolter's face. A broad-shouldered, balding fellow with gray hair and a round, bulbous nose narrowed his eyes to a slit when the sudden light blinded him.

"What do you want?" Berning asked. One of his soldiers on the bunk next to his woke up and slowly raised his head.

"I'm to report to you, colonel's orders. I've been assigned to your squad."

Berning nodded slowly.

"Good." He started to think. "Look for a place to sleep for now."

"Great," the soldier next to Berning, Lance Corporal Rudi Bongartz, said and grinned happily. His teeth shone in the dark like two white strips. "We can use as many helping hands as we can get when we put up the field showers tomorrow." He lit a cigarette. Bongartz always had a cigarette between his lips. Though each soldier was only issued a few cigarettes a day, Bongartz somehow managed to meet his needs. The lance corporal was tall and slim with black hair and a skin tone dark for Central Europeans. He expressed himself in simple words.

"Great idea, Gefreiter Bongartz. Well then."

"No," Kolter answered curtly and calmly.

"No what?"

"Just no. Sergeant, I didn't go through the toughest training in the world, and I didn't fight with the best soldiers of our times just to install some showers now."

"Er, what do you mean by no...?" Berning, who was obviously younger than Kolter, felt as if he had been hit in the face by a wooden plank. He felt completely blind-sided and didn't know what to say. Something like this had never happened to him before.

"Senior Lance Corporal, when I give you an order... "

But Kolter had already turned around, disappearing into the darkness of the barn, muttering, "I'm going to crash."

"Senior Lance ... er ... Lance ...," Berning called after him but Kolter apparently didn't care. Looking completely stunned, Berning stared at Bongartz, whose silhouette he could barely make out in the darkness. The Lance Corporal just shrugged and put out his cigarette butt on the floor of the barn.

Oboyan, Soviet Union, April 17th, 1943

Comrade Zampolit, the political commissar of the unit, waved his arms around wildly while addressing the hundred and twenty soldiers of the formation standing in attendance and praising to them the rule of the proletariat as the greatest achievement of the 20th century. An achievement that now needed to be defended against the Fascism and its brother, the Capitalism. He raised his index finger admonishingly, pointing out that this war wasn't about defending a stretch of land or even a city. This war was about nothing less than defending the freedom of every laborer and farmer. Comrade Zampolit spread his arms out as if he wanted to conjure up a storm and literally spit out his words while raging on about the German barbarians who, in an alliance of oppression with the Italians, the Finns, the Hungarians, the Romanians, the Bulgarians and the Japanese, had initiated crimes against humanity by forcing the free socialist labor councils to participate in this war.

Suddenly Zampolit calmed down and continued in a voice that was so soft that the comrades in the back rows could barely understand him anymore. The speaker's eyes blazed when he started to talk about Herbert Baum. He paused for a moment, searching the faces in the auditorium. Of course the name didn't mean anything to anyone in the room. So Comrade Zampolit told them the story of Herbert Baum, a German communist who had been brutally tortured and murdered by the Nazis because he had dreamed about freedom, equality and the rule of all workers. Therefore the Red Army, the armed ally of the socialist society of laborers, was not just on a mission to defend the motherland, Zampolit went on. This war was about freeing their brothers in Europe from the oppression through fascism and capitalism so that the liberated nations of Europe could be given the gift of socialism. It was about so much more than one's own life, one's family, one's country, Zampolit reminded them in an adamant voice. It was about the freedom of mankind!

Comrade Rjadovoi Arthur Petrosjan could barely keep his eyes open even though he had to remain standing, just like his comrades had to during this political instruction. What did he – an Armenian farmer's son – care about labor councils in Italy? Until two years ago, he had never left his hometown, and now he suddenly had to fight Germans thousands of miles away from home. Arthur didn't understand any of it; he didn't understand this war. Moreover, he simply didn't see this as his war. Naturally he would never show his lack of interest here in public. He fought hard against his exhaustion and lack of sleep; after all, the instructors had woken up his company in the middle of the night and made them work like slaves ever since then. His eyelids were so heavy that they trembled, but in front of him, next to Comrade Zampolit, were the officers of his unit. They would punish any hint of fatigue with a beating – or worse.

Thus Arthur continued to fight the necessity to get some sleep. His head was filled with thoughts of his home. At home right now he would probably be feeding the pigs and chickens while the babushkas were preparing a true feast: roasted pork, bread, eggs, cheese. Here all Arthur got to eat was dirt. Or German bullets if they sent him on another one of these suicide missions. He felt his rage rise up. Why had those Socialists made him leave his village? Why should this whole thing concern him? He didn't give a damn about any ideologies – why, he didn't even know how to spell ideology! So what if these Germans invaded this country? Arthur didn't care. So others would rule the country where his family's farm was. In the end that wouldn't change anything, and life would go on. The rage tightened Arthur's throat. He felt the blood rise up to his head, and his heart began to beat wildly. He would have liked nothing better than to walk up to the comrade at the front of the room, who was blabbering something about some Paris Commune right now, and smash his fist in the speaker's face. And then Arthur would go home to his father, his mother and his grandmother, who always exhorted him to go to the Tukh Manuk chapel to worship the black boy. Grandma was so religious.

Arthur wanted to go home, and now that he had suppressed his rage successfully, he almost started to cry. His stomach felt queasy. Yes, he really wanted to go home. Dad needed his help on the farm ever since Azerbaijani bandits had broken all his fingers. His hands hurt all the time, and now he even had even to work the farm all by himself. It really hurt Arthur to have to abandon his family. But most of all he longed for Sesede, that black-haired beauty with her full bosom and well-rounded hips. Oh, now Arthur's thoughts were going off in a totally different direction and his body reacted immediately. He wanted her, oh, how much he wanted her! She had already let him lie between her legs once – the night before he had to depart. And she had promised him she would become his wife when he returned. Yes, even his parents had given their consent! Now Arthur wanted to go home more than ever.

Outside Mezhove, Soviet Union, April 18th, 1943

Orders issued! The platoon leaders, the staff sergeant, the HQ platoon leader and the commanding officer stood next to the command tank of the company, a Panzer III that looked a little like a not-fully-grown Panzer IV and whose main gun was only fake. But the hull of the tank came with all kinds of communications devices. Yet its exterior betrayed the fact that it was the command tank because a rather striking frame aerial was wound along the edges of the hull on a structure behind the turret.

The company commander, an experienced soldier who was approaching fifty and whose face was covered with old gashes, glowered at the faces of his non-commissioned officers. A map that showed the whole European territory of Russia and even parts of Asia had been spread out at the soldiers' feet, and the commander had a long baton in his hand. He kept tracing the front line drawn on the map – the eastern front – with the tip of the baton.

The German Army had to maintain a front line of more than 1 500 miles from Lake Ladoga in the North to Maykop in the South. Between Oryol and Belgorod – both cities were in the hands of the Germans – the area around the industrial city of Kursk controlled by the Russians jutted out like a rock ledge into the territory occupied by the Germans. Engelmann sensed that his vacation was over.

"The division has gotten its marching orders," the commander began. "All platoons will therefore be on alert and ready to move without delay. Prepare yourselves for transport with the Reichsbahn from Stalino towards the front line as of April 21st. All units will follow tomorrow morning, but let me say this for now: We'll be taking part in an operation to straighten out the salient of the front line near Kursk; the code name is Operation Citadel."

"What plans do they have for us?" Engelmann inquired.

"Roughly, in two stages: occupy the city of Kursk, then advance into the interior of the area."

"Von Manstein wants to straighten out the front line in order to free forces, huh?" Engelmann mused out loud. The other platoon leaders nodded in silence and stared at the map.

"The plans call for a pincer movement from the north and the south via Olkhovatka, or more specifically Prokhorovka," the commander replied, pointing his baton at the towns marked on the map, which were both situated right behind the front line in Russian territory.

"The projection of the front not only gives us the option to straighten the front line," the commander further explained, "but also to lock in and destroy masses of hostile forces through the pincer movement."

Frowning, Engelmann rubbed his chin. "The Russians should be able to calculate that we'll attack right there," he said. "And anyway that's not Manstein's style at all. Didn't the field marshal always preach vast counter attacks against the flanks as being our only option?"

The commander shook his head vehemently. "Not von Manstein," he retorted. "It was the chancellor himself who pushed Citadel through – against quite a bit of resistance coming from the officer corps, or so people say."

"Is that starting up again..." Engelmann mumbled, shaking his head.

"No. Von Witzleben's right." The commander's face beamed conviction and optimism. "We have to act. Gentlemen, we'll take back the initiative in the East."

Engelmann wasn't really convinced about that yet.

Lucerne, Switzerland, April 18th, 1943

The day that opened up over Lucerne already began with rain at dawn.

A brawny man named Thomas Taylor, with wide shoulders and freckles, looked with tired eyes through the window of the tiny apartment at the Reuss River, which divided the city into two parts and now swallowed up millions of raindrops. Taylor wiped his face with his right hand and noticed that he urgently needed a cup of coffee now, but as usual the boys from military intelligence hadn't prepared a thing. Taylor was just glad that they had at least remembered to set up a bed for himself in the apartment.

These damn theoretics! He cursed silently. *Next time these dickheads can take care of their shit on their own!* The air was filled with the stench of cold cigarette smoke. Taylor took a drag on his cigarette and exhaled the smoke in long trails.

The young man – Taylor wasn't even in his mid-twenties yet – then glanced at his watch and stretched while his lips grimaced. He had to hurry … and felt awful. No wonder, considering the odyssey he had been on during the last few days. He ran his hand through his red hair and blinked a few times.

Oh well, if nothing else, the rain outside'll wake me up. Again he stared out of the window. A genuine downpour burst over Lucerne. Loud raindrops pelted the roofs of the buildings.

Crap! Shit! He cursed again, flooding his brain with English four-letter words his father had taught him. Then he reached for his clothes and started to get dressed: shirt, pants, tie. He would have preferred to wear a uniform but that probably wouldn't go down too well here in Switzerland.

Why was Taylor here? He had asked himself that question quite often and had always come to a very satisfying conclusion: because he was the best in what he did. Taylor had made himself more and more indispensable for his unit over the years, mainly due to his multinational background and multi-language skills – and of course his capabilities as a soldier, which shouldn't be forgotten, either. Taylor, born in 1920, was a German with a Scottish father, and he had lived in Poland – back then before the Reich. Because of his background he not only spoke German fluently but also English and Polish, was well acquainted with the different cultures and traditions of these countries and could therefore pass as a Brit, Scot, Irishman, Pole or maybe even as an American at any time. Due to his German citizenship – having been born on German soil and having a German mother – and the attraction the military held for him, he had signed up for service in the Wehrmacht in 1938. Then pure chance helped him: Because of an inquiry directed to his unit, his former division commander introduced him to Oberst i. G. von Lahousen, a colonel in the General Staff Service who was looking for soldiers and civilians who spoke Polish. And that is how it came that he witnessed the invasion of Poland not just as a common infantry soldier but had been planted near Breslau even before the war began as a member of the Kampfgruppe Ebbinghaus – a special combat formation – in order to occupy and control important industrial facilities until the German Army arrived. And then everything happened really fast: When the German Reich established the first command unit in the form of two companies in October of 1939, Taylor had been there from the beginning. He was happy to be able to serve in the unit, which had grown to the size of a division and was by now famously known as the "Brandenburgers". On the one hand, Taylor simply felt a higher calling than to just waste away as cannon fodder in some foxhole on the front line. He enjoyed the thrills of his adventurous profession and – this may have been the most important point of all – he wanted to make himself as indispensable for his country as possible, and an individual soldier could only really manage to do that in a special forces unit. Thomas had already encountered the racism of some Germans, and even though everything pointed toward improvement at the moment, he was still afraid he might meet with a harsh fate some day. Anyway, he felt like a German and did what he considered to be his duty to the Reich.

How it came to this situation here in Switzerland, though, was a simple story: Military intelligence needed someone who could pass as British as well as Swiss for a special mission, and since this military intelligence, which originally created the Ebbinghaus Unit, had always worked closely together with the Brandenburgers, they naturally looked for qualified personnel there and finally ended up with Sergeant Thomas Taylor. Now Taylor was certainly not Swiss but he was blessed with an important talent: He could imitate others perfectly – certain individuals with their personal quirks and their very own style of talking or even whole dialects and accents. Anything Taylor had ever heard even just once, he could reproduce absolutely convincingly. Ever since last autumn, his imitations of Himmler, Hitler and Göring had been smash successes with his unit.

In any case, this was how it came that Taylor had been transferred to the Military Intelligence Division in Stuttgart, where he had been prepared for his mission intensely and as part of this preparation also had occupied himself with Swiss radio programs and movies for hours on end. Two days ago the German Reichsbahn had transported him from Stuttgart to Constance, where he furtively crossed the border to Switzerland at night – just as he had learned it in his reconnaissance training. He had then helped himself to a bicycle in a small border town and ridden the bike all the way to Lucerne, where an apartment prepared by military intelligence had been waiting for him.

So far, so good, Taylor thought. Of course he was glad that he hadn't had to spend the worst months of the year in Russia, especially since "Ivan" – the German nickname for the Russians – had turned the area where Taylor's company had operated at his departure into a hellish inferno. Yet at the same time it bothered him that he wasn't with his comrades during such hard times, and he desperately hoped that they wouldn't hold it against him.

Again Taylor looked out of the window while the raindrops ran down the glass pane. If it hadn't already happened last night, a murder was taking place right now in Lucerne, and therefore the United Kingdom would have to do with one less spy in the future. Or the

Soviet Union. Military intelligence wasn't totally sure where the spy came from.

What a dirty game! Taylor thought spontaneously. Well, that's what came with being a human being – a dirty game in all walks of life.

*

It still hadn't stopped raining. Everywhere thick drops of water splashed into the Reuss River, but at least it wasn't too cold. Thomas Taylor walked across the Chapel Bridge with its wooden roof towards a thick tower right in front of the other side of the river. The tower looked pretty much like – Taylor couldn't think of a more apt description – an erect penis emerging from the water of the river. In the meantime a light-colored coat concealed his P08 pistol from being detected. He would know in a moment whether he had to use it or not. A thin, middle-aged man with bony cheeks and thick glasses, wearing a dark coat and a dark hat, was waiting at the end of the bridge, half-hidden by a building front.

Taylor glanced around, but apart from himself and this guy there wasn't a soul anywhere near.

Why should there be? Sunday morning, it's raining … who the hell would go out of the house right now? Here he sighed to himself. *Oh, right – me.*

He approached the thin man. For a short moment their eyes met.

"Beautiful weather it is, young friend", the man said in English with a German accent and stared at the dark river.

"Indeed it is. So Dora gave me the day off," Taylor replied and also stared at the water. *What imbecilic crap the Brits come up with! He mentally shook his head.*

"Okay, so you're the new guy?"

Now their eyes met again, and Taylor answered, "Let's skip the small talk and get down to business."

"As you wish, my friend." And with these words the thin man gave Taylor an envelope.

"I fear my sources are vanishing. Nevertheless your government should consider handing this over to your friends as well," he added in a serious voice. "The Germans are up to something."

"Haven't you heard? Germany is practically beaten ... it's just a matter of time." It almost caused Taylor physical pain to utter such a blatant lie, but then he was just playing a part.

"Well, we'll see." With these words the conversation was over for the other man; he turned around and disappeared in the pouring rain.

Taylor stared after him for a moment. "Goodbye, Mr. Rössler," he whispered. At least Taylor had not been forced to use his weapon, which meant three very gratifying things: First of all, the damned military intelligence had finally done a good job; second, the Reich now had an excellent new source of information, and third, they could now send the Brits as much manipulated information as they wanted to. Or the Russians – as already mentioned, military intelligence didn't have all the facts yet. Finally Taylor glanced at the envelope. Only a single word was written on it and he had not the faintest idea of its meaning: *Citadel*.

North of Ponyri, Soviet Union, May 2nd, 1943
Heeresgruppe Mitte – 47 kilometers north of Kursk

"Sergeant Berning?" A messenger reached the swale on the forest floor that Berning's squad had settled in. The starry sky and the brightly lit moon kept the night from being pitch dark.

"Here!" a bright voice with Austrian roots to it called out. Only seconds later the messenger had identified its owner. "Sergeant Berning. Orders from the platoon leader! Reconnaissance Patrol Berning! Report to the company commander at 23:15 hours!"

The sergeant repeated the order at once – just the way every German soldier had been trained to do. By repeating an order, the information burned itself into the recipient's memory, and it allowed the other party to verify that everything had been understood correctly: „Reconnaissance Patrol Berning, at 23:15 hours to the company commander."

The runner confirmed the order and disappeared back into the darkness as quickly as he had appeared. Berning, however, turned around to his men whom he could only make out as dark silhouettes by now. Nevertheless he sensed their stares, their serious faces and the tension in the air. The officers had drummed into them long and urgently how important this upcoming operation was – and now it would actually start. Berning felt an unpleasant twinge in his stomach. In no way did he feel up to what was about to happen.

As the squad was inside a secured perimeter, Berning didn't have to post a guard and could therefore gather all of his nine soldiers around him.

Again his eyes wandered from one steel-helmeted silhouette to the next. The night was quiet; the only sound was the chirping of the insects. It was almost frightening – the silence before the storm. Berning knew that the enemy was about three miles away from here, not more. Three miles to the north – and he would encounter human beings who would try to kill him. Berning was afraid, terribly afraid, but he didn't want his men to know that. He sensed the expectant looks on their faces. Yet, he had always hoped to survive without having to shoot at anybody. It had worked in the past, but what about now? Now there was this reconnaissance patrol!

"Okay, men. Let's do this!" he began, repeating the usual phrase because he couldn't think of anything better to say.

He didn't feel good; it was as if his whole body was struggling against the upcoming mission. Berning briefly almost felt the urge to throw up but he was able to suppress it. In the end he added a personal note to the phrase. "Everybody is okay?"

He made out nodding heads until a shrill voice squealed, "Bochum!" It was Rudi Bongartz cheerfully replying to his question. The young lance corporal was a guy one could only describe as being totally nuts. Bongartz was always in a good mood, even in the midst of the worst combat. And he was a very good-natured, caring person. Yet in combat, without any hesitation, he nevertheless killed everything with bullets, knife and fist that didn't wear a German uniform. Rudi hadn't always been in Berning's squad but he had already experienced several combat missions. And he was a total und unconditional fan of the VFL Bochum soccer team that

47

currently enjoyed considerable successes in the Gauliga, in which the team had even ranked number three last year. Rudi was the heart and soul of the squad, and no matter how tough the times were, he always managed to get the boys back on track.

With that, the ice was broken. The soldiers grinned, visibly relaxing. And Bongartz even topped it by saying, "Yeah, so what? Number seven and we just got started, I'm telling you. We're on our way! Just wait and see! Bochum, buddies! Bochum!"

Kolter, who was sitting at the side, grinned while stroking the shaft of his gun.

But now the queasiness in Berning's stomach returned. As the reconnaissance patrol, they would form the tip of the spear in Operation Citadel – a doubtful honor in his eyes.

"Well, all right, men." The sergeant cleared his throat several times; then he issued his preliminary commands in short sentences so that while he took care of issuing the commander's orders, his squad could do the preparations: Check the ammunition supplies, hand excess material to the 1st squad, inform the neighboring squads about the planned activities, and so on. And above all: hand over the pay books!

"And, Bongartz?" Berning ended his instructions.

"Yeah?"

"You'll get us another round of coffee."

North of Ponyri, Soviet Union, May 3rd, 1943
Heeresgruppe Mitte – 75 kilometers north of Kursk

Slowly, very slowly, the night gave way to dawn but the sun was nowhere to be seen yet. Berning's squad had received the order to advance to the so-called Hill 241, a small mound about two miles in front of the German positions, and to see if the area behind it, a vast, open space surrounded by woods, was occupied by the enemy. In the worst-case scenario, the men of Reconnaissance Patrol Berning were to make contact with the enemy and dig in on the hill before noon when the engineers would show up to clear the mine barrier assumed to be in this open space. That was the way dozens of minefields within the direct zone of attack of the German troops had been cleared last night. The mine-clearing activities that started this morning – therefore almost simultaneously with the attack – served the purpose of clearing minefields that were not directly in the path of the spearhead of the troops.

Berning's breathing turned shaky when his squad stepped out of the woods. The world around him still consisted only of silhouettes but the approaching daylight was getting brighter by the minute. No soldier under Berning's command had ever been killed before, even though he had been a squad leader already for over a year. That fortunate fact was not only due to his leadership skills: Often Squad Berning had simply been lucky; for example, they had been recovering in Northern Italy during the battles of the last winter or they had just been in the "wrong place" when their own division had been involved in active combat.

And now there is this reconnaissance patrol! Berning thought, searching the area with his eyes. They had reached a small, open space covered with shrubs. It bordered on a thick, wooded area with a swampy subsoil behind it that they had to cross, and after that Hill 241 became visible as a small mound which rose up over the flat land that stretched all the way to the horizon.

It's actually perfect for tanks, the sergeant thought, trying to let these thoughts distract him from his fears that had already accelerated his breathing and made his palms sweat. The wooden surface of his K98k – a repeating rifle – had become very slippery between his wet fingers. The rest of the squad walked directly behind Berning in a file. First there was Bongartz, a chain smoker who would have loved to have a cig dangling from his lips but who only got to carry the MG 42. The machine gun was already equipped with a 100 rounds belt, and a second one was hanging from his neck. Private first class, Obergrenadier Udo Feitenhansel, marched next to Bongartz with his K98k. Together with his MG gunner, Feitenhansel, and another soldier by the name of Schröder, Berning formed the vanguard; the remaining soldiers followed at some distance behind them, and Steffen Kolter was in the back. Kolter thought he was better than his fellow soldiers and showed it in everything he said and did. Yet, as a soldier, he *was* really damned good. For that reason Kolter served Berning as his second-in-command and was to lead the squad from behind if required. That was precisely what the sergeant had learned at the military academy in Sigmaringen.

Academy. Berning literally let the word melt in his mouth. *Academy is academy, and being out in the field is an entirely different story.* That's what the seasoned soldiers kept saying, and Berning, too, sensed that he would get to know the deeper meaning of this saying all too soon. He felt much too young and inexperienced for this mission because after all it was his first active reconnaissance patrol. And he didn't really want to do it either. He would rather be at home in Podersdorf am See in the Austrian Burgenland right now. This time of year he would spend the day at the lake with Gretel and sleep with her in her parents' barn at night – just like they had done last summer when he had gotten home leave from the front line. Berning noticed that thoughts like these aroused him, and so he had to shake them off quickly. The image of Gretel's plump breasts in his mind's eye faded when he turned around to his men and signaled for them to stop and crouch down.

At least they weren't the only reconnaissance patrol leaving the German positions right now. Without seeing it, Berning knew that to the left and right of him patrols like his own were setting out to investigate the remains of the extensive mine belt the Russians had laid.

"All right, men!" he said to his group. They looked at him, wide-eyed. They expected him to lead them in the best way possible, and at that moment Berning knew that he couldn't deliver. He wanted nothing more than to be able to get up now and just leave. His eyes glazed over and he stopped for a second. He actually had to fight back tears.

"Well," he stammered and started to get himself under control again. „You know the mission. We are under observation by the SMG team – the heavy machine gun team – up to that edge of the woods over there. Now we need to save time, so on the double. I'll show our objective on site."

In the approaching light of dawn one could barely see the edge of the woods that was about one hundred and fifty yards ahead. Berning noted a distinct, thin, broad-leafed tree whose trunk had been broken halfway up and whose leaves were therefore now lying in the dirt.

"This direction, the one I'm pointing at," he ordered. "One-fifty, broken tree. That's our objective. Double time at my command. Understood?"

"Broken tree, understood!"

"Got it, Sarge!"

"Jawohl, I understand!"

"Bochum!!!"

"Jawohl, tree one-fifty."

Berning looked around again. "Uh … at my command," he repeated while he pulled the sketch out of his chest pocket that he had prepared according to the commander's map the night before. He stared at the amateurish lines on the paper.

He went through everything again in his mind. *Positions, open space, woods, open space, hill. Why the hell did I take the sketch? I know the way!*

Finally Berning got up and gave the command. The soldiers marched off immediately.

*

The sun had risen and cast those merciless scorching rays down on the land that the Russian summer was known for. Wheezing, Berning was the first to reach the edge of the woods. He was a good runner but one hundred and fifty yards over broken ground with his weapon, ammunition and equipment was no easy task. His comrades followed behind him, exhausted.

"Secure the area in the woods!" the sergeant gasped and moved several yards into the woods himself.

"Report!" he immediately demanded while his men positioned themselves around him, using trees and hollows in the ground as potential cover, and readied their weapons.

"Report!" Berning yelled again and felt his voice getting hoarse.

"No enemy present!" several voices hollered.

"Understood," Berning confirmed and rubbed his sweaty forehead. His helmet started to slip and to bother him, and his clothes stuck to every part of his body. What the cold had been in the winter were the damned mosquitoes in the summer. Everything itched, and they kept swarming around everyone all the time. Berning waved his hand to keep the bloodsuckers from his face; then he turned to the SMG team at the other end of the plain, lifting his weapon over his head – the sign for "no hostiles in the area".

The team leader at the other end responded to the sign. Then the sergeant turned towards the dark woods. The treetops here were so close together that they formed a dense roof, and the vegetation on the ground was just as thick and thorny in many places. Berning took one step and knew: From here on they were on their own.

*

The early morning heat woke Arthur Petrosjan. Even before he opened his eyes, he felt his whole body itching. The insects were already awake. Arthur opened his eyes abruptly. Thunderstruck, he jumped up and grabbed his Mosin-Nagant, a repeating rifle made of wood. He was standing in a depression in the middle of the woods.

Da net že! he moaned silently. *Oh no!* His heart began to race. Sweat poured from his forehead, flooding his face. Arthur jerked his head and peered around in all directions. *Net!*

"Ory Raydovoy ikhaylo ic?" he whispered over and over again. "Ory Raydovoy ikhaylo ic?" Desperately, he called his buddy from Georgia but he didn't want to be too loud. He was aware of the fact that he was close to the German lines – and he found himself all alone! His platoon had marched on foot patrol through this section of the woods last night and had stopped for rest right at the spot where Arthur had just woken up. He actually had been supposed to secure the area but he had been too exhausted from the last days' activities. They had constantly been in action until late at night, only to be tormented with weapons drills by the drill sergeants who had had plenty of sleep in the camp. Arthur was sure that if the Germans didn't manage to destroy the Red Army soon, they'd manage to do it on their own.

And now he was scared. Had Comrade Sershant – the staff sergeant – noticed by now that Arthur was missing? What would he think? After all, Arthur had already messed up twice. This time they'd think that he had deserted! That he had gone over to the German side! This time they wouldn't just punish him with a beating. This time they would shoot him.

Arthur's eyes glazed over and his stomach churned. He had just thrown his whole life away.

Blin! He mentally cursed. *Shit!* Then he whispered the curse again: "Blin!" Tears ran down his face. Suddenly he heard a twig snap. He jumped, startled. Again it snapped. And again. Those were steps. Really close. Arthur hadn't lost his comrades after all. He climbed out of the depression immediately and followed the sound. He thought he still had a chance to get by with a simple disciplinary action.

*

No matter how carefully they moved through the woods, they could never manage it in total silence. Here and there a twig would snap or the ground would creak, but as a reconnaissance patrol behind enemy lines one should at least try to move as quietly as possible. Here in the densely wooded area south of Hill 241 this wasn't an easy thing to do, though. Where everything didn't just disappear in the muddy swamp, the shrubs were so thick that every step was a strenuous effort. Sergeant Berning and his men struggled through knee-high brambles, whose thorns bored into the flesh of their legs. What made things worse was the thick foliage at eye level. Young birch trees and tall shrubs blocked the view of anything farther than twenty yards away.

Berning glanced at his watch, a present his father had given him on his twenty-first birthday. They were late and had to hurry or else the engineers would beat them to the hill.

Suddenly a shrill whistle cut through the background noise, and the soldiers froze. Berning turned around and saw Bongartz, who was pointing the shaft of his gun in a northern direction – the troop's signal for "potential enemy ahead". Berning looked in the direction the gun pointed at – the heart of the woods where green thicket blocked his view. Yet then he also heard the crackling sound ahead of them.

There is something out there ... or somebody, Berning realized in his mind, and he was afraid that his weapon would slip out of his sweaty hands. He squeezed the wood so hard that his wrists hurt.

*

Arthur stumbled through the woods, forgetting everything he had ever learned in his military training. He had to think of his farm and his father who now had to get by on his own somehow. Arthur just wanted to get away. Out of these miserable woods, away from this fucking war. The queasy feeling in his stomach got worse. It was no longer only just the fear of being punished when he had finally found his unit again – of course, the most important thing was that *he* would find *them* and not vice versa, or else they would think he was a deserter. But at the same time his feeling of homesickness returned. It tightened his stomach and raised the urge to just sit down and cry. What the hell was he supposed to do? What was he doing here, anyway?

A thick row of hedges appeared in front of him; it was so dense that he couldn't see through it, and somewhere behind it he had made out these sounds.

"Blin!" he cursed under his breath because the noises had died down. But then he froze and raised his weapon. What if they were Germans? Fresh sweat formed on his brow and moistened his hair. His helmet slipped on his wet hair down to his forehead, blocking his view over and over again so that he had to keep pushing it back.

Hesitantly he took a step forward and stopped. He hadn't even chambered a round yet! And what if they were his comrades after all? How would they react if they saw him first – pointing his gun at them? How would Comrade Sershant react? Arthur's eyelids twitched. He mustered up all of his courage and marched through the bushes, shielding his face with his hands.

"Someone's coming through the bushes," Bongartz whispered, raising his gun. Berning's squad was completely petrified. Berning's hands doused his weapon with sweat, and his helmet slipped across his head. He turned to glance quickly at his men.

No! he thought. *Beginner's mistake!* All of his soldiers had focused only on the bush– everyone but Kolter, who had stayed in the area he was to secure – in the direction of six o'clock.

"Psst..." Berning whispered to get his squad's attention, continuing softly, "... watch your sectors!"

Did Arthur just hear a voice? He stopped and listened but now he couldn't hear anything in the area ahead anymore. He wasn't sure; after all, he had lumbered through the undergrowth like an elephant, and the noise of snapping twigs and the soil, which sank under his boots, had drowned out any sounds in the background. Was there really anyone behind these bushes?

Slušayu, he prayed silently. *Slušayu ... Slušayu ...* Arthur was a religious man. Though he didn't believe that God interfered with the fate of any individual person, at this moment he prayed to any higher power that was available to stand by him. Once again he gathered all his courage. He lifted his right boot, which was already full of mud, and took his next step, desperately hoping that he had gone to the chapel of Tukh Manuk often enough in his life.

A tiny fly buzzed in front of Berning's face but he didn't want to move to shoo it away. Keeping his whole body tense, he focused his gun on the bush and listened to the sounds that were coming closer. The silhouette of a human figure became visible behind the foliage. *A German? A Russian?* Berning couldn't tell, but he didn't want to risk taking a shot at a friendly. He silently hoped the figure would just turn around and disappear into the woods.

"Fire only on my order!" Berning whispered. The fly landed right above his upper lip. It tickled his skin and crawled into his right nostril. It was so disgusting that Berning felt like going ballistic but he remained frozen. Suddenly the bushes in front of him split apart, and a Russian stepped into view. The man froze as soon as he saw his enemies. And the Germans stared back – with raised weapons.

Arthur stopped breathing at the sight of the Germans. Gaping, he started to shake all over and began to hyperventilate. Carbon dioxide escaped from his mouth in quick breaths while his muscles cramped up.

Sergeant Berning stared at the Russian with wide eyes, unable to think straight.

Kapitulyáciya! Was the only word that popped into Arthur's mind. *Surrender!* After all, these Germans were good people! Educated people! They would treat him well! The warnings about the Germans' atrocities were nothing but propaganda! Suddenly he cheered up and was overcome with joy. He wouldn't have to fight any more, and who knows – maybe they would even send him home. What good was an Armenian farmer's son for the Germans anyway? Maybe he would go back home soon...

Arthur's right hand dropped the leather strap of his weapon that he had slung over his shoulder. There was a muffled sound as the Mosin-Nagant gun kissed the ground. Then he took a step towards the Germans.

"Stop, halt!" Berning yelled in German, English and Russian. Kolter, who had stayed resolutely in the area he was securing until now, turned around to see what was going on behind him. All he could see was a Russian soldier.

Arthur begged them desperately not to shoot him, but all he could speak was Armenian and a few words of Russian. He could tell that they didn't understand him. Sweat flowed down his back in streams.

Berning could tell that the man wanted to surrender. "Don't move, men!" he yelled, but Kolter had already pulled the trigger of his weapon. The projectile slammed through Arthur's upper torso. His face distorted into a soundless scream and he collapsed.

"Damn it, you idiots!" Kolter yelled at his comrades. "Do you really wanna wait until he stabs you to death?"

Berning was totally confused. Wondering, he stared at his men. "I think he ... he just wanted to surrender," he stammered. His mind was racing. Did they just commit a war crime? Did the poor man just want to surrender? Or did he really want to attack him?

It was Kolter who finally opened his mouth. "Surrender? Yeah, right, no way..." He couldn't go on because at that very moment a 7.62-millimeter bullet hissed through his body. Not able to believe it, Kolter stared one more time at the hole that suddenly gaped in his chest; then he fell forward to the ground and didn't move any more. At the same moment fire opened on Berning's squad from three sides.

"Fire!" the sergeant yelled. His comrades threw themselves down on the ground or jumped behind the closest trees for cover. Single bullets hissed through the undergrowth, tearing deep holes into the tree trunks. The wind carried Russian words over to the German soldiers from all sides – yelled orders and calls of the enemy. Toward the northwest, where the woods grew less dense, Berning could make out brown figures darting around.

A PM M1910, a heavy Russian machine gun with a shield behind the barrel and a gun carriage on wheels, started to fire and tore everything around Berning's troop into shreds. Short bursts of fire chopped up small and larger trees and blasted the branches around, while the impacts on the ground threw up small clumps of dirt. Berning saw how the shoulder of one of his men exploded and smithereens of flesh and uniform swirled around. Another soldier held his gun in front of his body to put the next cartridge into the chamber when a bullet made his K98k burst and tear into the man's flesh. Wooden splinters raced around and the weapon snapped in two. The defense line of Berning's squad broke apart. At the next moment the survivors of his unit just ran.

East of Stroitel', Soviet Union, May 3rd, 1943
Heeresgruppe Süd – 102 kilometers south of Kursk

Engelmann's unit with its panzers had moved into a small wooded area, awaiting the orders to attack sometime in the afternoon. Now all that mattered was how fast the engineers could clear the mine barriers ahead of them.

Every hatch of Engelmann's tank was still open. The first sunbeams already kissed the ground, and it was now unusually warm. Thus the men used the chance to let the heat caught in the tanks out and get at the same time a whiff of fresh air through the open hatches. They would be stuck for quite a while in their panzers, where a small microcosm of heat, stale air and the stink of gasoline was building up. The air was filled with sizzling tension. In light of the upcoming battle, the whole Heeresgruppe Süd – the Army Group South – seemed to pause for a moment. It would not be just a battle - it would be the decisive one! If they failed today, here at this place, then the whole German Reich would collapse, and every one of them could imagine what that meant.

There had been no shots yet, at least not in the section of Heeresgruppe Süd. Engelmann had opened both his hatch's lids and peered outside. He tucked his tank helmet in place, making sure that the throat microphone and the headphones were sitting correctly. Sitting on the right side in the front of the hull, Staff Sergeant Nitz's head protruded from the tank and stared at the battlefield-to-come with a serious expression on his face, while the assistant gunner, Corporal Eduard Born, stuck his somewhat feminine features out of the loader's hatch on the side of the turret. They all enjoyed the warm but much more pleasant air outside of their "tin can" while the gunner, PFC Theo Ludwig, and the driver, Sergeant Hans Münster, had already disappeared deep into the belly of the steel beast. As usual, Sergeant Münster was asleep.

Engelmann looked to the left and right with mixed feelings. First he saw his platoon's four other tanks to his left, whose occupants were waiting for the attack order just as tense as he was. The 3rd Platoon, also equipped with several Panzer IV, was to his right.

Well, at least that's something, the lieutenant thought because they had not always had so many of that type of panzer at their disposal – there had been times when there had not even been enough for one complete platoon. Unfortunately the Wehrmacht did not have sufficient resources to provide the type IV panzers everywhere they were needed: Therefore the 2nd Platoon and the company HQ had to make do with the much smaller, lighter and less powerful Panzer III, and then there was even a light platoon that had to report with nothing but Panzer IIs that had already been obsolete in

1939. It was the same situation throughout the whole battalion and even the whole regiment: The "IVs" made up no more than one third of all tanks. Engelmann sighed. He felt sorry for the poor slobs who had to show up here in a Panzer II, and he thanked God that he had been assigned to a Panzer IV platoon, though the Russian T-34s, these incredibly tough beasts with a huge main guns, were superior to even Panzer IVs. All one could do in a Panzer II was to pray when facing such an opponent.

Another indication, Engelmann thought and felt queasy. Each month the number of the superior Russian tanks grew while the German Army had to make tin cans like the Czech Tank 38(t) functional again to be able to at least motorize all units sufficiently. He did not need to read von Witzleben's appeal to the troops to understand how essential this operation was. The mystique of the German Army's invincibility had already dissipated in the Russians' defensive fire in 1941 when the Wehrmacht had stormed Moscow, and the allies of the Reich had wavered. The Wehrmacht needed this victory because now, in the third year of the war, the Russians had finally activated their gigantic war industry and were about to produce more tanks, airplanes, and artillery in one month than the German Reich did in a whole year. To that one could add the menacing invasion in the West that already hung over Germany like the Sword of Damocles. A second land-based front line would bring about the downfall of the German Army. Engelmann was certain of that.

He gulped. He did not want to admit it to himself but somewhere deep down inside he already knew that they

had lost. He could not even contemplate the consequences because he knew one thing for sure: A military
defeat would mean the total downfall of the German
Reich.

And then there was the bombing terror back home.
Soldiers of his regiment were being sent home increasingly often on furlough because they had suffered
deaths of family members who had been killed by
bomber raids – and Engelmann's own family didn't exactly live in a small village, either.

The lieutenant hastily shook off these thoughts. *There
simply has still to be some hope left,* he told himself, *there
has to be!*

He heard some static in the tank's radio. Nitz immediately disappeared into the belly of the tank.

"What is it?" Engelmann asked, feeling the subtle
sense of excitement begin that he felt before every combat. "Has it started?"

The signal was transmitted in numbers, and so Nitz
needed another moment to translate it into sentences
that made sense, using the radio log he had spread out
on his lap. Then he stuck his head out of the hatch again
and replied, „No. The Russians have captured half of the
engineer company directly in front of us."

"Holy shit!"

"Now we should use the alley near the 10th because
we don't know how far they got clearing our area. Sequence: 1st Platoon takes the van, then 2nd Platoon, light
platoon, company HQ, 3rd Platoon."

"Near the 10th ..." Lieutenant Engelmann repeated,
more to himself, "... near the 10th ...", while disappearing

into the turret of his tank Elfriede, where he had fastened his situation map to the wall. He stared at the territory it showed and the advance routes of the attack, sketched out in the map.

"Then we'll have to move toward the West."

"Would be better. It would be a shame if Elfriede were to hit a mine," Münster pointed out.

"Yeah, for all for us."

North of Ponyri, Soviet Union, May 3rd, 1943
Heeresgruppe Mitte – 75 kilometers north of Kursk

The remaining soldiers in Squad Berning were hunted down – by human beings and by bullets. Berning ran faster than he had ever run before in his life. He didn't even think about trying to coordinate the rest of his reconnaissance patrol to dodge the enemy while fighting. The young men were just running for their lives while the Russian voices behind them got louder and louder. The sergeant's head throbbed and fumed. His sight became narrower; all he saw were the trees and branches in front of him while the edges of his sight increasingly blurred into darkness. He wanted to get away from here, nothing else. He was not able anymore to think of fighting, or of his mission. All he could do was running.

At that moment Berning became aware of Bongartz on his right, how Bongartz, while running, grasped his machine gun, that big, heavy hunk of metal, firmly, suddenly turned around and kissed the ground. At the next moment the MG 42 spit out twenty-five deadly messages per second with loud bangs. With short bursts of fire, Bongartz got rid of the advancing Russians, who jumped to the left and right for cover.

Berning was now running on empty. The air exploded from his lungs in short thrusts. His breathing raced like a locomotive, and the colors of the images in front of him faded more and more. He knew they had left wounded squad members behind when they had stormed off but what was he supposed to do about it? He threw himself on the ground and quickly crawled behind a fallen tree trunk. Like a machine gun, he pulled air into his lungs and forced it out again. His sides hurt and he thought he tasted blood. Finally he risked a glance over the top of the trunk. He saw Bongartz jump up under heavy fire and leap with his MG behind a tree a few yards behind Berning, where he immediately pulled the second belt from his neck to reload the weapon. Berning could also see Private First Class Günther Schröder, whose legs were pulled out from under him at this very moment when several bullets pierced through his body. A screaming face dug itself into the lead-covered soil. In a distance, Kolter lay on the ground — without moving — as did two other soldiers, but they rolled back and forth like insects that had been sliced through the middle. Even farther behind him he saw soldiers in brown uniforms and the wide, bowl-shaped helmets that were so common in the Red Army. But he also saw Bongartz pull the cock of his weapon, open the cover, and insert the belt, ready to throw himself into the hostile fire of combat again. Bongartz bared his teeth while he pushed down the top cover of his gun. Next to his position, clumps of dirt flew up into the air. Berning also recognized PFC Feitenhansel and a few others, who finally stopped running when they heard Bongartz's "buzzsaw" start up again. Turning around, Feitenhansel fired one shot. Berning made up his mind. While Russian projectiles shaved off the treetops above his head, he finally realized that they *could* fight ... *had* to fight! They could do it! All he had to do was his job as a squad leader.

"I'm down to twenty percent, Herr Unteroffizier!" Bongartz yelled and decreased his bursts of fire. "The rest of the ammo is up ahead!"

Berning got up and aimed his weapon. He saw the Russians – two hundred, three hundred yards ahead of him – pushing forward fast under the fire of their machine pistols and rifles. Now he had to lay down suppressive fire with his MG while there was still any ammunition left. Then dodge under the cover of fire; keep the Russians down with single fire bursts and clear out to the south – back to their own positions. That was the only chance they had. Holding on to the handle of his weapon tightly, Berning put his finger on the trigger. He took aim: A Soviet soldier stood there out in the open and reloaded his PPSh. Suddenly there was a loud bang, and Berning felt like someone had kicked him in the stomach. His hands dropped the weapon immediately. Then he collapsed behind the tree trunk. His abdomen felt really warm and he sensed a pleasant fluid surround his crotch and legs like a mother's warm embrace. For a split second he surrendered to this pleasant sensation; then he suddenly realized that he had been hit. He could still hear that his own MG was suddenly quiet. Russian shouts danced in his head while he looked up at the treetops that were swaying lightly in the wind. Everything was green and getting darker.

Prokhorovka, Soviet Union, May 3rd, 1943
5th Guard Tank Army – 85 kilometers south of Kursk

Comrade Colonel General Nikolay Sidorenko frowned at the situation map that showed the whole Kursk salient. His adjutant had just added the last updates to it.

Sidorenko, in his mid-fifties, with short gray hair and stubbly cheeks, stood up and felt his stiff back. He rearranged his uniform cap that was sliding all over his head.

The latest developments indicated that he had been right after all – and at this moment in time Sidorenko hated being right. How often had he approached his superiors and pointed out the danger of the front-line projection in this section which reached like a balcony into those parts of the country occupied by the fascists? But until a few weeks ago the high command had not understood that the salient had to be reinforced. Large formations were approaching but were just not here yet. Again Sidorenko looked at the map. He could guess what these damn fascists planned to do. Using two wedge-shaped routes of attack, they would advance from the north and south via Olkhovatka, respectively Oboyan, towards Kursk in order to surround and destroy at least three Soviet armies. A brief grin ran over his lips. Sooner or later these damned Nazis would suffocate on their own arrogance. Just because they had been successful in surrounding whole troop formations of the Red Army in 1941, that didn't mean that the same trick would work again two years later. The brothers and sisters of the laborers' movement had had painful experiences with the Germans – and they had learned from them. Had they really? Sidorenko added up all Russian units that were gathered in the salient and calculated the assumed forces of the Nazis in comparison. A balance of power of one to one was in the making in the salient, truly not enough for an attack if one wanted to follow classic military strategy, but Sidorenko was realistic enough to acknowledge that a German formation was superior to its Russian equivalent in terms of fighting capacity and strength. Radios in every vehicle plus two additional crew members per tank as well as better training of many German non-commissioned officers were issues the Red Army had been tackling mainly by pure mass in the past. Sidorenko chuckled to himself. Would the fascists show up again in those ridiculous heaps called Panzer II even a spear thrower could riddle with holes? Sure! Yet the Nazis often more than made up for their technical deficiencies by applying their better tactical methods; therefore in the end, all that counted on the side of the Red Army were the numbers, and there was one thing Sidorenko knew for sure: What could a German Reich that was at war with over twenty different nations simultaneously on several front lines launch against the Union of Soviet Socialist Republics with its almost 200 000 000 inhabitants, its nearly inexhaustible resources and fossil fuels and its gigantic industrial facilities? It was obvious that the Soviet Union – and therefore socialism – would be victorious over the fascists in the end. The only question was how much blood and steel that victory would cost.

Here, in the salient of Kursk, things looked rather different though. The impending battle could end with a defeat even though a victory would neither serve the Nazis nor change anything in the overall picture. Still the situation was dangerous for Sidorenko. So he swore to himself in that instant to confront these hoodlums, murderers and oppressors, who considered themselves so very superior, right here – in Kursk, no matter how much blood it would cost. He made himself a mental note to talk to Konev as soon as possible. Konev had been made the commander of the Steppe Front two weeks ago when the officers of the Stavka finally realized the impending attack of the Nazis. Sidorenko reached for his glass, which stood next to the map on the table, and washed a mouthful of Merlot from Moldavia down his throat. Let the whole nation drown in vodka – for Sidorenko there had always been only one drink: red wine. Suddenly there was a knock on the door and a young officer, his adjutant, came back into the room, followed by several German soldiers, all officers and non-commissioned officers. Of course they had been disarmed, had hangdog faces and wore the uniforms of the engineer troop – as the black piping around the epaulets told Sidorenko.

"Tovaritsh Nikolay Sergejevitsh, mi podobrali eti nyemtzi w Ostrov," the officer informed him. *We picked up these Germans ahead of Ostrov.*

"Da," was Sidorenko's only answer. Then he nodded gravely and motioned his adjutant to step aside. He quickly pulled out his pistol and shot the sergeant on the left in the head so that bloody blobs splattered out of his skull and his limp body immediately collapsed onto the floor. The other Germans froze in terror and stared at Sidorenko with open mouths. Even the adjutant at the back was petrified in light of his superior's methods. The latter now grabbed the situation map and threw it at the fascists' feet.

"Mark the German staging areas for the attack!" he said in tolerable German.

Wide-eyed, the Germans stared at the map; then their eyes lingered on Sidorenko's face again. The Nazis hesitated – for just one second – one second too long! Sidorenko lifted his pistol and shot two bullets into the chest of the NCO in the middle. Like scalded cats, the two remaining Germans threw themselves on the floor and started to mark the Wehrmacht positions.

East of Stroitel', Soviet Union, May 3rd, 1943
Heeresgruppe Süd – 102 kilometers south of Kursk

Waiting – this never-ending waiting before the attack is the worst part of any war. Many people don't even know that a war consists mainly of waiting, not of combat. The soldiers wait for food, they wait for the next training segment, or they wait for the order to march off. And only very rarely, between the time in the rear echelon, between training, furlough and the eternal sitting it out in their positions up front, do the soldiers literally wait for combat. And that is the worst kind of waiting there is because while you wait, you still feel safe yet you know that in a very short time your life will be in

71

danger. Therefore this waiting is even worse than the battle itself because in combat, despite of all its cruelties, blood and death, a soldier is so charged up that he can no longer think about his actions but will simply act. If he gets killed in that state of mind, he at least no longer has the chance to ponder his miserable situation because he's too busy fighting. During the waiting phase, however, when all orders have been given, when every soldier knows his place in the upcoming battle, and only the right time for the attack has to arrive, he has way too much time to think about his situation, the war and everything else. Then you suddenly ask yourself why people have to shoot at each other and cause each other great suffering anyway when everyone could just live and let live. And then the question will come up as to why you have to battle other human beings who may not want this war and who don't want to lose their lives either. Then you ask yourself why the majority of human beings fight wars that the people really do not want at all, and you ask yourself what invisible powers make people who only want to live in peace attack each other.

Such thoughts also flashed through Engelmann's mind while he was staring out of the hatch of his tank at the area ahead, waiting for the order to attack that just did not come.

In the end the lieutenant crawled back into the belly of his tank to check on his men. Of course Münster was sleeping as always while Nitz was busy writing a letter to his brother-in-law. Born, one of the smartest soldiers Engelmann had ever met, used the light that fell through the open hatch of the tank to read a book with the title *The War of the Worlds*.

Aliens who attack earthlings? Engelmann, who had read the text on the backside before, wondered. *What a crap! As if we didn't have enough problems with our own species!*

Suddenly a loud whistling cut through the sound of running engines and calmly chatting soldiers. At first Engelmann noticed the noise subconsciously while thinking about Martians with tentacles. Much too late he realized the danger of the situation; by the time he did, there was a loud bang, and dirt and branches erupted all the way up to the treetops in the woods behind his panzer.

"Scheisse! Top down!" he yelled into his tank. Then he closed the commander's hatch himself. "Top down, dammit!" he moaned again. Finally all hatches were battened down.

Behind, in front of and next to Engelmann's panzer, the soil was torn out of the ground and blasted up into the air. Big chunks of dirt and rocks rained down on the tank while Engelmann and his crew listened to the orchestra of death. As long as they stayed in their tin can, they were relatively safe unless the artillery managed to land a direct hit, but then that would be bad luck. Outside there were screams that only penetrated the thick skin of the tank as dull sounds.

"It's not a coincidence that the artillery is spilling into our deployment area!" Engelmann yelled, barely managing to drown out the noise. Outside new eruptions tore fresh craters into the ground. A tree cracked under the ongoing fire and toppled over. Its crown landed right on a Panzer II but the driver swiftly stepped on the gas and pulled his vehicle out from under the branches.

"They know exactly where we are!" Nitz declared with resignation in his voice. "There goes our element of surprise!"

North of Ponyri, Soviet Union, May 3rd, 1943
Heeresgruppe Mitte – 75 kilometers north of Kursk

When Berning regained consciousness, all he could see was the ground that seemed to rush past him. It took him several moments to comprehend that he was leaning on somebody's shoulders who wasn't just carrying him but also running with him. Berning distinctly heard the man's gasping; he could hear the other man's lungs breathe in and out in quick bursts. The man's breathing was fast, it was racing as if it wanted to pass the man himself. When Berning was able to think clearly again and slowly started to realize what had happened and what had gotten him into this situation, the first thing on his mind was relief about the fact that the man who had thrown him across both shoulders like a sack of potatoes and whose back and legs were the only thing Berning could see was wearing a field gray and not a brown uniform. Then Berning listened but apart from the man's quick steps and the high-frequency breathing he couldn't hear a thing – above all no shots and no loud Russian orders.

The pain returned slowly at first but then it hammered itself deep into Berning's physical sensations. His right thigh was burning as if someone had poured acid on it, and his uniform pants were soaking wet. He gritted his teeth but he was close to crying. Then he also started to feel a sharp pain in his shin. He stretched his neck out as far as it would go, and out of the corner of his eye he could make out that the soldier wasn't only carrying him but also an MG 42 that was now sandwiched between the soldier's shoulders and Berning's shin, hitting it with every step.

"Bongartz?" Berning asked in a strained voice.

The exertion almost took Bongartz's breath away, and now he had to pay the price for running with his machine gun and his squad leader on his back. As good a runner as he was, he had reached his limits. He slowed down his steps and his breathing became louder. Each time he exhaled, one could hear a long gasp from the depths of his lungs.

"Don't worry, Herr Unteroffizier," he gasped. "We're almost there."

They reached the edge of the woods, to which the SMG fire team's area of action extended. Bongartz stopped and just dropped down on the ground. Berning crashed hard into the undergrowth and moaned while the lance corporal already struggled out from underneath him and the machine gun, groaned and jumped up.

"We're already in the penalty area," he sighed more to himself than to Berning and pulled off his *Stahlhelm* – his steel helmet with its distinctive coal scuttle shape. "How does that go again? Do you swivel your helmet twice?"

"Three times!" Berning groaned. "Three times, Bongartz!" The sergeant held his crotch with both hands. Though the pain was located more in the area of his thigh, he didn't dare to look down and check the extent of the disaster – he was too terrified of what he might see down there.

Bongartz jumped onto the open space – a dangerous attempt – held his helmet up and swiveled it three times back and forth over his head. Then he immediately dropped to the ground and remained there without moving; only his chest heaved up and down every second while his pulse slowed down. Moments passed – nothing happened. Bongartz got up and peered at the supposedly redemptive edge of the woods at the other end of the plains. Then he saw it: Between two groves of low pines a German soldier, who had camouflaged his Stahlhelm with tall grass, rose, took it off, too, and swiveled it three times.

Berning was still lying with clenched teeth on the exact spot where Bongartz had set him down. The lance corporal returned to his squad leader and picked up the MG. Then, grunting heavily, he threw Berning back over his shoulders and made his way to the German positions.

Berning noticed the sweat pouring from the back of Bongartz's head down into his uniform. They stepped out into the open space. The searing sun was shining more mercilessly by the minute. Then they saw it: East of their position, infantry soldiers tore out of the woods – as far as they both could see. Berning squinted because of the bright sun that was slowly moving south and marveled at the cumulative power of the 253rd Infantry Division. Carrying their weapons in stalking position, the soldiers focused on the area ahead. They marched at walking pace in long skirmish lines so that, in the case of an attack from the front, their collective fire power would be available. The roar of propeller engines already joined the tense silence at the scene; at the next moment a dozen German aircraft zoomed over the soldiers' heads while, all the way at the back, the mechanized infantry troops in their half-tracks emerged out from the underbrush.

The attack here in the North had started, and despite his pain Berning's face broke out in a wide grin. He had caught his million-dollar wound and would be able to go home.

East of Stroitel', Soviet Union, May 3rd, 1943
Heeresgruppe Süd – 102 kilometers south of Kursk

The enemy's artillery was still hammering mercilessly at the German positions even though the fire by now had moved farther south. The detonations of the shells could still be heard in Engelmann's panzer, and when the crew members opened the hatches of their panzers and peered out, they could even see the eruptions as tall as buildings shooting up into the sky farther back in the woods. The hostile artillery fire had not claimed any victims in the regiment since most of the soldiers had been able to protect themselves by staying in their tank. But now the Russians were probing the positions of the infantry, who, according to the first radio signals, was getting a beating.

"If the order to attack doesn't come soon, we won't have anything left to attack," Born mumbled, staring at the ceiling of the tank. Five men, stuffed into a tin can – that meant being crammed together like sardines in a very small space, so small that they couldn't help touching each other. That had its advantages, too, though: A tank crew grew together quickly, which also became apparent by the fact that the ranks often became blurred inside the armored vehicle. Even the soldiers spoke their minds more openly in the presence of the commander here than they would have done elsewhere.

Born restlessly shifted his weight on his chair, but it was either the wall of the tank that pressed into his back or the shaft of the machine gun that poked him.

"Don't worry, our planes will quickly put an end to this." The dull thud outside almost drowned out Nitz's claims that the dive bombers that had roared over their heads a few minutes ago were on their way to enemy' positions. It would definitely start soon: First, the German Luftwaffe had five hundred dive bombers plus escorting fighter planes alone in the area of Heeresgruppe Süd in the air that were raking the Russian artillery as well as bombing the defense belt at the front right now. Second – though it was not audible due to the Russian grenades raining down– the German artillery guns had also been firing at the enemy's positions for the past twenty minutes.

"When will it finally start?" Münster wondered aloud. "I mean we've had enough *Büchsenlicht* for quite a while now."

Engelmann glanced at his watch: *8:50 a.m. German time*. Here in Russia it was already almost noon.

Though he could have almost cited the battle plan by heart, he studied his map again. The more he could see the details in his mind's eye, the less precious time he would have to waste later, when decisions had to be made fast.

Engelmann frowned while his index finger traced the planned marching route.

After all the extensive preparations for Operation Barbarossa – the invasion of the Soviet Union – and after two years of war in Russia, the German Army still hadn't managed to acquire decent situation maps with Roman letters, which meant that Lieutenant Engelmann again had to struggle with Cyrillic letters in order to identify towns and roads. Of course that didn't make things any easier.

According to plan, they were to advance in northeasterly direction across the Lipoviy Donez, a narrow branch of the Donez River. Then, after two and a half miles, they would come to a Russian mine barrier that, according to intelligence, was abandoned – something Engelmann couldn't imagine since blockades without surveillance were useless. Behind the blockade there were two and a half more miles of flat plains that had to be overcome; so the terrain was very suitable for tanks. The first defense belt of the enemy was expected to be on the Osërovka – Shtsholokovo line, two tiny farming villages – actually more like large farm compounds. Once they had passed this line, they had to move on towards the road that led to Prokhorovka whereby the second defense belt was expected to be on the Lutski – Plota line, which was on the way. Both trenches were located in the only range of hills in this otherwise extremely flat country, which showed that the Russians too had done their homework. If everything went according to plan – and it never did – come nightfall, the

German forward troops would be behind the second Russian defense line.

Suddenly static came from the radio. Using his right hand, Nitz pressed the receiver, a speaker built into the mount for the head, against his ear as hard as he could. After a few seconds he confirmed that he had received the message, turned away from the radio and nodded. "It's starting," he informed the commander and the driver through his throat mic. Münster passed the message on to the gunner and the loader since neither was connected to the crew's range and both therefore had to be addressed directly – even by the commander.

"Okay," Engelmann replied while his mind was flooded with orders and rules of conduct for cases like this that had to be carried out now. Years of training and war had shaped him. "You know what that means. We're in combat mode." Throughout this campaign, Engelmann had had the good luck to lead the same tank crew, and over time his small community had developed its own ritual: At the beginning of any combat action or, to be more precise, when Engelmann determined that they were in "combat mode", the usual polite phrases and observations of rank were put to rest and everybody in the tank started to call each other by their first names.

Engelmann took a red tin can out of his chest pocket and shoved a piece of chocolate into his mouth. Then he gave his orders: "Hans, start the engine and step on the gas. We take the lead of the 1st platoon. Sequence behind us as follows: Müller two, Laschke three, Meyer four, Marseille five. Transmit via radio, Ebbe." That was Nitz' nickname. "Over and out."

As always, Nitz had already adjusted the radio system of the tank according to Engelmann's preferences: the commander's microphone and headset were switched to the intercom while Nitz could switch between the radio range of the platoon and that of the company.

"Müller two, Laschke three, Meyer four, Marseille five, jawohl," Nitz repeated and immediately spoke into the radio transmitter, "We're in the lead, sequence after us Anna 3, then Anna 2, Anna 4, Anna 5." Not every message was coded elaborately but of course the code names were part of the cover. Engelmann's tank roared when Münster started the engine, engaged the clutch and accelerated. Elfriede immediately raced out on the open space. The lieutenant opened both sides of the cupola and stuck his torso through the opening. No matter how dangerous this was, nothing was more important than being able to watch the battlefield directly with one's own eyes and ears. Engelmann immediately detected two black dots in the air; they were far ahead on the horizon and kept rushing down on the ground and then turning away. He hoped that the Stukas would eliminate most of the Russian defense before it could pose a danger to his platoon.

From all sides the tanks of III Abteilung of the regiment now rushed out of the woods on to the open plains while the Russian shells kept flattening the rear. Panzer IIs, IIIs and IVs rolled across the open space that seemed to stretch endlessly to the horizon and only up north was interrupted by smallish sections of wood and single hills. The chains of the steel beasts leveled the ground underneath, crushing shrubs, bushes and rocks. They moved straight to the mine barrier that had been placed in front of a row of hills and into which the engineers had been cutting paths for each company since last night. The infantry companies and engineers marched directly behind the tanks out of the undergrowth. The men's faces were distorted into grimaces and looked shaken. The Russian shells had given them a severe beating. The men advanced in the wake of the tanks to be deployed whenever the road had to be cleared of obstacles or hostile infantry forces had to be eliminated. Even to the right of Engelmann's platoon, the order to attack must have arrived as well. Far ahead in the distance, half-tracks were moving into formation. From the edge of the forest that had given them cover for the past hours a heavy tank battalion sped up onto the plains. Forty-two Panzers VI "Tiger", huge and sharp-edged monsters with a main gun that exceeded far past the hull, were to expedite the breakthrough with brute force and to clear the way for the military forces that followed. The steel predators spread out in the open space and formed immediately a wide skirmish line.

"Take your foot off the gas, Hans," the lieutenant groaned. He had to slow his driver down all too often. While they were losing speed, he watched the Tigers pass by and take over the lead of the attack. Thousands of tons of steel rumbled over the tortured earth in this section of the front line alone this section of the front line, and when the lieutenant saw the whole extent of the interaction of the weaponry – air force, artillery, ground forces – he was overwhelmed by a sense of superiority for a moment. What the German Wehrmacht presented here had no equal. What, if not a victory, did such efforts deserve? Suddenly he heard a loud bang as if someone had popped a balloon. One blink of an eye later, one of the Tigers was enveloped in black smoke. Engelmann recognized the cause at once: This was not a hit; this was a burning engine. And farther away by the swath in the woods, one of the heavy tanks was already no longer moving while the commander climbed out of his hatch, cursing. The new tanks still struggled with technical problems, though it wasn't as bad as it had been last year. Yet everybody's hopes lay in the new Panzer V "Panther" that had its first real action today. Thirty of these tanks had rolled off the assembly line just in time to support the operation.

*

After a fifteen-minute ride across easy negotiable terrain most forward troops had reached the abandoned mine barrier. Engelmann recognized the row of hills covered with small sections of woods in the distance, raising right behind the mines. Now the lieutenant's platoon was at the forefront of the front line again because the Tigers had moved east three minutes ago to use the passages that had been cleared for them. The fifty-seven-tons panzers would not join again until they had reached the other side, where the regiment in the wake of the Tigers was to penetrate the first defense line of the Russians. Engelmann's platoon not only formed the tip of his company; no, the company was also the spear head of the battalion, which was the spear head of the regiment. Therefore Engelmann would be the first to face the enemy and that was just fine with the tank commander. Of course he wasn't motivated by a death wish but he'd rather face the danger with his Panzer IV than have his comrades endangered who had to make do with IIIs and IIs.

When Elfriede approached the mine belt, Engelmann recognized the markings the engineers had set up: Metal rods in the ground that were connected to each other with barrier tapes showed the way. As was to be expected, the passages were very narrow; only two tanks fit through them side by side. That feature made Engelmann queasy.

If the Russians don't monitor this blockade, he thought, *they're wasting a huge opportunity.* But again: He couldn't imagine that. Turning to Nitz, he issued new orders: "Ebbe, let Müller come up on our side; then we'll be the first ones to pass through the minefield. Marseille will bring up the rear. Keep your eyes and ears open; I still don't believe that there are no Ivans around here."

Engelmann rested both arms on the edges of his hatch and squinted to examine the groups of hills that were standing in the glaring sunlight.

A well-placed sniper over there will end my life faster than I care for, he thought. For that reason some tank commanders hid in their tanks nearly all the time, but Engelmann needed a clear view. As a leader he had to collect information – the most valuable commodity in any battle; how else could he issue the right orders for the situation?

Engelmann's and Müller's tanks had to approach each other until they were only five yards apart so as to fit through the passage side by side. All they had left then on either side was a bit over three feet of space between the tanks and the markings. Slowly but surely the heat of the sun grew unbearable. Engelmann reached into his tank and pulled out his sunglasses, which he had hooked into the situation map, so he could see better against the blinding light.

"Careful, Hans, careful!" he reminded his driver, who was driving at a crawl down the 90-yards-long passage through the minefield. The engine of Müller's tank growled next to him. The commander's hatch was closed, and so he couldn't see Müller. Engelmann sighed. The two next tanks of the platoon were already approaching behind them. He didn't have a clear view of the row of hills ahead of him; many shrubs and groves made for ideal hiding places.

Usually this is the right time to address the Lord, Engelmann thought and had to smile. He – whom the war had turned from a passive Christian into a devout believer – was talking to God a lot these days; yet at the same time he didn't think it was right to ask the Lord for good luck in battle. Engelmann was firmly convinced that God would not hold His shielding hand only over the Germans but also over the Russians at the same time. Therefore the humans had to sort out their differences by themselves.

The two tanks at the front had already passed through the first third of the path when the commander's hatch of Müller's tank opened, too, and the master sergeant, a slender man with sunken cheeks, stuck his torso through the opening.

"Everything okay over there, Herr Oberfeldwebel?" Engelmann called to him.

Müller looked at the sky with a satisfied look on his face and raised both arms as if he wanted to bless the land. Grinning widely, he nodded.

"Great," Engelmann yelled at the top of his lungs though he could hardly overcome the thunder of the engines and squeaking of the chains. "Up ahead we'll fan out and take up position concealed by a hill!"

Müller nodded again. Engelmann disappeared in the belly of his panzer.

"Ebbe," he gasped, wiping away the sweat dripping out from under his cap with his sleeve, "general order: We'll fan out behind the blockade, goal at eleven o'clock, the three hills in the front, take position behind the elevations."

"Fan out, hills in front, position behind the elevations. Jawohl!" And with these words Nitz turned away and held the transmitter to his lips. While his voice sounded through the tank, Engelmann got up again and peered outside. Suddenly smoke rose from between the hills. Instinctively the lieutenant covered his head with both arms and ducked down slightly. There was a huge blast when the tank next to his was hit. Sparks flew while the shell ricocheted off the armor of the hull. Then Müller screamed, lifted his hands and sank back into the tank. Only then did the blast of the shot thunder across the plain.

"Shit, what was that?" Engelmann gasped, almost drowning in his own sweat.

"Eleven o'clock, four hundred!" Nitz repeated an incoming message. The lieutenant looked out of his hatch and saw the smoke rising from a group of pine trees between the hills.

"Pedal to the metal, Hans, and get us out of this passage!"

Münster nodded and accelerated. The engine roared up.

"Ebbe, to all tanks: Split up the rows of twos and hurry. If they catch us here, the whole passage will be closed off!"

"Roger, Sepp." Nitz turned one of the knobs to increase the volume on an angular radio that was sitting in a mount and looked a little like the "Volksempfänger" radios the Nazis distributed to the populace. Then, frowning, he let it rip. His words hurled out of his throat while he relayed the orders. The gun of Müller's tank already blasted away. Engelmann could see the eruptions of dirt that shot up into the sky way too far to the left of the assumed position of the enemy. The lieutenant narrowed his eyes to slits; then the blasts between the hills started up again. Flashes from muzzles enveloped the trees, and one blink of an eye later an eruption of soil and grass bushels exploded in the minefield to the right of Engelmann's tank.

"Damned bastards!" Engelmann groaned and held both arms over his head to protect himself while he was showered with clumps of dirt. Then he could clearly see a Russian land mine that had been torn out of the ground by the explosion. It was hurled more than one hundred and fifty feet through the air; then it hit the grass and bounced several times like a soccer ball before it came to rest.

In the meantime, Elfriede's engine grumbled even louder when Münster stepped on the gas. Groaning, the chains dug through the dirt. The smell of gasoline filled the air, and the speed of the tank accelerated to 15 mph. The terrain did not allow for more but by then they had reached the end of the swath anyway. Suddenly a machine gun started to crackle in the distance. Tiny feathers of dust sprang out from the ground in front of Engelmann's tank; then sparks flew around the hull. Engelmann ducked down, disappeared into her protective belly and quickly closed both parts of the hatch.

"Machine gun to the right!" he yelled and sat down on his commander's seat, which was in a raised position between that of the loader and that of the gunner.

"They want to blind us!" Nitz chimed in, grabbing for his MG now – he might still need to use it. Instantly smoke rose between the hills up ahead, the next Russian shell was launched. It exploded on the ground between Engelmann's and Müller's panzer even before the sound of the shot roared away over their heads. A wall of soil rose like a wave and spilled over the beasts of steel. Müller's tank fired back. Too short! Soil rained on the shrubs on the other side.

"Did Müller see the enemy?" Engelmann wheezed, holding onto the steel of his tank with both hands.

His question was directed at Nitz, who immediately got behind the radio.

"No!" he replied mere seconds later. "They're shooting with HE-explosives on the off-chance that they'll hit something!"

"Damned waste! Münster, turn to 11 o'clock in the direction of the enemy!"

Engelmann's tank reached the end of the passage, and at once Münster turned left.

Don't ever show the gun your backside! Engelmann thought. The Russian machine gun was still firing its load indiscriminately between the tanks.

"Sepp?" Born asked nervously and already had his fingers on the ammunition. "Should I load?" The machine gun knocked on the armor. From the inside it sounded like someone was throwing pebbles at the tank. Then Engelmann peered through one of the eye slits in the turret and realized that the enemy's position was only 270 yards ahead. His thoughts ran in circles: *These SOBs made us come pretty close! They probably know themselves that it's a suicide mission.* He still had no idea if it was a gun or a tank that had been positioned on top of the hills. Suddenly he saw the shield that was typical for Soviet anti-tank guns gleaming in the sun.

"Blast it!" he ordered. Born knew what he had to do. He grabbed the first round of a total of 87 and heaved it into the breech. Through his window, Engelmann kept his eyes on the enemy's position. Again the shrubs ahead of them started to spit smoke. The lieutenant didn't even have the time to tense his body. There was an ear-shattering bang as if King Kong himself had kicked the side of the panzer. A direct hit! Inside the tank, the crew members flew back and forth. Hans stalled the engine as he was thrown violently against the wall and the tank creaked to a halt. One moment later Müller's panzer fired a shot that finally stopped the guns up ahead. Now the wind softly carried the agonized screams of human beings in their death throes across the plain. Engelmann, however, couldn't hear them. His ears were ringing and his eyes were throbbing as if he were drunk. He pressed both hands against his skull and blinked. Groaning and cussing under him, Münster pressed the electric starter and brought the engine back to life. Fortunately the Panzer IV was able to take quite a beating as long as the hostile fire power was limited. Although the anti-tank gun hit had torn a deep scar in the turret, it hadn't penetrated the plating.

"Report!" Engelmann barked with hoarse voice.

"The engine is okay! I think we got lucky."

"Müller caught a severe hit," Nitz reported after a short conversation with the next tank. "A wound in his neck is bleeding profusely. Meinert's taking over Anna 3."

"Copy that," Engelmann confirmed, chewing on his lower lip. Müller was a generally popular soldier of the platoon – and he had a pregnant wife and three kids at home.

"Ebbe, the platoon shall take up defense positions, once they are through the passage, and call for transport of the wounded through the company command. We have to get Müller to the back."

"Copy that. Defense positions and transport of the wounded." Nitz squeezed himself behind the radio again.

„And, Ebbe?"

"Ja?"

"Laschke should go to the right and take up position there."

"Roger." The staff sergeant immediately contacted the other units of the platoon and forwarded the orders while Hans continued to step on the gas so that Engelmann's as well as Müller's tanks approached the hills from the left. The lieutenant would have liked to go back outside but there was still a hostile MG troop roving around through the hills up ahead. Engelmann was brave but not suicidal. However: If the Russian MG shooters had been thinking the same thing, then they would have already taken a hike. So now it was important to push farther forward quickly because by now even the last Russian soldier had probably figured what was closing in over the Soviet front line right now.

North of Ponyri, Soviet Union, May 3rd, 1943
Heeresgruppe Mitte – 75 kilometers north of Kursk

When Bongartz and Berning finally reached their own trenches, a radio message had been sent to the platoon leader, Staff Sergeant Claassen, via the heavy machine gun team, detailing the events the reconnaissance patrol had encountered. Consequently the battalion had sent a whole company to clean out the woodland that originally had been just circumvented when the front troops pushed forward.

Aside reserve troops of the operation, the Schnelle Abteilung 253 still had time until tomorrow, anyway, before they would definitely move forward. Less than twenty minutes later additional infantry soldiers started on the double. If there were still any wounded comrades to rescue, they couldn't lose any time. Lance Corporal Bongartz was ordered to take Berning into the area designated for the wounded via the command post.

*

Bongartz had carried Berning and his machine gun all the way back to the command post, where a number of soldiers now looked up and stared at the sergeant's blood-soaked pants. The lance corporal was completely pumped out and sweating whole waterfalls. Trembling, he pushed the air out of his lungs while Berning's face cheered up considerably. The thunder of shots in the distance as well as fire nearby filled the air while here the platoon, after having moved to an open forest, prepared to cover the return of the reconnaissance patrol again.

Moaning with exhaustion, Bongartz put the sergeant down and guided him very carefully on his legs so he could help him to sit gently on the grass. But when Berning's boots touched the ground while he groaned and made a face. Bongartz suddenly lost his balance and fell back into the grass due to the counterweight of his machine gun. Berning just remained standing. Pushing his Stahlhelm back onto his neck, Bongartz stared at his squad leader who was standing firmly in front of him. Berning could tell that the lance corporal was raging. His face was distorted with fury.

"You can still stand on your feet?" Bongartz asked, stunned. But Berning didn't understand what he meant. He looked down and noticed that the projectile had torn his pants, which were now soaked with blood. He was genuinely surprised that the pain had decreased noticeably.

"YOU CAN STILL STAND UP?" Bongartz's eyes turned into narrow slits; his hands turned into fists. Though he could barely breathe, his rage seeped out of every pore. It was the first time Berning witnessed the usually so debonair lance corporal being in such an angry mood.

He took a step towards Bongartz. He winced but the pain was bearable.

"YOU CAN WALK?!" Jumping up, Bongartz looked as if he wanted to punch his squad leader in the face.

"Calm down, will you, Bongartz," Berning stammered, visibly afraid of getting beaten up. He waved with his arms and stepped back.

"Why don't *you* calm down? Do you have any idea how many men we've just left behind?"

Berning's deep blue eyes stared at Bongartz. His lips formed a soundless "Oh", and then he understood. All of a sudden he felt feverish and dizzy. He rubbed his eyes with trembling hands.

A harsh voice interrupted the chaos. "Berning!" The platoon leader, Staff Sergeant Mauritius Claassen, stepped between the two soldiers. The stocky noncommissioned officer, a man in his early forties who sported a thin mustache, focused his dark eyes on the sergeant, who was trembling all over. Then Claassen looked at the sergeant's torn trousers.

"What are you doing standing around here, Sergeant?" Claassen was not amused. "Your whole squad has been eliminated, and you just stand here and wait for a change in the weather? Are you out of your friggin' mind? Why didn't you report to me immediately?"

Berning stared at his platoon commander with eyes glazed over. He no longer had his body functions under control. His joints were quivering as if he was in the middle of an earthquake. Finally he opened his mouth, wanted to say something but didn't know what. He knew that from the troop's point of view he had failed miserably. And again Berning felt sick. The dizziness and the seasick feeling in his stomach, telling him that he was about to throw up, hit him like a kick in the groin. He sensed – as he had done when he had been with the reconnaissance patrol that morning – that he was totally out of place here, that he neither belonged in this uniform nor in this part of the world. He wanted to go home, nothing else. All he desired was to get away from these shooting Russians and his yelling comrades who were never satisfied, regardless what he did.

He wanted to go somewhere else where he was accepted the way he was. Yet the fact that the platoon commander was tearing his head off in front of the lance corporal was the least of his concerns.

"Bongartz!" Claassen enunciated. "You've done a good job, son." He nodded sincerely at the lance corporal. "Report to Staff Sergeant Schredinsky, 1st Squad."

Bongartz lowered his head. The expression on his face showed how much the loss of many good comrades hurt him. He nodded slightly and trudged off towards the 1st Squad's site while putting a cigarette between his lips.

"Oh, and Bongartz?" Claassen called after him.

Stopping in his tracks, the private turned around. "Herr Oberfeldwebel?"

"VFL Bochum against Alemannia Gelsenkirchen last Saturday: six to three."

For one second the lance corporal's face lit up but the smile disappeared again just as quickly.

"As I said, Herr Oberfeldwebel. We still manage to get the fourth place!" With these words Bongartz disappeared in the shrubs.

Claassen smiled for a second and whispered something like "fucking son of a bitch." His face hardened,
and he turned to Berning, who was still standing there
like an idiot.

"So, you will now report to the military physician
ASAP."

Berning nodded.

"And afterwards, I want a word with you ... and you
won't like it!"

South of Osërovka, Soviet Union, May 3rd, 1943
Heeresgruppe Süd – 97 kilometers south of Kursk

In 1941 the German airplanes had still controlled the airspace over Russia, but these days had long since been
over. Milch's military branch had lost a great part of
their fighting power due to the mismanagement of his
predecessor as well as the progressing wear-and-tear after four years of war. And while German fighter planes
were desperately spraying into crowds of thousands of
the Allieds' planes back home, the pilots of the Luftwaffe on the Eastern Front were increasingly aware that
the Soviet Air Forces were gaining more power by the
day while the Luftwaffe was losing ground perpetually.
In a tremendous effort, the Germans had managed to
round up enough aircraft for Operation Citadel. Those
would be of course missing on other fronts for the dura-
tion of the battle, but at least, over the battlefield in the
Kursk salient, the German Reich once more dominated
the air.

Lieutenant Engelmann looked up at the sky while his Panzer IV, Elfriede, advanced across the vast Russian steppe. Behind him and next to him were his platoon, his company, his battalion.

He could hardly believe it when he saw more than seventy panzers of the types II, III and IV rush by in small wedge-shaped formations and fan out as broadly as several miles towards the first Russian defense ring. Even three self-propelled anti-aircraft guns that were supposed to fight enemy aircraft moved with the steely masses of III Abteilung. Right in front of Engelmann, merely a mile ahead, 34 Panzer VI Tiger steamrolled across the plain – six others had broken down due to technical defects and were immediately picked up by the maintenance platoons. As the fighter planes of the Luftwaffe circled over Engelmann's head, Stukas kept flying north to hammer away at the Russian lines there, or south for refueling and reloading ordnance. Engelmann hoped that the capacities of the German Air Force would suffice to support the whole operation on this level because nothing was deadlier for a tank jockey than the enemy's air dominance.

The Tigers lumbered on mercilessly. At times the high grass here on the Russian plains covered them up to the tracks. They formed a wedge of tanks so as to break through at one point with brute force. Here and there Russian artillery fire dribbled between the German panzers; then huge balloons of dirt flew up as high as the trees and exploded in every direction. But the shrapnel and rocks filling the air could not hurt the big steel beasts and their smaller brothers. Now and then the crews inside just heard the patter of dirt against the metal skin that sounded like sudden rain pouring down.

Engelmann reached for his field glasses to look into the distance, which wasn't all that easy while the tank was moving. Yet it was enough to get a quick glance. Here and there a wooden hut or worn-out path as well as a single tree or a little clump of wood were scattered over the land. Engelmann could make out several connected buildings in the distance that looked like a collective farm. That was Osërovka. Smoke was already billowing between the houses. One blink of an eye later thick smoke also started to rise from the adjacent woods. The Russians had opened fire but over this distance they could only scratch the Tiger's paint job. New waves of soil spilled over the German tanks as the front row came to a stop and started to return fire. The recoil of the 88-millimeter guns made the tanks rebound with every shot. One could literally see the strain, the enormous pressure of the explosions caused by the ignition of the rounds, put on the steel. Yet, the Tigers stayed intact and transformed the positions in the enemy's first defense ring into a smoldering mess of debris. Explosive projectiles tore anti-tank guns in half while armor-piercing ones had no problem whatsoever penetrating the armor of a T-34 head-on either. Engelmann had his platoon stop under the cover of the Tigers and take position. Far ahead a buried T-34 turned into a ball of fire. The turret of the tank was ejected above the flames and thrown up into the air. Engelmann found the Russian tactics of burying their tanks, making them into stationery arms, fatal because this way the T-34s lost the necessary mobility they needed so badly to stand a chance against the superior Tiger.

Up ahead the Tigers turned the horizon into a series of geysers that spit out pitch-black smoke. The battle didn't even last five minutes; then the last Russian gun was silent. The engines of the heavy tank battalion roared, and the vehicles dashed towards the lane that had been cut into the Russian defense line.

"Stay with it, Hans," the lieutenant ordered although he didn't have to give that command at all because his driver was already accelerating to the max. Engelmann peered at the area ahead and squinted. Despite his sunglasses and the fact that the sun was behind him, the day was so bright that he had problems observing the battlefield. At the same time, they had to be especially careful now. The Russian infantry certainly would not risk a battle with the Tigers but would let themselves be overrun by them so as to attack the weaker tanks or the infantry troops that followed. Equipped with mines, hand grenades and anti-tank rifles, they definitely posed a danger to Engelmann's platoon.

The first Tigers were already emerging through the hole in the front line up ahead.

Engelmann's brow was covered with sweat, and the breeze blew dust into his face that immediately stuck there. He put his head into the tank for a moment and looked at his men, whose shiny faces were fully focused on the action. The heat lingered inside Elfriede, mixing with the smell of gasoline and sweat to form a highly unpleasant atmosphere. Yet the crew members had other, more serious problems. At that very moment their tank reached the shattered defense line.

"The old man says we should go to the right and up to five hundred meters into the depths of the trench positions," Nitz repeated the commander's orders he had just received via the radio. "Old man" was a regularly used term for commanding officers.

"Roger," Engelmann confirmed. "Hans, you heard the man?"

"Yep, Sepp!" At once Münster turned right.

"Ebbe, let the others fan out and follow. Take up position in the current sequence, hundred meters from tank to tank."

"Copy that. Follow and position!"

"Keep your eyes and ears open. Get ready to use the MG."

Nitz was still busy operating the radio but Loader Eduard Born nodded and then petted the handle of the co-axial machine gun as if he wanted to commit it to the upcoming battle.

Closing the commander's hatch, Engelmann eased his body behind one of the narrow eye slits. In the meantime his tank drove along a row of trees behind the Russian trenches, moving away from Osërovka again. The other tanks of the platoon followed and in turn were followed by the 2nd platoon with its IIIs.

Engelmann pressed his face against the eye slit but he could hardly see anything besides tree trunks and tall grass. He gripped both flaps of his hatch with his right hand but then he paused.

Lord, thou art in heaven..., he asked the Lord for protection, took a deep breath and pushed the hatch open again. Cautiously he stuck his head out over the edge of the protective steel and checked the surroundings. Lumbering, his tank ploughed through the soft soil.

"Careful!" the lieutenant moaned into his throat microphone. "Don't get stuck, Hans!"

Nodding, Münster looked through his tiny eye slit attentively at the small section of the world it allowed him to see. Chewing on his bottom lip, he accelerated up to twelve miles per hour. The faster they zoomed across the soft ground, the better!

Engelmann kept peering through his turret at the surrounding area. Apparently they had surprised the enemy after all, because the lieutenant could make out several open military trucks at a single farm; anti-tank mines were sitting on the beds of the vehicles still wrapped. And two trucks with howitzers already attached were burning near Osërovka.

Did the Russians intend to position a second mine barrier here and pull back their artillery behind the second row? Engelmann didn't get around to pondering that question because just at that minute a projectile shot past Elfriede, almost touching the tank, sliced the trees next to it in two like matches and finally exploded far away on the plains. The echo of the shot followed in the blink of an eye, booming across Engelmann's tank. The lieutenant immediately recognized the cloud of smoke that rose from a cluster of bushes on the open plain nearly half a mile ahead.

They're not bushes at all – that's another buried T-34! It hit him in a flash. He reacted without hesitation. "Armor-piercing round!", he yelled, and then: "Hans! Drive around that son of a bitch! To the left!"

Engelmann's panzer turned to the left with a jolt and sped up. The lieutenant held onto the edges of his cupola with both hands while sweat dripped into his eyes. He blinked several times and shook himself.

"Loaded!" it rang out from the belly of the tank.

"Three o'clock, seven hundred, buried tank, fire!"

But Elfriede remained silent.

"Where, Sepp?" Ludwig asked instead, staring through the optics of the turret at a wide field covered with shrubs. The lieutenant leaned back in the tank. "That group of bushes, the one that is higher than..." he said with a hectic voice. The T-34 shot a second time. One moment later behind Engelmann's platoon a Panzer III went up in flames and came to an abrupt halt.

"Scheisse, shoot, just shoot!" Engelmann raged and drummed on the edge of his turret with both hands.

Behind him, a machine gun began to saw. Russian soldiers, who apparently had glimpsed a chance to escape between the trees near Osërovka, where taught mercilessly the mistake in their idea. They fell to the ground, screaming, when the MG salvos pierced through them and everything around.

Finally Ludwig fired. There was a loud bang; the whole tank shook, then sparks flew, and the ragged branches that had concealed the T-34 in its pit were peeled off.

"Goddammit, it just swallowed the shell!" Engelmann groaned, wide-eyed. He didn't even have to order Born to load the next shell; Born did it on his own. Instead he ordered in a harried voice: "Step on it, Hans! We have to get behind that bastard!"

The engine creaked and raced; the tank accelerated to its max. The tracks dug themselves into the soft ground, leaving deep scars in the soil. Simultaneously about 1.2 miles east of Engelmann's position, the vanguard of II Abteilung broke through the defense belt. Several Panzer IIIs rushed onto the open field and tackled the half-buried beast from the other side.

The Russian tankers probably know full well that they're dead. They just want to take as many as possible along with them, Engelmann thought not without admiration. The thought of what might happen to him one of these days entered the lieutenant's mind but the action around him quickly demanded his full concentration again.

Münster had Elfriede storm out onto the plain – away from the trees near the first defense belt – as fast as the tin can could go. Meinert's panzer was right behind them.

Again the enemy tank blew out smoke while sending another shell on its way. Engelmann's fingers cramped up until they started to hurt. He couldn't make out where the shot had landed but it hadn't hit anything; nothing else mattered. Meanwhile the noose around the T-34 was getting tighter – Engelmann and Meinert from the left, the Panzer IIIs from the right.

Defying death, they raced towards the Russian tank. Due to the III's 5-centimeter gun, they could only penetrate it in close combat or from behind – a dangerous game. It was as if ants were attacking a stag-beetle. By now the crew of the T-34 also knew where to find the targets that were easier to slay. Its turret slowly turned towards the Panzer IIIs. Meinert fired. He missed; the projectile went left.

Oh no! Engelmann groaned silently and rubbed the stinging sweat from his eyes.

"Loaded!" The voice came from inside his tank.

"Fire!" Elfriede shook once more when the main weapon was fired. A hit exactly between the turret and the hull! A dream shot! Again sparks rained over the enemy's tank and catapulted the branches that served as camouflage up into the air ... and again the damned beast just swallowed the projectile.

These goddamn Russians and their goddamn tanks!, Engelmann cursed to himself. He felt like crying. The enemy was not only clearly superior in numbers but also some areas of technology. They had already surrounded the hostile tank halfway and their next shot would be fired at its tail, where its protection was the weakest. Yet now Lieutenant Engelmann noticed that their hit had had an effect after all. The turret of the T-34 didn't turn any further and the barrel suddenly pointed diagonally at the ground. The turret was jammed! At the same time the IIIs had reached the disabled tank. The Russian crew already knew what was coming. All the hatches of the T-34 sprang open almost simultaneously but it was too late. From less than 200 yards distance the Panzer III nearest to the wounded beast shot it a shell under the turret, aiming from a slanted right angle, so that only burning flames instead of men jumped out of the hatches.

Engelmann slumped down in relief. There was still fire behind them but it was just here and there. The first defense belt had been broken. The command tank, which had stayed near Osërovka with the 3rd platoon, attacking Russian reconnaissance tanks, was now driving onto the open plain at a distance of a mile, now in Engelmann's view.

Then the company's commanding officer reported via radio: "First trench taken. We'll catch up with the heavy tank battalion right away. 1st Platoon will take the lead."

*

The Tigers had already crashed the Soviets' second defense belt and had challenged them at several points to find the perfect spot for a breakthrough. Here the Russian trenches were concealed by tall grass between small groups of hills and strewn with fresh craters from the German artillery shells. Stukas dominated the sky and dove farther ahead down to the ground, where they devastated enemy tanks with bombs or board cannons. Engelmann's units came to a halt at some distance behind the Tigers. Again the iron cats of prey were supposed to break through the defense as part of the wedge-shaped tank formation while the lighter panzers remained in their wake.

Up ahead between the hills, trails of black smoke rose up into the air – everywhere where there had been once an anti-tank gun position or a buried tank. Still the defense was even fiercer here. The enemy artillery now started to focus on the Tigers and enveloped them in waves of soil. A massive belt of anti-tank guns was still firing away full blast. The Russian shells tore glowing scars into the outer layer of the armor of the Tigers but the Russians would need a whole truckload of good luck to disable that kind of monster from a distance of more than half a mile. Groaning, the German panzer beasts swallowed one hit after another without showing any signs of slowing down while thinning out the Russian defenders in the trenches with each shot.

Engelmann looked to the right where the tank forces of the 6th Army were rolling up all the way to the horizon. Far behind them, the troops of the infantry and *Panzergrenadiers* followed; they had just reached the first defense ring and were clearing it at that very moment. Engelmann bit his tongue. The wedge-shaped formation they were driving in here contained the great risk of getting too far away from the following troops during the attack, thus the risk of becoming isolated by enemy counter thrusts against the rear guard increased. But on the other hand, a fast attack was necessary, or else they would give the Russians too much time to move their reserves to the Kursk salient. The first radio messages about the general situation indicated, however, a rather sobering picture of things in the south so far, and that was what gave Engelmann a headache. He had realized from the beginning that it would be a tall order, but part of him had still hoped they could change the outcome of the war here in the Kursk salient. Yet he also knew that there was nothing else he could do but continue and give it his best shot. He had no influence on what happened at the other sections of the front line, anyway.

Parts of the right flank had already been left behind early in the afternoon. The XI Armee Korps of the Armee Abteilung Kempf had gotten into heavy defensive fire while crossing the Donets and was now stuck on the east bank of the river. While the center of the attack was supposed to slash its way through to the Seym River via

Prokhorovka, following it to Kursk in the form of the 6th Army's mechanized forces, it was the job of Kempf's formation to push through Rshavez and Korotshka to Skorodnoye to seal off the salient to the east against Soviet counter attacks. If they failed to seal it off, the right flank of the 6th Army would be exposed, which could become rather unpleasant. Engelmann frowned. He didn't like it when his fate depended so much on other people but that was just how it was when you were a soldier. The only hope he had was that the plan would succeed as a whole.

Unexpectedly one of the Tigers stopped in the area ahead with a loud bang. A shell had hit its bogey wheels, and now the tracks were dissolving. The other tanks continued to let their guns do the talking, turning the Russian trenches into one single wall of fire and smoke. Looking through his field glasses, Engelmann could make out fleeing soldiers, and then three Russian airplanes showed up. They came roaring in from the northeast, flew once over the battlefield in a wide curve and turned around. They were targeting the Tigers! The flaks were already firing behind Engelmann's back, but the versatile Iljushin Il-2 "Shturmovik" were too fast and agile for them. They rolled over and flew loops while being enveloped in bouquets of exploding flak shells. They had definitely come to hunt for the Tigers; yet Engelmann also didn't feel comfortable standing immobile on the plain while the dive bombers were around.

"Eiserner Gustav in the sky! Hans! Start the engine and follow the heavy battalion at a medium distance!"

"Yep, Sepp," Münster's voice rang out in Engelmann's headset. Then Elfriede's engine came audibly alive. The tank immediately started to move, and the rest of the platoon followed.

Several German fighter planes already appeared in the air over the battlefield and took up hunting. Screeching, the Shturmoviks switched to nosedives. Rockets were ejected from under their wings and pulled long contrails after them while heading for a group of Tigers. The board cannons of the planes added a dash of 23-millimeter projectiles to the assorted rockets. The bullets from the aircraft guns didn't faze the Tigers. They bounced off, sparks flew, and then they scattered in all directions. A well-aimed rocket, however, could be deadly. Long columns of soil shot straight up into the air when the rockets hit the ground and exploded, but one Tiger also took a hit. Black smoke enveloped the steel monster. The tracks stopped and the beast ground to a screeching halt. Then the tank burst into flames.

Once the planes had gained more height again, the German fighters were already on their trails and started the dogfight. Only seconds later a burning IL2 crashed on the ground. It came down in a grove and went up in flames in an enormous explosion that exterminated the surrounding trees.

In the meantime the Tigers had finished firing at the second Russian defense belt and started to roll out again in order to break through the line. Engelmann took a glance at his map. Behind the cluster of hills they would come to more open fields before reaching the road to Prokhorovka.

"Always stay close to the Tigers." Engelmann said it more to himself than to his men.

Münster accelerated the tank to 13 miles per hour while the tracks toiled through the soft soil. The Tigers farthest ahead were already disappearing between the hills and behind the columns of smoke. Engelmann's panzer now passed the tank with the loose tracks that still stood in one spot without moving and had to wait for the Panzergrenadiers and infantry soldiers who were advancing. Then they passed the burning tank. Engelmann could feel the heat that blew towards his tank and had to look away. Despite the planes in the sky, the thundering sound of the artillery, the deafening clatter of the engines, and the screeching of the tracks it was as if he could barely hear – more like a feeling rather than a clearly defined sound – the screams of the men burning inside the iron juggernaut. Of course that was impossible and of course the soldiers in that panzer were already dead by now, but every time when Engelmann was on the battlefield, he got this feeling. He had heard the screams of crews imprisoned in flames several times before – first they were loud, strong and blood-curdling; then they became weaker and weaker until the sounds died – and with them the soldiers. That was the most gruesome thing Engelmann had ever experienced. He desperately hoped that, should he ever be hit by a shell, the explosion would kill him instantly and he wouldn't fry in agony in his tank. In addition to the flames, it was the heat that was any tank crew member's worst enemy. The sun was still beating down mercilessly on the battlefields close to Kursk and was partly responsible for the fact that the temperature in Engelmann's tank had risen to more than 120 degrees F. Every member of his crew was soaking in his own sweat, moaning under the nearly inhuman conditions.

Finally the panzers of the III Abteilung reached the defense belt that had been blasted wide open.

"Ebbe, keep your eyes peeled!" Engelmann ordered. "Fire at enemy infantry forces!"

"Copy that."

"Hans, full speed ahead. I want to get behind the trenches as soon as possible!"

Engelmann was firmly convinced that Russian infantry soldiers were still lying in hiding between the burning tanks and destroyed anti-tank guns. Yet they wouldn't show themselves but instead would pit themselves against the forces that followed without tanks. A sense of doom made him sick to his stomach and he felt the urge to disappear into the protective belly of his tank immediately but he forced himself to stay outside above the cupola. He needed a clear view now more than ever, and the value of his own sense of hearing on the battlefield shouldn't be underestimated, either. Though Engelmann's ears already hurt and were ringing from the day's battles, he didn't want to stuff cotton balls into his ears the way some of the other soldiers did. Then he might as well go back inside his tank, cover his ears with his hands and sing loudly.

The III Abteilung passed through the second Russian defense belt without any incidents and then caught up with the Tigers, which crossed a deep plain scattered with a few farms and groves. Again the tall grass covered the enormous tanks up to their turrets, but the relentless tracks ground their way through the thicket. Now they came to a dense forest on the right flank; it divided this section of the front line from that of the II Abteilung, which from now on, as expected, had to make its way to the road that led to Prokhorovka without a heavy tank wedge shielding them. A few miles farther north the forest ended or at least became considerably less dense and once again turned into small hills that were covered with shrubs. The road was somewhere behind them, and the forces would reunite there. Engelmann grinned. At least they actually seemed to accomplish that day's operation goal.

But the Russians were not defeated yet, and they demonstrated that fact in an emphatic manner because up north, where the hills started, two T-34s suddenly stormed onto the open plains and immediately started to fire. Without air or ground support, the two tanks once again showed the Russian fighters' high degree of willingness to make sacrifices that had often given the Germans a tough time. The armor-piercing shells exploded between the Tigers and directed their attention to the Russian tanks. The heavy panzers turned and adjusted their main guns.

Engelmann, who once again could feel relatively safe in the wake of the heavy tank battalion and thereby became a mere observer of the battle, trembled when he saw the two T-34s. Squinting, he witnessed the fate of the vehicles that shone in the sun; they looked like pyramids with gun barrels.

Two T-34s against almost 30 Tigers, he reflected and nodded respectfully at his Russian tank comrades, *that's as if Germany would fight a war against England, France, the Commonwealth States, the U.S.A. and Russia all at the same time ... Whoa, wait a minute! Ha ha ha. Geez, we're fucked!* A desperate grin tucked at the corners of Engelmann's lips in the face of his own gallows humor while the Russian tanks were shot to pieces in the area ahead. Then he froze. The Russian soldiers hadn't sacrificed themselves in vain because just then dozens of black dots appeared on the northwest horizon, rushing straight ahead towards the backs of the Tigers. An AP projectile already penetrated one of the German panzers and killed every soul inside it. Now the others realized that they had been lured into an ambush and started to turn around.

A rookie mistake, Engelmann mumbled silently before tensing his body and mentally preparing himself for the battle.

"Hans! To the left and onto the open field! Russian tanks in the strength of two companies approaching from the north-northwest. Take us as close as seven hundred fifty!"

"I've already seen them," the driver groaned and carried out the order.

"Edi, AP round!"

Squinting, Engelmann focused his senses on the approaching tank formation. The enemy presented nearly forty tanks that assembled for a counter attack and now stormed onto the plain. The Russians wanted to decrease the distance between them and the Tigers because they knew one thing: Once the Tigers had turned around, the Russians had to get much closer to them in order to penetrate the armor of the German panzers while the Tigers could eliminate medium-sized battle tanks even at a distance of 1.2 miles. Regarding Engelmann's Panzer IV, it was just the opposite, however; in this situation Elfriede was the weaker opponent and therefore forced to risk dangerously close combat. But the lieutenant had no choice. Forty T-34s against thirty Tigers – so he couldn't just sit and watch.

"Ebbe, let the platoon fan out and attack!"

"Apropos the old man says to fan out and attack." Nitz's mouth twitched into a quick grin and he tugged on his mustache. Then he passed Engelmann's orders on to the platoon.

"Thanks a lot," Engelmann grumbled.

Of course, part of the training of a tank commander was knowing the strong points and the weaknesses of various tank models of the enemy, but Lieutenant Engelmann had never been content with the few training sessions at the tank academy. Instead he had always studied the T-34 and others in his spare time as well. He knew that he couldn't wait until the experiences of the battlefield taught him the correct range and parameter values because he might not live to see that day. If he wanted to survive the war, he had to know his enemy; and yes, he did. Engelmann didn't have to waste any precious seconds looking at the tank identification handbook or armor-shooting tables.

Seventy millimeters turret, forty-five millimeters bow at sixty degrees; that totals ninety millimeters, the data raced through his head. He also cited the penetration capabilities of his own gun: *Ninety millimeters at five hundred meters, eighty at one thousand.* After the dozens of tank battles he had been in so far, he had gained enough experience to develop the following rule of thumb for himself:

750 meters – four tenths of a mile – were a sound distance when going up against T-34s and comparable tanks. This definitely gave him the chance to do damage while not being close enough to the enemy to be able to throw his cap at the turret of the Russian tank and hit it. In the area ahead, the T-34s sped towards the formation of Tigers and shot with everything they had, but most of the German panzers had already turned around and offered the Russians nothing but the massively armored fronts. Tank-piercing projectiles were exchanged between the two formations; then the first tanks went up in smoke or exploded directly. At a blink of an eye, a third of the Russian forces were lost, but the Tiger crews had to pay with blood, too.

Now Engelmann and the 9th Company attacked the enemy from the side while the rest of the battalion just reached the plain.

"Theo, up there, the one on the right next to the two shot down. Seven hundred!"

"Roger," Ludwig yelled. His voice was almost swallowed up completely by the battle noise.

"Fire!"

And Ludwig fired. The round hit the tracks of a T-34, bursting them. Unable to move, the enemy tank stopped. Unable to move but not yet unable to fight.

"Load and take another direct shot at it!" Engelmann ordered and struck the edge of his hatch several times with his fist. The T-34 that was hit slowly turned its gun towards Engelmann's platoon – but it was too slow. Ludwig already fired again with the main weapon; this time Ivan bought the farm. It started to spit smoke and sparks; then it fell silent forever.

"Hans, to the right. The smoke's blocking my view!"

Münster immediately turned the tank to the right and gained several yards. Engelmann ducked back down into his turret and closed the hatch; now things out there were starting to get too dangerous for him after all. Most of the other German commanders had withdrawn into their tanks, too. Peering through an eye slit, Engelmann tried to look past the thick plumes of smoke that concealed the battlefield in front of him. All around him loud explosions and detonations. The Tigers fired their main weapons, and behind Engelmann the tanks of the 9th Company fired away. As far as the lieutenant could see, most of the Russian tanks had been destroyed. He heard the detonations of the last T-34s that were shot to steel lumps at that very second. Then for a moment there actually was something like silence – at least if one ignored the noise of the engines and the fires crackling. Two despondent crews of T-34s and a lighter, smaller Soviet tank were trying to save themselves by escaping between the wrecks of all of their dead brethren. Turning around, they stepped on the gas while the Tigers sent their deadly farewells after them. Clumps of soil flew high up into the air; yet the Russians got lucky.

Suddenly a new enemy showed up on the scene: A KV-2, a heavy tank with a gigantic turret that by itself was as high as a tall man, entered the battlefield at the northern end of the plain and promptly kicked a Tiger's butt with its 152-millimeter main gun. The others turned around and engaged in combat. Armor-piercing shells hissed past the KV-2 and tore the trees behind it to shreds. Engelmann swallowed hard. It was a giant of a tank, and even though it was alone and the Germans had five hands full of Tigers, they now all faced a murderous battle.

"Ebbe, have the platoon gather around our position. We'll avoid the open space on the left, stay at the edge of the woods for two thousand meters and then attack the flank of that SOB!"

"Are you serious, Sepp?" Nitz hardly ever questioned his commander's orders but now, in the presence of their new opponent, his voice rang with concern. "I mean, we've got the Tigers. That thing'll tear us to pieces!"

Engelmann didn't want to die, either, but after all they *did* want to win the war – for their fatherland, for their families.

"I'm serious, Ebbe!"

Nitz slid behind the radio. Engelmann's panzer started to move, and at the same time one of the commanders of the other Tigers appeared to anticipate a great opportunity to earn himself an Iron Cross. He broke out of formation and stormed towards the enemy tank that was swallowing two 88-millimeter rounds as if the Germans were shooting at it with water pistols. Of course a Tiger could have been a threat to the KV-2, but not at a distance of over one and a quarter miles and with 110 millimeters of armored steel protecting its bow. The KV-2 had cleverly positioned itself at the edge of the forest so that it could only be tackled from the front.

While the Tigers kept firing in the background and actually tore a track on that Russian tank behemoth into pieces, the panzer that was approaching fast shot mercilessly, too. The KV-2, on the other hand, had concentrated on the approaching enemy forces and covered them with a cloud of dirt every twenty seconds. Engelmann's tank raced along the edge of the woods, his platoon directly behind him; yet they were still too far away. Suddenly a Junkers Ju 87 "Stuka" shot across the battlefield, easily recognized by its wing tips, which curved upward; even Engelmann could identify it through his eye slits.

"Thank God!" he groaned, and the Stuka turned around to get into the right position to attack targets near the Russian wrecks. The Tiger that had broken out of formation had also reached the destroyed Russian tanks by now and used the burning steel wrecks as cover from the KV-2. The pilot of the Stuka flew closer but he was too slow. The KV-2 had used up all the life it had had in it, allowing the Tiger to finish it off with one targeted shot between the turret and the hull. An explosion ripped the side of the tank off, creating a huge hole out of which smoke emerged.

Done. A sense of relief spread through Engelmann's body. Then he froze. *Why doesn't the Stuka turn back?* His eyes widened, and a nanosecond later the guns of the aircraft were spitting death and destruction. The lone Tiger in the middle of the Russian wrecks accelerated while dozens of projectiles rained down on it.

"Shit!" the lieutenant cursed.

"He thinks it's a Russian!" Münster groaned.

When the dive bomber had reached the interception point of his nosedive, it turned about and gained in altitude, while a 550-pound bomb came loose from under its belly and detonated to the right of the Tiger. The impact of the explosion shook the steel beast but it didn't manage to penetrate it. The Stuka rose higher but then it already turned about again.

"He's gonna attack again!" Münster gasped. All the soldiers on the battlefield were condemned to doing nothing but watch and pray – all except for the crew of the Tiger. Hatches opened and hectic crew members scrambled out of their tin can. They carried a large red cloth and climbed up onto the hull of their tank, where they hurriedly spread it out. The cloth was not just a simple piece of fabric but the new flag of the German Reich with black-white-and-red stripes that now covered the rear hull. Nevertheless, the pilot prepared for his next attack. Spellbound, the soldiers stared at the sky – too spellbound to flee. The Stuka flew a wide arch. Then it came back … and turned away.

North of Ponyri, Soviet Union, May 3rd, 1943
Heeresgruppe Mitte – 75 kilometers north of Kursk

Platoon Leader Claassen had not exaggerated when he promised Berning an unpleasant conversation. The doctor had bandaged the young sergeant's wound — just a graze wound on his thigh — and handed him a note that was not marked with any color, meaning that he was fit for duty and had to report back to his unit. On the way there he was already overcome with worry and fear while the battle far off was underway.

Berning had enough of the military men who thought they were somebody just because they could yell and issue orders. He didn't want to be in a war, and he didn't want to be shot and killed. The light burning sensation in his thigh kept reminding him how real the risk of death was here. Berning didn't want to be a sergeant any more, either; all he wanted was to get away – go home. His father had signed him up for NCO academy because they got free meals and accommodations there and because his family didn't have much money. But he hadn't imagined that war would be like this – now that he had had a taste of battle. And nobody seemed to like him here anyway. He felt lonely and left behind. And as he stood in front of his platoon leader who informed him at the top of his lungs how incompetent he was and that he was a disgrace to the whole NCO corps, Berning was close to tears while all the misery that had bottled up inside of him made his lips quiver.

Together with Obergrenadier Heinz-Gerd Bauer, the private first class everybody called "Hege", Berning was now cowering in a hole they had dug near the edge of some woods near an open field; the hole was to serve them as a trench in the case of a Russian attack. Here they roughly secured the direction to the south, but tonight they didn't have to worry about anything because the German attack formations were still quite far ahead of them. In the distance he could hear the artillery fire of two armies entangled in their violent clash, while the sun was even now getting ready to leave this part of the planet.

Every time, one of the huge explosions illuminated the sky, it was like lightning twitching over the firmament far ahead. The scenario was eerie but quiet.

Some of the soldiers in the trenches were chatting calmly, talking about their girls back home or smoking cigarettes, always anxious to cover the glow with their palms to give a sniper no target in the upcoming darkness.

Claassen obviously wanted to push Berning to the limits. The sergeant had no other explanation for the fact that his platoon leader had assigned him to the squad of this madman – this Staff Sergeant Pappendorf – after his 3rd Squad had been disbanded. Pappendorf was a noncommissioned officer everybody feared – crew cut, always a dapper appearance, and he was able to quote any regulation like a minister could quote from the Bible.

In addition, Pappendorf was a veritable slave driver, a bastard who abused his men until they broke down. At first there had been complaints about him, but his soldiers had soon realized that this would only cause more pain for them. Berning had already had problems with this guy when he himself had still been a squad leader, since in Pappendorf's mind he never conducted himself correctly enough and never behaved well enough. And now? Now he was completely at that bastard's mercy!

Pappendorf had assigned Berning – after a major dressing-down about trivialities, like the way his Stahlhelm sat on his head – to the MG team as its leader. At the same time the sergeant was to accompany the squad as an assistant squad leader, though Berning didn't want to lead anybody any more. It only meant that he would make even more mistakes and his life here would become even more loathsome.

And so while dust slowly settled and colored spaces turned gray, Berning sat in his foxhole with stomach pains and timid thoughts and just didn't want to carry on anymore. Next to him, Hege leaned against the wall and stared at the open field. The private first class with the bad teeth was apparently lost in his own thoughts.

"I still wonder what were those things we saw earlier," the soldier interrupted the silence.

Berning didn't react.

"Never seen anything like it. Could they have been these new Panthers?"

Berning just shrugged. *How am I supposed to know?* He thought. Two hours ago two gigantic tank destroyers had broken out of a lane in the woods to their left and lumbered towards the front line. The soldiers of the reconnaissance squadron had never seen anything like them, and since then Hege hadn't been able to get rid of the sight of these tremendous things. On the rear half of the hull, which had a length of more than 26 feet, there was an immovable turret of monstrous size from which a giant barrel protruded that was so long that it reached even farther than the hull. From the bottom of the hull to the top of the turret, the tank surely measured at least nine and a half feet. That thing was even larger than the new Tigers and had thrilled the soldiers here in their trenches. They desperately needed sights like this one after the mixed war years of 1942 and 1943. However, apparently Hege now realized that the sergeant didn't feel like talking and fell silent again.

The thunder of the artillery had moved back very slowly during the past few hours, becoming softer. Berning had no idea how the attack was going, and neither did he care.

Southeast of Lutshki I, Soviet Union, May 3rd, 1943
Heeresgruppe Süd – 89 kilometers south of Kursk

The Russian plains ahead of Kursk were already veiled in darkness. The moon now appeared behind thick cloud formations and softly lit up the front sector. Lieutenant Engelmann looked up at the firmament. It was getting cloudy and looked as if it might rain the next day. In the southeast, where the XI and XXXXII Armee Korps had already been stopped by heavy Russian defensive fire only a few miles behind the eastern bank of the Donets, the artillery was still rumbling, but in the area covered by Panzer Regiment 2 it was quiet right now.

Fortunately Engelmann didn't have to worry about the safety of his unit since the infantry forces had already passed them when dusk set in. Now the infantry forces positioned themselves half a mile farther up the road. Lieutenant Engelmann leaned against his tank and stared up at the sky. A few stars sparkled between the clouds. Just at this moment an uneasy feeling took hold of him. He sighed deeply. Even though he had never believed in the success of this operation, somewhere deep inside of him there had been hope that Citadel might be successful after all and could turn the war around once again in favor of the Wehrmacht. But now, on the evening of the first day, it became apparent that even though the Russians had been surprised, they definitely were not undersupplied and would be able to stop the German attack at the front line after a few miles of territorial gains only.

Although the 16th Panzer Division had accomplished its goal for the day by breaking through the second defense belt, this was pretty much the only successful action. In the southeast, Kempf's army was still stuck at the eastern bank of the Donets. As long as no more successes were achieved there, Engelmann's panzer division couldn't advance, either, for otherwise it would get too far ahead of the rest of the troops, thus exposing their flanks. So now they had to dig in by the road to Prokhorovka and wait for reports of success from the southeast.

It's so fucked up, Engelmann thought, contorting his face while shaking his head. *We're sitting here on the doorstep of Prokhorovka, the next interim goal on our way to Kursk, and all we can do is wait.* Every hour they were giving the enemy by waiting would let the Russians hole up better and bring in more reinforcements. Every hour of waiting diminished their chances of success, but there was just no other alternative.

Things were even worse up north. The enemy's forceful rocket launcher batteries had prevented the German forces from advancing just about everywhere. Only some elements of the XXXXI Panzer Korps as well as the XXIII Armee Korps stood in the trenches of the second defense belt; all the other formations were stuck somewhere in the first defense belt or even before. The situation *was* fucked up. Engelmann let out another sigh while his men's low voices and the faint rustling of clothes reached his ears. His soldiers had prepared a hole as cover under their tank, where they just had finished eating and were now getting ready to catch a few hours of sleep. Münster farted loudly, and while Nitz cursed him out, the originator of the fart and Ludwig cracked up. Apart from that, Nitz's complaints about his backache, which wouldn't let him get comfortable, dominated the background noise.

Engelmann was glad to have a crew that worked together so well in all areas, but as much as he'd like to, he couldn't feel cheerful today. Again he had spent a day on the battlefield where he had been forced to kill other human beings. He, the bright graduate with a degree in German literature, should instead be in school now, teaching young students things – things with meanings. Here in the war, though, the only thing he taught his young men was how to eliminate lives even more effectively. Yet as a tank commander, his position in the war machine was rather merciful because most of the time he didn't even come to see the consequences of his actions. Of course he did see the burning tanks, and naturally he could imagine what their crews went through. But he didn't have to kill anyone face to face, didn't have to watch how another human being's eyes became lifeless when he slew a stranger at short distance or rammed a bayonet into his chest. Engelmann shook his head and hoped that his service to his country would end soon. After four years of war it had to end at some point, but he was sure about one thing: As long as the Reich ordered him to fight, he would be at its service. That was the schizophrenia of his life and he was aware of it.

Again laughter rang out from under his tank. Engelmann envied his men for being able to be so cheerful despite the events of the past twelve hours and their overall situation. Certainly they had made some progress today, but as always in this war every success also had its dark sides: Today many good men had had to pay the price for Mission Citadel, good comrades … friends. Engelmann sighed once more. Then he decided to send a few more prayers to the Lord before going to sleep himself. With that intention he walked some steps away from his tank and disappeared behind an old broadleaf tree. He was aware of the fact that the number of atheists was growing steadily and that especially the war was promoting such convictions; that was why he always prayed in solitary. After all, he didn't want others to think he was crazy.

Dear God, he prayed in silence, *again I can't ask your forgiveness for the things I did today because I did them fully aware of their consequences. No matter what the military chaplains may say – I do know that my soul is condemned.*

But I want to ask you once again to at least protect the innocent and to punish the guilty in this cruel war. Please hold your protective hand over those who are righteous men.

Engelmann was sure that no one could ask more from the Lord in a war. Yet he still had another request: *Dear Lord, I also want to ask you to particularly watch over Elly and Gudrun. Elly is really a good person who deserves nothing bad and no war, either. Do with me as you think is right but please protect my family.*

Engelmann stepped back out from behind the tree and returned to his tank. While praying, he had neither folded his hands nor made the sign of the cross. In his opinion such rites and symbols that had been invented by institutionalized religions weren't necessary in order to talk to God.

124

The lieutenant stared at his tank, which shone in the moonlight. All the scars the last day had carved into it seemed to shine, too – for example the hit by the anti-tank guns from the previous morning had merely put some dents into the steel, discoloring it. Yet even this sight added to Engelmann's worries. Again he sighed because he sensed how limited the resources of the Wehrmacht were. On this day alone the Tigers here in their section had been reduced by a quarter of their numbers while two Panzer IIIs in his division had broken down, and the whole light platoon had stumbled into an ambush at the second defense belt and been destroyed. Those were casualties they would miss dearly tomorrow. Certainly they had also driven more than fifty Russian tanks to hell in this area alone, but tomorrow a hundred new tanks and the day after tomorrow one hundred fifty more would drive up, while the German army would fix some of the battered tin cans the best they could. After all, soon the Russians would produce more tanks per month than the Reich in a whole year – and they even had enough military personnel to fill every single one of them. It really *was* a fucked-up situation.

Prokhorovka, Soviet Union, May 4th, 1943
Kursk Front – 85 kilometers south of Kursk

Konev was dead. Killed in action on the very morning of the attack, not suspecting a thing while inspecting a Katyusha regiment that had been bombed by German bomber aircraft.

And now the Stavka had assembled all armies in the Kursk salient under one front. In the morning they had made Colonel General Sidorenko the commander-in-chief. The Russian officer poured over the situation map while sipping his glass of wine. He had just sent his adjutant and the other officers outside because he needed a moment for himself. Sidorenko emptied the glass, raised it and looked at the curved glass. Overwhelmed by a sudden rage, he threw it into a corner where it broke, jangling.

Sidorenko knew exactly what the Stavka was up to. He had more enemies there than was good for him, and now that the high command of the Red Army had totally missed out on the attack of the Germans in the Kursk salient, they wanted to blame him for the Germans' victory after the fact! Then they would shuffle him off to some insignificant post, maybe as a Gulag commander in Siberia? Sidorenko snorted. Surely a triumph of the fascists in Kursk wouldn't affect the overall Soviet victory. The Germans were simply not the equal of the superior Red Army. Here in the Kursk salient, however, things looked different. Sidorenko had no more than twelve armies in the salient, whereas the fascists apparently attacked with five armies – though covering just two sections of the front line while Sidorenko's formations had to cover the whole salient, which of course was defended by additional Nazi armies on the other side as well. Four of his armies were guard armies, so they were better equipped and trained and therefore had considerably more combat strength, but all of the guard formations were concentrated south of Kursk, and now, right in the middle of the battle, Sidorenko could hardly order major troop movements. The situation was totally fucked up. If only Konev had listened to him at the beginning of March when he pointed out the risks the Kursk salient held! But it wasn't until mid-April that the high command came up with the idea of reinforcing the front line here – much too late. Though two armies were moving in, the first soldiers wouldn't arrive before next week.

So he had to win this battle using the means available to him right here in the salient. He didn't have a lot but as of now Sidorenko made a decision: He wouldn't yield, and he wouldn't give up, either. He would win this battle – the battle of Kursk even though the situation was difficult for the Russians: The German attack forces mobilized a concentration of troops at one location like it had never been seen before. That impressed Sidorenko. He had calculated from the battle reports and the reports of the scouts that alone in the south thirty divisions had lined up on a front line that was only one hundred kilometers wide. If the scout reports were even roughly correct, then the fascists were mobilizing more tanks – and surely as many airplanes – for the attack at the Kursk salient than they had deployed for the attack against the whole motherland in 1941.

Sidorenko rubbed his eyes and yawned. It was already past midnight, and he had been up for more than twenty hours. Again the Russian officer inspected the situation map closely that his adjutant had just updated. It didn't look good: Though Sidorenko had been able to stop the fascists front troops almost everywhere, the Germans would fall asleep with a smile on their faces if they knew the price he had paid. Sidorenko had been able to deal with the Nazis only by using massive artillery – especially his rocket launchers.

In the afternoon he also had instructed his artillery to fire their ammunition reserves, which could only be used if so ordered. He had done this because he hoped to nip the German attack in the butt that way. But the damn Nazis did not seem willing to give up yet. Now his batteries were down to fifteen percent of ammunition in many places, in some parts of the North they were even down to five percent. Therefore he planned to re-arrange things tomorrow: He would take away large shares of ammunition supplies from the armies that were holding the western front line of the salient and supply the batteries in the North with those shells. At the same time he would concentrate his armored forces in the South where he intended to take the initiative, while up north he could only hope that well-aimed artillery blows against German attack attempts would remind the fascists of the hellfire of the first day, thus keeping them from advancing.

Disgusted, Sidorenko spat on the ground. He could puke when he thought of all the failures of his high command. The idiots in the Stavka had refused to listen to him and instead had preferred to concentrate their forces in the North and South for the great summer offensive, as well as at the Kalinin Front west of Moscow, where the fascists were supposed to start a major attack operation under the codename Citadel. What was Kursk, a small town in the middle of nowhere, to the generals? All they thought about were the fronts! Now Sidorenko had to deal with a shortage of ammunition and bad equipment, just like in 1941. Of course fresh artillery ammo was on its way but it was not here yet. The command kept rambling on about the Great Patriotic War of the socialist brothers, but here in the Kursk salient he felt more like a capitalist who had invested all his money in the wrong stock.

"Bah!" Sidorenko detested the Stavka's incompetence but for the time being he had to make do with what he had. Again he looked at the situation map while exhaustion pressed against his eyelids. He knew that if the fascists continued with their attack at the break of dawn, they would march right through. He would be unable to shower them again with such a barrage. He also knew that he didn't have enough qualified soldiers to brave both the enemy's wedge-shaped lines of attack. His idea for the battle was therefore to go for a decision in one single battle in the South, where he would crush the Nazis' attack troops with massive tank forces. If he warded off one of the attacks, he would prevent the pincer movement of the Germans and therefore the encirclement of four Soviet armies. The Russian officer pondered this idea for a few moments. Then his mouth widened in a satisfied smile. He had found his location for the decisive confrontation: Prokhorovka!

Lucerne, Switzerland, May 4th, 1943

Sometimes the Brits were very fast, Taylor had to admit. The Russians, too. When the German attack on the Kursk salient had started yesterday morning, the "island monkeys" had understood quickly that the plans that had been leaked into their hands were fake. Or else the Russians had understood it. Thomas just had not expected them to be too cowardly to do the dirty work by themselves.

No, they actually sent the police of Lucerne on Taylor! That was a clue that he was dealing with the Brits. After all, the Russians were still washing their dirty laundry themselves.

It's almost embarrassing, Taylor thought, grinning, while he hastily pulled on his clothes. *At least they still let me have fun!*

The news that his cover had been blown had reached him a few moments after he had sent the whore packing who had charged him one third of his monthly pay for a little sex.

Oh well, Switzerland is an expensive place! Thomas pushed the magazine into his P08, grabbed the knee joint and finished loading his weapon. *At least the military intelligence is paying me for this crap!*

The news had come via the telephone military intelligence had installed in the apartment before Taylor's arrival. Again he had to acknowledge that the spies of the Reich had done a good job for a change this time. So there was an officer at the Federal Police Department in Bern who liked to fatten his mediocre paycheck. He had immediately tipped off military intelligence about the request of the Swiss Federal Office to the police of Lucerne to provide them with personnel for the apprehension of a German spy.

Now Taylor had to disappear before the federal comrades in their democratic way could slap a death sentence on him. He pulled the ski mask he had knitted himself over his face so that only his eyes were still visible. The fewer people who saw him, i.e. could recognize him, the better! He checked his watch. Four minutes had passed since the phone call.

Time to get going! He told himself as he glanced out of the window one more time. Down on the street he saw Swiss police officers in their dark uniforms with the strange-looking caps gathering under the light of a lantern.

"Fuck!" he groaned in English; just another term he had learned from his father. Then he opened the door to the apartment and stormed outside onto the stairway with his pistol drawn. Two police officers downstairs already expected him; they were apparently waiting for their colleagues. Without hesitating, Taylor pulled the trigger of his Luger twice and gunned down the Swiss officers.

Two guys less that can stand in our way when we march in, he reflected and ran down the long hallway towards the back door. It was still dark but it wouldn't be long before the first sunbeams gleamed down on the roofs of the city.

Shouts and barked orders mixed with the moans of the two dying men as more police officers came charging through the entrance. Sirens began to wail and engines revved up. Taylor, however, had received the information soon enough before the police had been able to surround the building. He pushed the back door open with all his strength and ran out into the darkness. He had checked out potential escape routes hundreds of times before and knew the system of narrow alleys twisting between the medieval buildings like the back of his hand. Taylor finally bolted across the street and disappeared in a tiny alley; hectic yelling behind him while boots ran over cobblestones. Now the police officers approached the building from all sides and surrounded it but Taylor was long gone. He squeezed himself through narrow alleys and only crossed the main streets sprinting, where it couldn't be avoided. After three minutes of running and side-stepping he had gained enough distance to his former apartment. Finally he stopped between some tin garbage cans next to a closed restaurant, an old building with thick stone walls. He lingered for a few moments, caught his breath and rubbed his armpits that were dripping with so much sweat that puddles had formed beneath them. But he was in good enough shape that a little chase like this one didn't really put a strain on his body. Yet now that he finally had the time for it, he gave in to the adrenaline that was flooding through his body. What a great feeling it was when the sensations were heightened and fear drove his body to a top performance! Taylor did his job just for moments like this one! Just for these moments!

He turned around and then went through his mental archives of the city. He was good at remembering whole maps and city structures down to the smallest details; sometimes all he had to do was take a quick look at the object in question. He immediately knew how to proceed. He only had to walk a quarter of a mile through an extended alley that ran behind a row of businesses; then he would come to the park and, after that, to the cemetery where he had set up a campsite. Yes, Taylor had taken precautions precisely for a situation like this one. He ran this route quickly, crossed the narrow park that was currently used for growing potatoes thanks to the "Plan Wahlen" developed for agriculture and nutrition in Switzerland. Finally he reached the Friedental Cemetery, a large, eerie churchyard with silhouettes of countless gravestones that rose up from the ground like anti-tank barriers. A light breeze blew across the terrain and made Taylor shiver because he was soaked in sweat. For one quick moment, for just a second, he paused to catch his breath. Then he marched purposefully to the northeastern end of the cemetery, stepping on flowers and stomping on graves until he reached an old crypt overgrown with shrubs. Dawn was breaking while sirens howled in the distant city. He had to hurry because after his bloody deed the federal blokes were certain to block the roads and search every corner of Lucerne to find him. Taylor left the crypt behind and instead scrambled into the bramble bushes just to be embraced by their thorny arms.

"Bloody fuckers ..." he cursed when the thorns penetrated his pants, but in the end he found what he had been looking for: a small wooden box he had hidden in this spot more than a week ago. Taylor pulled the box out of the shrubs and took out its contents: a fresh set of clothes, a scarf and a hat, Swiss chocolates and another clip for his gun. He changed quickly before returning the box with his old set of clothes to its hiding place. Without wasting any time, Taylor hit the road. His destination was a military intelligence safe house north of Remigen in the Canton of Aargau, which bordered to the German Reich. He wanted to and had to put the distance of over thirty miles behind him as fast as possible.

*

The sun was already settling in the West when Taylor, who once again had managed to obtain a bicycle and had cycled the whole distance without a break, reached a small wooden cottage nestled deep in the woods. He immediately recognized the building made of lateral braces from a photo he had once seen. Thomas was dripping with sweat and hungry, too, because the chocolates hadn't done much to fill his stomach. And the last mile or so on the rough and bumpy forest terrain had been an agonizing ordeal. Now he hurled the bike on the ground in front of the cottage and fished the key, he had gotten in Stuttgart way back, out of his wallet.

He immediately stuck the key into the lock on the door, which let him in while he tucked a cigarette between his lips – his last cigarette, he noticed with chagrin.

The interior of the cottage was furnished sparingly; a table and two chairs made of dark wood as well as a cot were everything his accommodations had to offer. Naturally no weapons or anything else were stored here that could alert anyone who might search the cottage.

Instead Thomas merely found an envelope with a handwritten note inside. He glanced at the few lines. Though any layman would only see a love letter from a certain Juan to his sweetheart Luise in the document, Thomas recognized the real meaning of the words contained in the note. Instead of being sent back home, he had received his next order, which would lead him to Bern.

Still better than the Eastern Front! Yet he had to think of his comrades who were fighting for their lives somewhere in Russia right now. Then he noticed that the guys from military intelligence actually had thought of him: a tin can filled with tobacco and even a pack of cigarette paper sat on one of the chairs. Taylor's face broke out in a wide grin.

West of Ponyri, Soviet Union, May 4th, 1943
Heeresgruppe Mitte – 71 kilometers north of Kursk

Berning's company had been marching all afternoon. Now it was night again, but they would follow the front troops that had penetrated the Russian buffer zone near the mountain range around Olchovatka.

It seemed to Berning that the battles had proceeded considerably more smoothly on this second day of the operation – only a little artillery fire had filled the horizon and now, instead of constant shelling, one could only hear the thunder of guns now and then. Berning hoped that the Russian resistance had been broken and that the remaining Ivans had fled because he knew that the Russians liked to be overrun by the mechanized units just to take up the battle with the infantry that followed.

His boots stomped down the tall grass while he and his comrades crossed a wide open space in a skirmish line, which meant that all soldiers of the company advanced staggered next to each other in one long row. Looking first to his left and then to his right, Berning saw the silhouettes of soldiers who moved forward tense. He could hear the sound of gear banging against other gear and the constant rustling of grass and brush under the men's boots. They reached a rather large forest that needed to be crossed. Then, at the other end of the woods, they would take up position and spend the night there.

Berning didn't want to go on.

His belt with all his gear on his back was pulling him down, creating pains in his tailbone. And on top of that, the handle of his spade hit him in the back of his knees with every step he took. Every inch of his body itched, especially where dried or fresh sweat met countless mosquito bites. Berning inhaled and exhaled audibly; then he sighed deeply. It felt as if the weapon in his hands was getting heavier by the minute.

Thoughts of home flooded his mind, making everything even worse. He would much rather have spent the past hot summer day on the shore of Lake Neusiedl, so shallow that one could walk right through it from one end to the other.

"Berning," a voice called him.

He remembered going to the lake with his classmates after school, swiping grapes from the fields, and returning home in the evening with a sunburned back. Those had been wonderful, happy times when Berning hadn't had a care in the world.

"Berning!"

And of course he also had to think of Gretel and how he had held her breasts in his hands for the first time. They had protruded from her body like mounds of firm, hard flesh.

The hours he had spent with her in the barn during his last leave had certainly been the most exciting times of his whole life. Gretel and Franz Berning had always been inseparable. They had gone to school together before the National Socialists had come to power. They had also spent most of their afternoons and weekends together. Berning had helped out on Gretel's parents' vineyard estate, and Gretel had often been in his mother's kitchen, helping her with the pork roast or the vegetable soup. Last year in September they had swiped a bottle of Sturm from the basement and drunk it by the lake at night. Oh, how much trouble they had been in! Yet they seemed to be made for each other. They knew it; their parents knew it. Only this stupid war didn't seem to know it!

"BERNING!"

The sergeant thought he had heard a voice. The landscape of Lake Neusiedl dissolved into thin air, and suddenly the tall grass of the Russian plains was back. A figure was rapidly approaching from his right. It passed all of his comrades, and it was not until the figure was only one yard away from Berning that he recognized Staff Sergeant Pappendorf, whose whole face was panting with fury and who looked as if he was about to blow a fuse.

"BERNING!" he sputtered with rage, towering menacingly over the sergeant. Pappendorf's distorted face came so close to Berning's that their helmets collided while the staff sergeant intimidated him with a crazed look like that of a bird of prey right before its nosedive. "What the hell's wrong with you? You really are the worst sergeant I've ever met!" His voice boomed across the open plain while he spit out his words at Berning with a wet undertone.

All the Austrian could do was stare back.

"We're not in school where you can just doze off, you useless imbecile!"

The soldiers to his left and right were already gazing while the whole formation of the squad had come to a halt. Once again Pappendorf banged his helmet against Berning's Stahlhelm.

The sergeant wished that the ground would open up and swallow him.

"You can be damn glad that we're in the middle of a military action, you gun full of blanks! Otherwise I'd make you do push-ups until your skinny little arms snap! Keep your mind on the mission, will you?"

"Jawohl."

"Jawohl what?"

Berning felt like rolling his eyes. Even he knew that you used ranks sparingly out in the field, but Pappendorf obviously belonged to the species of non-commissioned officers that wanted to take any opportunity to bathe in the glory of their rank.

"... Herr Unterfeldwebel," Berning whispered and then lowered his eyes with feigned humility.

Stretching his head forward, Pappendorf breathed directly into Berning's ear, "You're nothing but a grunt! A pitiful little private with the wrong insignias on his shoulders!"

Then Pappendorf looked up. His short hair barely reached past the edge of his Stahlhelm, and his uniform was impeccable even though they were out in the field. The Eastern Front Medal, a round, silver-colored piece of metal with the Prussian eagle on it, sparkled on the left side of his chest – in the second buttonhole. Though he had been wearing the medal for a year now, it looked as if it had just left the embossing machine. Underneath the eagle was the swastika because the Wehrmacht wasn't able to replace all medals that quickly. Next to it, the silver wound badge dangled from his chest.

In addition, Pappendorf wore the EK I – the Iron Cross 1st class. The staff sergeant had even buttoned the collar that hardly anybody wore on the front line into his field blouse as the Wehrmacht regulations dictated. Several seconds passed while Pappendorf glared at Berning.

The sergeant had no idea what he was supposed to do. "What … what can I do for you, Herr Unterfeldwebel?" he finally stammered hesitantly.

Pappendorf lifted his nose so high that he could only see the sergeant out of the corner of his eye. Then he turned around and marched straight back out into the dark. Berning stared after his squad leader with pure hatred in his eyes.

What a slime ball, he thought. *Risks the lives of all of us just to play his power games!* Berning's contempt for this human being grew with every second while sweat ran over his hands, making the wood of his weapon slippery. The whole squad was still standing there without moving while the other squads had long since moved on. This bastard was really playing a dangerous game.

"Sergeant Berning?" Pappendorf's voice echoed across the open space.

Berning sighed. "Here, Herr Unterfeldwebel."

"Come here! On the double!" the squad leader's voice ranted.

Oh no! Berning immediately started to move. While he was running, his gear pressed into his back even more and kept banging against his arms and legs. He was already black and blue in those spots where the spade or the bread bag or the canteen kept hitting his body.

"Come on, move it!" Pappendorf drove him on.

Berning ran ahead of his comrades who were mere shadows in the dark down the row and finally reached his squad leader, whose outline was as straight as a candle, except for the fact that this candle was holding a submachine gun.

"Man, don't run in front of the weapons!" Pappendorf yelled, gesturing wildly. "Do you want to be gunned down by your own men when the Slavs come?"

Berning groaned and stopped, breathing hard. Pappendorf stuck his nose up into the air as high as if he wanted to touch the clouds. "Stay with the mission, Sergeant!" he admonished Berning in a threatening voice.

"Jawohl!" Berning was breathing so hard that he could barely get out this one short word. The combination of the strain of the short sprint and his fear of another confrontation was too much. He lowered his head, and his fingers clamped down on the shaft of his weapon while he desperately wished he was anywhere but here.

"JAWOHL WHAT?" Pappendorf yelled, spitting wet words into Berning's face. This guy obviously didn't care that they were in the middle of a war.

"Jawohl, Herr Unterfeldwebel!"

"There you go!" The staff sergeant looked at Berning for a moment before adding sharply, "What's wrong with your first assistant machine gunner?"

The question was harsh and caustic, and Berning had no idea what Pappendorf was talking about. He hesitated for a second and stared at the ground. Then he looked up with eyes glazed over. "I don't understand … err... what you mean, Herr Unterfeldwebel."

Pappendorf exploded. "WHAT THE HELL? ARE WE AT THE COUNTY FAIR HERE OR WHAT? IF YOU LET YOUR AMMUNITION BOXES RATTLE AGAINST EACH OTHER JUST A BIT LOUDER, EVEN STALIN IN MOSCOW CAN HEAR YOU!"

His words rolled across the open space like the shock wave of an explosion, echoing back and forth.

Berning just stood there like a dog in the rain; he didn't move.

"So stop it, will you, Sergeant?"

Berning nodded, turned around and ran back to his position.

He heard Pappendorf's voice yelling "Jawohl, Herr Unterfeldwebel!" behind his back; it sounded disappointed. Then Berning reached the left tip of the squad where he had his place with the MG fire team.

Wiping his face with his right hand, he could hear Pappendorf yelling, "Well, comrades! Thanks to your new assistant squad leader we fell behind the platoon. So: Double time! My speed; everybody keeps up with me!"

Double time? In the dark? HERE AT THE FRONT LINE? Berning couldn't believe what he had just heard. *Does this guy think we're still in basic training or what?*

Then he heard the high-frequency clatter of gear at the right that was so typical for running German soldiers.

Now they can hear us at least as far as Washington! But even this quick attack of black humor couldn't hide his true state of emotions. His stomach hurt even more, and his homesickness pressed into his guts, torturing him. Now the soldier on his right started to run, and Berning started to move, too. Breathing hard, he ran across the bumpy grass field and could feel the pressure points on his feet while his pulse began to quiver.

All of a sudden the air was full of hissing and whistling sounds in the distance. It sounded like airplanes taking off. The noise was coming closer at the speed of light.

"A Stalin organ!" somebody yelled. Then all hell broke loose around Berning. Countless rockets hit right into the marching area and threw up soil as if a giant's rake was digging up the land. Berning threw himself on the ground and covered his head with both hands. He could feel the air around him being sucked in by the explosions. Then it dispersed, thumping in all directions, tearing on his uniform and gear. The whole spectacle took no longer than about twenty seconds. Then the detonations gave way to the screams of dozens of soldiers in pain. Berning raised his head slowly but all he could see were the silhouettes of soldiers lying on the ground and in fresh craters. The first assistant machine gunner lay next to him, screaming, trembling and flailing like a fish out of water. There were more screams: from his right, from his left, from everywhere. Then Pappendorf started to yell, drowning out the rest of the noise. "Berning, come over here right now!" he yelled hectically.

Lutshki I, Soviet Union, May 4th, 1943
Heeresgruppe Süd – 87 kilometers south of Kursk

The southern front-line sections of Operation Citadel were in the grip of the dark night that had ended the attack movements of the day. Lieutenant Engelmann – who had still been pessimistic about the further progress of the operation – had witnessed how a single day could change the fortunes of war: On the first day of the operation, the land gains had still been modest, and the German Army had clearly failed to reach the goals for that day almost everywhere –Engelmann's division had made one exception to that rule. Today, however, they seemed to have faced a totally different enemy.

There had hardly been any Russian artillery fire at all, and enemy airplanes had been driven away from the airspace much more successfully. In the evening, the formations of the Wehrmacht were able to report considerable progress in almost all sections, and indeed this second day of Operation Citadel literally spurred the German soldiers on and even gave the skeptics the necessary confidence that they were on a mission that wasn't doomed right from the start.

In the face of their success, Lieutenant Engelmann had also seen a little light at the end of the tunnel. But then his regiment had done its share, too. Today they had moved north on a section of the road to Prokhorovka where the infantry and Panzergrenadier forces of the division had taken the villages of Kalinin and Lutshki I.

In the course of the battles around these two villages, the III Abteilung of Panzer Regiment 2 had to fend off a counter attack of enemy tanks of the British Churchill model. Engelmann's platoon had survived all three combat actions without any losses; the 9th Company had lost one Panzer III; the III Abteilung had to deplore three tanks, one of which only had engine failure, though. This battalion alone had destroyed 23 Russian tanks and 36 artillery guns.

And the attacks on the other sections had been more than satisfactory: Formations of Kempf's army had blocked the road from Belgorod to Korotcha and moved up north far enough to gain again a coherent front with the units of the 6th Army. That paved the road for another push tomorrow.

Lieutenant Engelmann had used his tarp to get comfortable underneath his tank. While Nitz was already snoring loudly next to him, Ludwig was writing a letter to his father, Münster was stuffing himself with a margarine sandwich and Born was reading the last chapters of his science fiction novel in the light of a candle, the lieutenant had spread out his situation map and was studying the area once again. He put a piece of chocolate into his mouth and pulled his blanket all the way up to his shoulders. It had cooled down, so Engelmann had also wrapped a scarf around his neck to protect it from the cold while a few drops of rain fell on the area around Prokhorovka. Tomorrow morning at 0400 German time the Luftwaffe would fly a massive attack against the city and enemy anti-tank gun batteries in front of it. Then, at 4:30 a.m., they would advance along the road up to the city limits, under cover of the Tiger panzers, and hopefully take the whole city before dusk set in. Of course military intelligence had not overlooked the fact that the

Russians were gathering large tank units around Prokhorovka, including many guard formations, but that was fine with Engelmann. Somewhat thrilled by the success they had achieved today, he hoped they could already deliver the decisive blow tomorrow, ending the fight. With a little bit of luck they would then, after taking Kursk and stabilizing the front line, return to the rear echelon. And then there were the Tigers that had taken over much of his work and had always stood between his own unit and the enemy like armored shields. Since the mechanics had worked on the broken-down tanks since last night, doing overtime, for tomorrow Engelmann could count on 34 Tigers again. Not bad!

He took another glimpse at the map. The city was surrounded by a powerful defense ring while enemy forces along the road leading up to it had most likely been positioned there to stop the German attack columns by seizing their flanks. Engelmann knew what they had to watch out for. The territory gave the defensive forces an advantage, and he couldn't count on the German Air Force eliminating every single emplacement. Tomorrow wouldn't be easy, but the united firepower of the artillery, the tanks, the infantry and the air force would get them through it with flying colors.

Finally Engelmann folded his map and put it aside because Cyrillic letters and tactical symbols were already dancing around in his head. He turned on his back and stared at the belly of his tank. Of course he could be sitting in a cozy farmhouse with the company commander, drinking beer, but in the presence of the enemy he preferred to stay with his men.

"Herr Leutnant?" Born's voice interrupted his thoughts. Turning around, Engelmann saw that Münster and Ludwig were already asleep.

"Mhm?" Engelmann looked into Born's large blue eyes.

"Can I ask you a question?"

"Sure."

"Even if it is a … well … critical question?"

"A critical question?"

"Yeah..."

"What do you mean by that?"

"I mean a critical one … a question you may not want to hear."

"Now you've made me curious – why don't you just come out with it?" Engelmann smiled, pleased that his men trusted him so much.

"Well … I've just been thinking about all this. About the war … about what we're doing here."

"Yeah, I've noticed that."

"I've been reading this book, Herr Leutnant." He pointed to the German edition of *The War of the Worlds*. "Have you read it?"

"No, that's not my kind of thing. I prefer realistic classics."

"Anyway, it's about creatures from outer space that attack human beings. They're from Mars and they want to settle on Planet Earth and claim it all for themselves."

"I see."

"When I think about it, it strikes me that in this war..." He hesitated. Not that long ago it would have been extremely risky to talk about certain things – particularly critical things – and even today the Reich was certainly

146

not a democracy with a guarantee of freedom of speech. But then Born dared to say it anyway. "... Well, in this war *we* are the Martians. Okay, Poland attacked us first, it was all over the radio and the newspapers, and of course we had to react against those who had declared war on us."

Engelmann frowned while Born continued. "But why Russia? Why are we here?"

Engelmann nodded slowly. Questions like this entered his mind more frequently than he cared for, and sometimes the answers he came up with were anything but comfortable. The lieutenant sensed that Born had to speak his mind about something that was threatening his inner peace.

„You know," the corporal continued, „when we kill Russians in a battle – like we did today – then sometimes I think that they're just people, too, who are fighting for their lives. Who are defending their country – against intruders. For a long time I used to think that we were the good guys. But now – well – for a while I've been suspecting that we're the bad guys in this war. The attackers, the Martians."

Engelmann thought for several seconds because he didn't want to smack the man down with slogans. Instead he wanted to give him a well-founded answer. "We're in a war, Herr Stabsgefreiter," he finally replied in a tone of voice that indicated that he was choosing every word extremely carefully. "Unfortunately there are no good guys in a war. There are only people who kill each other. I know religious faith doesn't mean anything to you but trust me, the God I believe in doesn't like this war any more than we do. But it seems to be necessary because apparently we human beings can't live together in peace. Maybe first the cruelest wars have to be fought that afterwards mankind can live together in peace. So to put your mind at ease, all I can tell you is: We Germans are neither the good guys nor the bad guys. You always have to look at everything in the big picture: the great war, the Treaty of Versailles, poverty and starvation. Let me tell you honestly: I was no friend of the Nazis and I like the NSDAP the best where it is right now: as political marginalia without any recognizable influence. I think our new government is doing a lot of things better, especially here in the East. Now we're conducting a war again, no longer a campaign of complete destruction, and we stick to certain rules, as absurd as that may sound when it comes to fighting for your life.

One of the subjects I studied at the university was how societies work. Believe me, wars don't start because one man points a finger at another country. Wars are preceded by millions of actions, events and things whose combined effect nobody can predict. That's why I unfortunately can't give you a complete answer. It looks like the 20th Century is to be the century of wars. So we just have to accept the situation the way it is, and it doesn't matter any more – that is maybe the saddest part of it – who was originally responsible for the outbreak of the war. These days all that matters is surviving and saving our *Heimat*. That's all it is about."

Born smiled. "Thanks, Herr Leutnant. That's exactly why I asked *you*."

Engelmann had to smile, too, while his own words echoed in his mind. His answer may not have been satisfactory but at least it was sincere. Suddenly he wished for one thing: When he became a teacher sometime in the future, he wished to have students like Eduard Born.

West of Ponyri, Soviet Union, May 4th, 1943
Heeresgruppe Mitte – 71 kilometers north of Kursk

"Come on, get the radio operator!" Pappendorf yelled but this time there was no hatred in his voice; it sounded just frantic. The staff sergeant crouched on the ground, bending over a young soldiers whose chest had been torn to pieces by a large metal splinter and who only lay there, twitching, while bloody foam bubbled out of his mouth. Berning could see the wound only in the light of his flashlight, and he could barely make out Pappendorf's bloody hands that were fishing a sketch of the area out of the map case hanging from his shoulder. He then spread out the piece of paper over the abdomen of the wounded soldier. Berning was unable to do anything but stare at the torrent of blood that was flowing out of his comrade's body. His fingers shook, he felt his legs cramp up, and he had left his weapon at the spot where he had been surprised by the rocket attack.

"Berning, Come on, man! The radio operator!" Pappendorf shouted without looking up from the sketch. The sergeant started to run. The air was filled with cries of pain, with screaming men wrestling with death while some of his comrades were slowly struggling to get up.

"Werner?" Berning gasped, stumbling between the dead bodies and wounded or dazed soldiers. PFC Werner was the radio operator of Pappendorf's squad, which meant that he had to carry a 40-pound backpack around with him at all times.

"Werner?" he whispered in a trembling voice. He looked around. Hege looked dazed, shook his head and grabbed his machine gun to check it for damages. Farther away, another comrade lay on the ground, moaning and holding his leg. Berning took his flashlight and walked up and down the rows of men. Then he noticed a square-looking silhouette on the ground lying beside a crater. He took one step towards it and let the beam of his flashlight roam across the object he had discovered. All that was left of Werner was a bloody torso, half a leg, and his head down to his lower jaw. The rocket explosions had strewn the rest of his body all over the place. Berning puked like a horse. He threw up disgusting chunks of food, garnished with stomach acid, into the grass while getting dizzy. He closed his eyes and turned his head away while his shaking hands fumbled to feel the radio. He clenched his teeth and wanted to scream while his fingers dug the radio out of the chunks of flesh. He could feel the warm blood stick to his hands and lower arms. More undigested food rose from his stomach and up his throat but he kept his mouth shut though it was filling with vomit. With tears in his eyes, he swallowed and yanked on the backpack. Suddenly it came loose. He ran back to Pappendorf and put the radio down next to him without saying a word.

"Find the platoon's frequency!" Pappendorf muttered in a voice that was astonishingly easy to understand despite all the screaming. Again Berning stared at the soldier with the splinter in his belly, whose eyes were wide open while he was coughing up blood. Berning couldn't tear his eyes away from him.

"Jesus Christ, Berning! Find the platoon's frequency, will you?" With these words Pappendorf, who was busy drawing something onto his sketch with a pencil, brought Berning back to the present. The sergeant shook himself quickly like a wet dog. Then he looked at the bloody instrument panel of the radio that was miraculously undamaged.

"Is ..." He was unable to get out another word.

"Berning!" Pappendorf yelled but the sergeant just stared in all directions, mesmerized, taking in the contours of all these wounded, dead and uninjured soldiers.

"BERNING!" Pappendorf bellowed, straining his voice.

"Jawohl?"

With his pencil Pappendorf pointed at a dot on the sketch. "Grab the MG and a soldier. I want a secured area here ahead of the woods. Then come back. Move it!"

Panting, Berning set out to do as ordered. He got Hege and another soldier. Then he took both to the point Pappendorf had indicated on the map, where he found an indentation in the ground near two pine trees. He positioned the fire team there and ran straight back to Pappendorf. Again he couldn't tear his eyes away from the disaster the Stalin organs had created. When he had reached his squad leader, he stopped without saying a word.

The sketch, which was smeared with blood by now, was still on the abdomen of the wounded soldier. His hands were shaking but apart from that he just lay there, blinking.

"Has the area been secured or why are you back?" Getting up, Pappendorf stared directly at Berning. His eyes were steely, and the sharp undertone, for which the staff sergeant was known, was back in his voice.

"Yes..." Berning was unable to think clearly. His ears hurt and his head was spinning.

"Well, then report it, will you?"

"Jawohl ..."

"Jawohl, Herr Unterfeldwebel!"

"Jawohl, Herr Unterfeldwebel!"

"Jawohl what?"

"Jawohl, the secured area has been set up!"

"HERR UNTERFELFWEBEL!" Pappendorf roared, spitting his words into Berning's face. "THE SECURED AREA HAS BEEN SET UP, HERR UNTERFELDWE-BEL!"

"Jawohl, Herr Unterfeldwebel."

"Then start to take care of the wounded! The platoon is sending a squad that will help us transport them to the casualty area."

"Yes..." Berning's lips trembled. "Jawohl!" he stuttered, getting himself under control just in time. He looked around, completely lost. Then he froze when he noticed Pappendorf's penetrating look.

"... Herr Unterfeldwebel!" he added hastily. Then he fished the large package with the first-aid kit from the lining of his field blouse without knowing at first where to go with it.

Finally he squatted down beside Pappendorf, tore the package open, and brought his shaking fingers to the thick metal splinter that was sticking out of the soldier's chest.

"Not him!" Pappendorf bawled. "He's kaputt!"

Berning stared at his squad leader wide-eyed. Then he looked at his comrade on the ground. The wounded soldier was spluttering blood and his eyes looked feverish. His face was deathly pale.

"NOW GO, BERNING!" Pappendorf's roar hit the sergeant like a hurricane. He got up and ran off – panic-stricken. He had no idea where to go or what to do. His fingers gripped the bandages and smeared the radio operator's blood all over them. Then he heard that same noise in the distance: airplanes that were taking off. Berning stopped in his tracks and looked up at the sky while the sound was becoming louder and louder. He was unable to move.

Suddenly someone threw himself against Berning with full force. He lost his balance and fell on the ground. He felt Pappendorf's arms pushing him down.

"Sergeant, get down, man!" the staff sergeant yelled. Within the blink of an eye, the howling concerto of the rockets ding down started again, and the area west of Ponyri turned into pure hell for the soldiers of the reconnaissance squadron.

Lutshki I, Soviet Union, May 5th, 1943
Heeresgruppe Süd – 87 kilometers south of Kursk

In the light of the rising sun Lieutenant Engelmann, looking out of his cupola, witnessed the combined power of Luftflotte 4, one of the primary air fleets of the Luftwaffe that crowded the sky with seventy-five Henschel Hs 129 ground-attack planes, twin-engined one-seaters with a futuristic design, on their way to Prokhorovka. Engelmann knew that the "can openers" would make his job a lot easier. The Henschels were, for good measure, also accompanied by a group of Ju 87s. gesetz

The most impressive of them all, however, were the twelve heavy Heinkel He 177 bombers. They were giants with one propeller on each wing and a big glass cockpit at the nose. Protected by the other planes, the bomber squadron flew in the center of the formation that was itself accompanied by fighter planes. Therefore nearly two hundred German airplanes were swarming in the cloudy sky on their way to the enemy lines.

Engelmann was quite aware of the fact that the He 177s' mission was not to dump their three tons of bombs per plane over the Russian trenches but rather over the city itself. He hoped that there were no more civilians there; at the same time he knew all too well that today would most likely claim innocent victims.

*

The German planes were already small dots on the horizon when Panzer Regiment 2 received the order to attack. At 4:32 a.m. German time – here in Russia it was already early morning – the thirty-four Tiger tanks of the heavy tank battalion went into motion, crushing the

154

road to Prokhorovka as well as the area to its left and right with their tracks. Once again the III Abteilung started to move in the wake of their big brothers. The 6th Army was on the way to its first goal, which was to be taken today. In the East their flanks reached the Donets, and therefore the troops of Kempf's army that were farthest toward the front, while in the West the mechanized troops of the 2nd Panzerarmee progressed towards Beloye. This mass of forces in a relatively small space allowed the German Army to form a closed line. In the North it lined up with two more armies that pushed forward in the direction of Olchovatka to finally penetrate the Russian lines completely.

*

The territory to the left and right of the road to Prokhorovka was a wide open space only interrupted by a few groves, and in addition it was rather hilly. Every few hundred yards a farm or a tiny village hugged the road, but there were no more civilians around.

To the right of the road, the III Abteilung tore through the field while the I Abteilung used the road. The Tiger battalion marched ahead, fanned out widely, thus placing itself almost completely in front of the regiment.

Engelmann looked at his map. They were only a few thousand yards away from the southern bank of the Psel River, which flowed around a bend here before it forked off to the North where its source was. Now they came up to a narrow branch of the Donets that was no more than a brook. The panzers of Engelmann's platoon crossed the water while the Tigers in front of them were already plowing through the next open space over a length of several miles. On the horizon a small village appeared that sat enthroned up on a hill. The road twisted and turned uphill all the way to the buildings. Engelmann looked out of his turret at the area ahead of them and saw the black smoke columns that rose up everywhere in the village and on the surrounding hills. Over there the Luftwaffe had already raged and now the German artillery was busy to produce more match-wood. With every one of Engelmann's heartbeats, dozens of shells fell on the houses, tore off roofs and churned up the ground. Huge pillars of dirt rained down on the village but even that couldn't break the Russian resistance. Their guns, which were positioned everywhere between the buildings and the surrounding hills, boomed already, tickling the Tigers. The latter returned the greetings and silenced several enemy guns with their blasts while the "Ratsch Bumms", as the Germans called the Russian 76 millimeters divisional guns M1942 based on the sound they made, blasted at the German steel colossuses from the hinterlands. Engelmann stared at his map and tried to translate the Cyrillic letters into something he could understand.

"That village up there should be Bele … Behlenkin … Belenkino … to hell with it! You know what I mean. Hans, take up position behind the narrow mound 60 yards in front of their positions. Ebbe, let the platoon gather to our left and assume attack position. Be prepared for Russian counter attacks!"

"Yes sir, the platoon to our left," Nitz confirmed and squeezed in behind the radio. Engelmann's tank moved towards the position he had ordered and stopped there.

The Tigers ahead of them also took up their positions. In the meantime the Russian resistance was almost completely extinguished.

Engelmann took a glimpse at his watch. *Already past 9 a.m.*, he groaned silently. Despite the fact that there hadn't been much enemy fire today, things progressed slower than planned. Still, he intended to reach Prokhorovka before nightfall. Biting his lower lip, he looked ahead. Thick clouds hung over Belenikhino. If they got any downpour, everything would quickly turn into mud here, and then the offensive would progress even more slower.

Engelmann put a piece of chocolate into his mouth while his mind continued to race. Behind Belenikhino the regiment would turn north and surmount the hills this side of the curve of the Psel River before moving on to Prokhorovka. The schedule was extremely tight, and the lieutenant worried that it would be already now difficult to stick to it.

"The Panzergrenadiers will be here in twenty minutes," Nitz, who had overheard a radio message, announced.

"They'd better hurry up," Engelmann mumbled. Since any built-up area was a very dangerous territory for tanks, the plan of operations had the men of Panzergrenadier Regiment 64 conquering the village under cover of the tanks while the German artillery moved into positions directly behind the front troops so as to reach all the way behind Prokhorovka in the ensuing combat actions.

*

Engelmann watched the Panzergrenadiers that approached the village platoon by platoon. The soldiers advanced, disembarked and under cover of the half-tracks that could give sufficient suppressive fire if needed due to their mounted machine guns. Behind III Abteilung numerous artillery guns took up position on the hills that blocked the view at the landscape farther away. Engelmann glanced at Elfriede's interior. Though it wasn't that hot today, the air inside the tank was stale again. Münster slept in a bath of his own sweat while Ludwig and Nitz were lost in thoughts. Eduard Born was absorbed in a new book. The cover read *The World Set Free*.

Shots were fired from the distant village. Russian snipers had holed up there and fired with long guns and small anti-tank rifles. Wherever an enemy position was discovered and no German soldiers were around, the Tigers sprang into action. One of the heavy tanks blasted a whole house into the air with an high explosive projectile while the foremost Panzergrenadiers reached the buildings on the outskirts and at once separated from their half-tracks.

To Engelmann, his comrades looked like ants that were making their way into the village. He could see tiny figures dropping like flies or disappearing into houses. Soon fresh smoke columns joined the long plumes that already hung over Belenikhino. The Panzergrenadiers advanced building by building and had soon cleared the whole southern part of the village.

The radio hissed. "I Abteilung reports retreat movements. The Ivan's infantry's leaving the hills in the East," Nitz informed them.

"Roger," the lieutenant replied while his eyes kept looking ahead. How glad he was to be able to sit here in his tank instead of having to trek through the enemy villages with his submachine gun and pistol! Yet the Russians didn't seem to measure up to the Panzergrenadiers. Though some shots could still be heard in the area ahead, the firing was no longer as intense as it had been a few minutes ago. Only here and there the noise of a gun or a mortar could be heard, while now and then one of the half-tracks fired a blast that echoed in sound waves across the land. Nitz pressed the receiver of the radio to his ear when a new radio message came in.

"Nine one, copy that," he confirmed, turning to the lieutenant. "Sepp, the Panzergrenadiers report: enemy resistance has been broken. The Russians are withdrawing from the village."

That was quick, Engelmann thought, glancing at his Swiss watch. *11:02. We've caught up a bit.*

"We should get ready," Nitz forwarded the next radio message.

"Okay. Then wake up, all of you, and put the books away!"

Born closed his book but of course Münster snored on blissfully.

"Hans! Wake up!" Engelmann repeated firmly. No chance – the sergeant was sound asleep. Engelmann climbed down into the belly of his tank, grabbed Born's book and slapped Münster on the head with it. The soldier woke up in an instant and was directly alert.

"Man, I was just dreaming about my girlfriend," he complained softly, rubbing his eyes.

"Now, everybody – get ready!" Engelmann ordered. Just then a hectic voice came through the radio, filling the interior of the panzer. It was only then that the lieutenant noticed how loud it had become outside. He stuck his head through the hatch and saw the trouble they were in.

"Russian counter attack!" he yelled. Everybody in his tank immediately began to move. Hans started the engine while Ludwig already reached for the shells.

To the left and right of the village, dozens of light and medium Soviet tanks rushed onto the plain. They tore across the land at breakneck speed, quickly shortening the distance between them and the German tanks.

The 88-millimeter guns of the Tigers already responded, turning some of the attacking tanks into metal scrap, but that didn't seem to daunt their comrades.

Ignoring their casualties, the Russian tanks tore on while constantly firing. Huge columns of dirt rained down on the Tigers and then on the panzers of III Abteilung.

"Hans, get moving! Close in three hundred meters to the Tigers, then keep left!"

"Copy that! Step on it, then left!"

"The platoon shall follow us and take up attack positions on the left next to the Tiger with the perforated side skirt. We'll tackle anything that goes for their left flank!"

Münster accelerated, and Elfriede started moving, groaning and moaning. The whole platoon followed behind Engelmann. Radio communication among all tanks was a much underrated advantage in combat the Russian tankers didn't possess. But once again they approached in numbers that made ran cold sweat down the spine of every German tank crew member. There was still no end to the flood of tanks streaming over the hills and onto the flat plain. Engelmann had already counted fifty vehicles and and there were still coming more. Instead of deploying shrewd tactics, they just flooded the battlefield, and in the end this tactic might even be successful. Engelmann bit on his lower lip – a bit too hard, because he suddenly tasted blood. While he held onto his hatch' rim with both hands, his mind continued to race.

The Russian tanks just smashed right into the formation of the Tigers at full speed, forcing the Germans into a dangerous close combat. The enemy tanks formed a wide skirmish line without any flank security.

Engelmann had an idea. "Ebbe!" he yelled into his throat microphone.

"Sepp?" Nitz responded.

"Radio message to the commander: Suggestion! The 9th breaks out of the Abteilung, bypasses the heavy battalion on the left side and attacks the enemy's flank."

"Break out, left side, into flank, Roger!"

"Hans, step on the gas and turn left now."

"Yep, Sepp."

Ahead of them, one Russian tank after another took a beating and turned into a bonfire of steel, gasoline and human flesh. Yet the sheer mass of enemy forces had its effect. The left track of a Tiger was torn apart after having already been hit three times in the side skirt. Then the ammunition supply of another tank exploded, lifting the turret and hurling it several feet up into the air. The heavy steel construction crashed down next to another panzer with a loud bang, propelling soil and bushels of grass up into the air. The Tigers continued to fire while maneuvering skillfully to form a wedge so as to present their armored fronts to both Russian attack fronts that were streaming over the hills to the left and right of the village. Finally the flood of tanks to the left came to an end but around seventy enemy tanks had already entered the open field. Armor-piercing projectiles burst between the vehicles of the III Abteilung, while the German artillery was firing full power in the background and aimed their guns almost directly at their visible targets. More Russian tanks – mostly T-34s – rolled from the right onto the battlefield, but some of them went off-track and ended up in the village, where they, pinned between the buildings, were easy prey for the Panzergrenadiers. Again it became obvious that most Soviet tanks had no radios because the Russians had apparently not yet noticed that the village was no longer under their control. Now they paid a high price for their ignorance. From all sides German soldiers stormed towards the clumsy tanks, climbed up the hulls and threw grenades through the hatches or fired through the eye slits. Mines and sticky bombs were also in high demand. Engelmann could see the small dots that crept all over the enemy tanks right before the steel monsters came to a halt.

"The old man agrees," Nitz called out to Engelmann. His voice was almost drowned out in the fighting ruckus. "He's giving his orders to the other platoons now."

Again Nitz pressed the receiver to his ear when another message came in. "1st platoon leads the raid!" he yelled.

"As always." Engelmann looked ahead where the forward troops of the enemy's tank formation crashed into the rows of Tigers and fired at them. The two steel fronts jammed into each other and went for hunt with armor-piercing rounds. That was the moment when the battle turned confusing. Dense clouds of smoke surrounded the tanks of both factions that met for a deadly dance. While the German vehicles attempted to stick together in small combat units and were thus able to keep their positions, the Russians drove around aimlessly and attacked anything within reach. The Soviets paid the price for their tactics or the lack thereof, the Germans paid equally for their lack of numbers; ten Tigers had already been hit and went up in flames. Yet the combat zone was also littered with smoldering and smoking olive-colored wrecks.

Now the tanks of the Panzer Regiment 2 also caught up with the Tigers in order to aid their big brothers. Panzer IIIs and IVs, even several Panzer IIs joined the action and fired everything their ammunition supplies allowed for. To the right of the village, several self-propelled assault guns took up position and destroyed no fewer than three T-70 – tiny, pyramid-shaped tanks.

"AP round!" Engelmann shouted. Born grabbed one of the shells and inserted it in the chamber.

"Loaded!" he screamed, almost drowned out by the deafening noise of fight. With full speed, the tanks of the 9th Company broke out of the formation of Tigers, navigated towards their left flank, then turned to the right.

The command tank stayed in the wake of the 2nd Platoon. Though the motto of the German Wehrmacht was actually "leading from the front", in light of the weak tank armor and the gun that was merely a dummy, nobody blamed the company commander for doing this. At least he was present during the attack. The transmission power of his radio would have sufficed to direct his troops from the artillery positions in the back.

"Step on it, Hans," Engelmann ordered and disappeared through his hatch. They were about to get into close combat, so he wanted to be sure to have at least several millimeters of armored steel around him.

Münster steered Elfriede in a wide turn into the flank of the Russian tanks that had kept some distance between themselves and the Tigers, which provided them with the opportunity to fire at the Germans from the hills. Squinting, Engelmann peered through one of his eye slits. Now it was important to immediately eliminate the enemy forces that were already aiming their guns at 9th Company. Since the commanders of the Russian tanks were unable to communicate with each other, the Germans had the opportunity to surprise and shoot at as many tanks from the side as possible.

"Ebbe! Our platoon tackles anything that tries to stops us. Allocation of targets from left to right. The other platoons are to take care of the rest." In combat, Engelmann sometimes turned into a company commander but he also did it because the real commander let him – and because Engelmann simply was a good company leader. Nitz's words chased each other as he passed the orders on to the other panzers.

"Three o'clock, eight hundred..." the lieutenant started his target address because one of the enemy tanks suddenly turned in a tight turn to present his front to the 9th Company. Ludwig activated the tank's turret traverse and aimed the barrel at the Russian tank.

"Get rid of it!" Engelmann called out.

Münster stopped. Ludwig fired but he missed the target. The AP projectile exploded in the grass, and tons of soil sprayed in all directions. Immediately Born loaded another shell. Laschke's tank fired and destroyed the target while the two other tanks of the platoon were focusing on other targets to the left. In the meantime the vehicles of the company started to mingle. Panzer IIIs and IVs rolled into battle in a wild mix, deployed and considerably cleaned out the rows of Russian tanks. Then, without forewarning, one Panzer IV of the 3rd Platoon blew up in a large detonation that turned it into a chunk of metal scrap engulfed by flames.

"Where did that come from?" Münster groaned but Engelmann couldn't see anything through the narrow eye slits. At the same time all hell broke loose over the 9th Company. The German tanks were surrounded by thick columns of dirt while a Panzer III from the 2nd Platoon was hit in the road wheels, throwing its tracks off. It came to a stop and no longer moved.

"Guard tank at eight o'clock, 1 200!" Nitz, who had just received the message over the radio, yelled.

Shit! Engelmann moaned silently, *they know the same tricks we do!*

"Turn, turn, turn!" he yelled at the top of his voice.

"They're Shermans!" Nitz added in an excited voice while hysterically turning the adjusting screws of his radio. Münster turned the panzer around. The next tank of the 3rd Platoon was already going up in flames while its hatches popped open and men frantically started to climb out of the death trap, their tank had suddenly transformed into. Looking through his eye slits, Engelmann could clearly make out the loader whom he had shown a picture of Elly and Gudrun the day before. Now the man was crawling out of his tin can. His uniform was on fire and he threw himself onto the ground. Then the lieutenant saw the Russian tanks that had so cleverly stabbed them in the back. About fifteen Shermans – items on loans from the U.S.A. to the Soviet Union – came up behind the German panzer company. The Shermans were slim battle tanks with a broad turret that sat enthroned almost exactly in the center of the hull; their fronts and tails were slanted sharply. Engelmann had never run across these tanks on a battlefield before and didn't really have their data at hand because he had thought that these lend-lease tanks were used only rarely. But rare or not – here they were, and Engelmann had to waste precious seconds checking his charts. His eyes widened in surprise: Though these tanks were not armored all that well, none of his platoon's tanks could withstand their 75-millimeter guns – not at this distance.

The Germans and the Russians fired, and there were casualties on both sides. Then the 9th Company got unexpected support. The artillery batteries positioned less than a mile away started to fire directly at visible targets, and today the boys were veritable sharpshooters. The first salvo tore up the side of a Sherman, blasted the turret – including the red star – of another tank away and turned three more armored fighting vehicles into burning infernos.

Wrecked tanks, metal scrap and bodies burned to a crisp, were scattered all over the battlefield; and now that the Germans had destroyed seventy percent of the attacking forces, the Russians realized that they had been defeated and started to withdraw. Under fire, the Russian tanks retreated behind the hills, while the Shermans that had crept up through a thin section of forest were completely annihilated. Engelmann's tank fired the last shot of this battle and hit the remaining Sherman right in the middle of the hull while it was trying to drive backwards into the woods. The round penetrated the armor and extinguished all life inside.

Engelmann would have liked to lean back in his turret and take a break but it wasn't that simple. What was important now was to take up position again, to regroup and to request support to look after the wounded and dead. But then the order to pursue ASAP, issued by the regimental commander, Colonel Rudolf Sieckenius, came in over the radio. Engelmann sighed.

Of course it was sensible of Oberst Sieckenius to use the dynamics of the attack to advance directly to the hills of the south bank in the Psel River bend, but Engelmann was so exhausted from the battle that he felt like just going to sleep under his Elfriede. The lieutenant had dark rings under his eyes when he looked at his crew's sweaty, serious faces and nodded slowly.

"Let's go then," he said, faking enthusiasm and clapping his hands.

*

The rest of the day was one long sequence of smaller tank skirmishes. Engelmann's unit didn't make it as far as the goal of this stage, Prokhorovka. The forces farthest at the front were stopped right before the city limits. But they had conquered the hills west of it that were so important. The Russians had defended each one of their positions bravely and fiercely in murderous combat. Again and again small enemy tank formations had regrouped for counter attacks and drained the energy of the 16th Panzer Division. Constant dripping wears away the stone. Above all, enemy infantry forces let themselves be overrun, over and over again, just to engage German soldiers and supply corps troops that followed on foot in fights. For this reason Engelmann's unit had to turn around twice to go back to places they thought they had already conquered and fight there once again.

In the evening they finally got the order to stop the offensive and make camp so the exhausted soldiers could rest and repair the tanks, some of which were badly damaged and most of which were out of fuel and ammunition.

The forces of the Panzer Regiment 2 alone had achieved a three-digit number of hits that day, and the Tigers could celebrate almost as many. Baffled, Engelmann shook his head and wondered where the Russians got all these tanks from.

Yet he knew this much: Tomorrow just as many or even more enemy tanks would await them. The Russians were still rallying their armored forces near Prokhorovka.

The 16th Panzer Division, however, was battle-weary and had already lost more than a quarter of its panzers because they were either destroyed or immobile in the workshops. The Tigers only numbered twenty-two tanks by now. Engelmann had also suffered a loss: Meyer's tank had been hit and, apart from the radio operator, who had suffered severe burns and been taken to the field hospital, every man had been killed in action. Engelmann sighed. Here it was again, that pessimism in his heart. Suddenly he wasn't certain at all any more whether Citadel could be brought to a successful conclusion.

Ponyri, Soviet Union, May 5th, 1943
Heeresgruppe Mitte – 72 kilometers north of Kursk

The enemy's rocket blasts had hit the reconnaissance squadron hard – especially 2nd Platoon. Claassen, their leader, was in the field hospital and after he had lost already a leg, it was still uncertain that he would live to see another day. Staff Sergeant Schredinsky, the leader of 1st Group, was dead, as were six of his ten men. Two others were severely wounded. The attacks had been mere minutes apart – a few minutes had been enough to extinguish twenty-one lives and to cripple twenty-seven others forever. Pappendorf, the highest-ranking surviving sergeant of the platoon, was now the platoon leader of a unit that was hardly any bigger in size than a reinforced squad. He was in charge of seventeen soldiers, all of whom were enlisted men, all except for Sergeant Berning.

Berning sat at the kitchen table of an abandoned farm-house in Ponyri and ate a sandwich with cold cuts. Next to him was Hege, who had field stripped his MG on the table and was cleaning its parts. He had been working on them for hours – just sitting there without saying a word, polishing the parts that were already shining. The rest of the platoon that occupied the two rooms of the cottage was silent as well.

Some of the men were cleaning their gear or weapons; others just sat around, smoking a pipe or cigarette or eating their rations. Bongartz had already littered the wooden floor under his legs with twelve cigarette butts; his thirteenth cigarette was stuck in the corner of his mouth. Everybody was lost in thought. No one said a word. Pappendorf, however, was not here; he was in a briefing with the company commander and the other platoon leaders to discuss the further course of action. Two hours ago the reconnaissance squadron had been replaced in the front line by a reserve company and had then proceeded to Ponyri on foot where the men would stay at least until nightfall.

Now and then Berning looked over at Bongartz but the lance corporal never returned his glances. Bongartz was the only one left here that Berning really knew.

Suddenly the door opened and Pappendorf walked in, his arms behind his back. Berning noticed that the staff sergeant was not only scrubbed clean but that there was no dirt on his uniform anymore, either, and that the blood had been washed out. It had turned into pale red stains. He stood there, dressed according to regulations, clenching his teeth and eyeing his men sharply. Everybody looked up and froze. Grimy faces, glued onto soldiers whose boots were covered in mud and whose uniforms looked as if they were made of forest dirt, stared at their platoon leader. While chewing on a thick piece of bread, Berning looked at his comrades. Suddenly he noticed that Pappendorf's eyes were focused on him again.

Startled, Berning jumped up, realizing his mistake.

"Attention!" the sergeant yelled. All of the soldiers obeyed, standing straight.

Berning saluted and reported, "Herr Unterfeldwebel! Unteroffizier Berning reporting the platoon waiting for further orders."

Ordinarily the soldier with the highest rank would now tell the soldiers to stand at ease but Pappendorf didn't. He just stepped slowly into the room. Every step of his metal-plated boots clicked audibly on the planks of the wooden floor. Pappendorf's gaze lingered on Berning.

"Tell me, Herr Unteroffizier," he said in a conniving voice, „tell me why I see thirteen soldiers here that aren't doing anything useful."

Berning stared at his new platoon leader while sweat was forming on his palms again.

But Pappendorf wasn't done yet. "And also tell me why you are one of these soldiers that aren't doing anything."

"I ... err ... I'm eating ... so I'll be ready for action..."

"SHUT UP!" Pappendorf interrupted him. "Being a lazy good-for-nothing is one thing. But what's even worse for me are the Pharisees! Don't you tell me anything! You're just loafing around here, nothing else!"

"I..."

"Why does my platoon look like a bunch of Slavic farmers that don't know anything about water and soap? Herr Unteroffizier?"

Berning didn't know what to say. *Because last night we were shot to pieces by the Russian artillery, you son of a bitch! Because we had to deal with death and suffering! And – God-dammit – because we're in a war!*

Pappendorf glanced at his watch. "Berning, you've got exactly ten minutes to get yourself and the platoon cleaned up so well that it could be presented even to the Führer himself."

"Jawohl!"

"Jawohl, HERR UNTERFELDWEBEL, Berning!" Pappendorf brawled.

Berning could kick himself for forgetting it again.

"Jawohl, Herr Unterfeldwebel!" he yelled.

Pappendorf stared at him.

What else does this guy want from me? Berning wondered.

"What does a German soldier do when he gets an order?" Pappendorf asked in a sharp voice.

Berning hesitated, thinking it was a trick question. "He ... carries it out?" he finally stuttered.

"DO YOU TAKE ME FOR AN IDIOT OR WHAT?! He'll repeat the order, Berning! He'll repeat the order!"

Everybody in the room just stood there as if frozen and endured the scene while Berning felt a sense of rage spreading throughout his guts. His right hand twitched slightly.

"I have the order … to get the platoon cleaned up so well … that it could be even presented to the Führer himself..."

Berning avoided Pappendorf's eyes. Spontaneously he added another "Herr Unterfeldwebel."

His platoon leader nodded and checked his watch again. "So, Sergeant, the first minute is already over!"

With these words Pappendorf clicked his heels and left the room. Berning folded his hands over his head and felt his breath racing again. He paused for a moment. Then he ordered, "Well, come on, guys. Get going! Clean yourselves, your uniforms and boots up! Move it!"

He wouldn't have had to tell the soldiers anything. They stormed out of the room, out of the farmhouse, and ran to a narrow brook that flowed near the farm. While everybody was leaving the room and Hege was hastily reassembling his MG, Bongartz suddenly walked up to Berning.

"Goddamn Nazi bastard," the lance corporal mumbled and threw his glowing cigarette butt on the ground, stepping on it.

Berning just nodded and looked at Bongartz, who was getting ready to leave and clean himself up, too.

"Gefreiter Bongartz?" the sergeant said spontaneously, feeling the need to talk.

"Jawohl?" Bongartz stopped and turned around.

"That business with the reconnaissance patrol … well, I mean..." Berning didn't know how to start, and he also didn't really know what he was trying to say.

But Bongartz smiled softly, went over to him and gave him a friendly pat on the shoulder. "It's okay, Herr Unteroffizier. You're a good guy."

His smile was wide and sincere, and Berning had to smile, too. So he did have a friend here, after all.

Southwest of Prokhorovka, Soviet Union, May 6th, 1943
Heeresgruppe Süd – 86 kilometers south of Kursk

The casualties of the past days had forced the command of the 16th Panzer Division to reconsider their options. Now the 16th moved toward Prokhorovka, side by side with the 5th and 7th Panzer Divisions, while complete infantry and Panzergrenadier divisions followed. In the meantime the XIII Armee Korps went around the city, crossed the railway line to Belgorod with its divisions and aimed for a shot at the Russian defensive line in the south. Lieutenant Engelmann had never seen so many military forces concentrated in such a small territory before. Tens of thousands of soldiers were moving in a sector that was only a few miles wide, and there were times when the German troops actually outnumbered the enemy during the infantry campaigns of Operation Citadel. If it hadn't been for the massive enemy tank formations that seemed to sprout out of the ground like weeds, Engelmann really could have believed that the Wehrmacht had a long-term chance of winning this war after all.

Due to the large number of casualties – the workshop companies had been able to repair dozens of tanks and vehicles last night – the tank wedge in the section of

PzRgt 2 could not be accomplished as planned. The Tiger battalion with only 23 fighting vehicles left was too decimated to stand in the front alone. At this point General Paulus intervened personally because he didn't want to see the new German "wonder weapon", the VI Tiger, completely sacrificed in this important mission. He stated, "If the Tiger is to be not only a military success but also a psychological one, it must not only participate in Citadel but also survive the operation."

Therefore the Division Commander von Angern developed the plan to enforce the massive tank wedge with several medium-sized Panzer IVs as well as comparable captured tanks in order to continue to move enforced firepower and as many tanks as possible to the front line. Today that tank wedge was to move onto the plains between the south curve of the Psel River and Prokhorovka and challenge the armored Russian troops stationed there to the decisive battle, while the infantry formations were supposed to occupy the city center.

In preparation for this move, a raiding patrol had already taken hill 226.6 during the night. The hill was intended to serve as a "nest" for the artillery observers in the battle of the next day. And now, at dawn, the German tanks got going again.

*

So now we're at the farthermost front line, Engelmann thought while his tank – in a row with the remaining members of his platoon, other Panzer IV platoons of the regiment, two T-34s painted gray with a *Balkenkreuz,* as well as the rest of the Tiger panzers – was moving towards the possibly largest tank battle of all times. The armored forces of the division advanced to the plains north of Prokhorovka where, according to reconnaissance, 800 Russian tanks had gathered. The German Wehrmacht had 720 tanks and assault guns to face these concentrated Soviet forces. One thing was certain: At the end of the day, one of the two adversaries would have lost the majority of his armored troops in the Kursk salient, which would finally decide the battle of Kursk.

Just in these minutes a Russian radio signal with the message "Stal! Stal! Stal!" was intercepted. *Steel! Steel! Steel!*

It was beginning.

The German airplanes were already in the air and involved in combat with Soviet fighter planes. With screaming engines, military planes crashed onto the ground where they perished in gigant explosions. The Russian fighter aircraft were massively present in the sky and prevented most German dive-bombing attacks.

"Does it have to be so damn hot?" Münster whined.

"The I Abteilung reports contact with the enemy – T-34 in battalion size attacking from the north-northeast." Nitz put an emphasis on "east" by pulling the rod long as a piece of jerky.

Nodding, Engelmann looked over at the Tiger tank to his right that was throwing up a dense dust cloud while squashing the grassy landscape. Dozens of hits had scorched the skin of the steel behemoth, leaving deep scars.

Again the sun burned mercilessly. The commander of the Tiger, who also was riding with his head out of the hatch, looked over to Engelmann and grinned. Then he disappeared into his metal beast while the first Russian artillery shells hit the wedge-shaped lines of attack.

Detonations tore up the ground and whirled soil over the tanks. Engelmann glanced at the terrain once more and disappeared into his tank as well. The area up here, northwest of Prokhorovka, was one big flat open space without any cover whatsoever. No trees, no rocks, no hills as far as one could see.

And now they would face the 5th Guard Tank Army on this terrain – battle-hardened, well-trained and moti-vated tankers in tough tanks.

Every muscle in Engelmann's body tensed up.

"The téte of the 5th Panzer Division has run into a tank trench near the bank of the Psel River, and they are stuck there under Russian anti-tank fire," Nitz reported.

Peering through his eye slits, Engelmann could al-ready see little black blocks with tails of dust clouds on the horizon. His eyes widened. There were hundreds of Soviet tanks out there in front of them. And hundreds of German tanks to oppose them.

This will be a massacre, the lieutenant thought. *Dear God, please let us survive this day alive and well.*

Looking down for a moment, he noticed that the mus-cles of his arms trembled and burned.

"Hans, stay close to the Tiger on our right. He's our life insurance." Engelmann was ready for the battle.

"Yep, Sepp."

Still tearing up the ground between the German tanks, the artillery now claimed its first victim. A Panzer III got a hit in the track, which ripped apart immediately and brought the tank to an abrupt halt. Yet the metal front kept on rolling towards the Russian tank armada.

"The 7th has encountered enemy T-34s and KV-1s," Nitz informed Engelmann. The 7th Panzer Division moved on the left flank of the 16th. The black blocks up ahead gradually grew larger. The thunder of artillery fire rolled over the plains.

"I Abteilung is in a gun battle with one hundred and twenty Russian vehicles." Nitz forwarded the message as coolly as if he was talking about the weather. "The 7th is getting its ass kicked. Twenty-four panzers finished so far." Nitz looked directly at his commander, although that was not easy within the confined tank.

"Now it's us or them."

The blocks ahead of them turned into silhouettes of tanks; then the Tiger to Engelmann's right fired without slowing down, which was forbidden and foolish. Engelmann couldn't tell where the shot had hit. The impacts of armor-piercing rounds mingled with the hits from the artillery shells.

"AP round!" Engelmann ordered.

Born confirmed the order and loaded the first shell.

"I Abteilung has been penetrated! Enemy tanks are right in the middle of our formation!" Nitz groaned.

Instinctively Engelmann looked to his right but all he could see was Elfriede's armored skin. Yet even from his cupola he could only see the right edge of the II Abteilung.

"The 2nd reports sixty tanks directly ahead of us – a total of one hundred and twenty sightings." Nitz snorted loudly. "Order from the old man: Set targets yourselves according to the formation; then fire. Light and medium tanks. Tigers will deal with the heavy ones. 1st Platoon has permission to fire. 2nd and 3rd Platoon: Stay back and take care of enemy forces breaking through." Again Nitz concentrated on the messages coming in over the radio.

"Ebbe, the platoon is to look for targets on its own. BTs, light as well as T-34s, max. We'll leave the big ones to the Tigers. Fire at your own discretion!" Engelmann gasped while Nitz already passed the message on. When the next signal came through, the staff sergeant looked up.

"What?" the lieutenant asked.

"The commander of the Tiger is on the line."

"And?"

"He wishes us *Waidmannsheil*."

The two steel fronts raced relentlessly towards each other and wrapped each other in a curtain of shells.

Olive and grey tanks were hit, stopped abruptly and spit flames while the human beings inside were burned alive. For hours and hours, as far as one could see – and even farther – the battlefield was covered with the crowning achievement of the human art of killing. Tactics and thinking did not matter anymore. All that counted was steel and fire.

The two fronts interlocked, and then the tanks tore each other apart at close distance. They opened each other like tin cans and smashed the vulnerable crews to a pulp or they burned their flesh off their bones. After battling for an eternity, the Germans finally proved to be the more efficient destroyers of the day. With over three hundred and thirty tanks hit, the 5th Guard Tank

Army sounded retreat and the battle was decided. History would only register the German Wehrmacht as winner and the Red Army as loser, but the plains northwest of Prokhorovka on this day were lined with the remains of 1 780 tankers of both sides, of no interest to anyone anymore, just laying as charred clumps of human flesh in the smoldering wrecks of their tanks.

Southwest of Prokhorovka, Soviet Union, May 6th, 1943
Kursk Front – 86 kilometers south of Kursk

Though Sidorenko had had some hope of deciding the battle in Prokhorovka with his mechanized troops and tanks, in wise premonition he had already ordered his staff to be moved to Lgov, west of Kursk. He knew that Prokhorovka was the gateway to Kursk; and once the Germans pushed it open, Kursk would be defeated as well. For that reason Lgov had been the better choice from the start because he could continue to coordinate the forces from there after the fascists had completed the encirclement. In the end, the Nazi forces in Prokhorovka had simply been too powerful. Now Sidorenko was lying on a hill at the edge of the woods behind the cover of a tree; from here he could oversee almost the whole battlefield. His adjutant was waiting in the car parked at the other end of the woods, with his uniform probably soaked in sweat because the Nazis were already very close by. Still, Sidorenko had wanted to witness the combat action with his own eyes, and that was why he had stayed here. Now he was watching an open field that reached to the horizon and was covered with smoldering tank wrecks. Five hundred – maybe even six hundred – destroyed armored fighting vehicles lined the battlefield, while the remains of the socialist forces retreated. The Germans chased them in a closed front, pushing their own troops mercilessly. Sidorenko saw many of his tanks shot to pieces while fleeing. No more than a few hundred at the most would make it, and these already had their orders: Gather in the areas the 60th Army was holding. But Sidorenko could also see the masses of burning Nazi tanks; even some of the Tigers that the Soviet tankers were so scared of were now blazing in the fire. It had been a good idea to order his troops to always make it a priority to go after the Tigers. Every Tiger tank they killed would show that these monsters were not invincible, after all. Actually Sidorenko himself could count sixteen Tiger wrecks right ahead of him looking through his field glasses.

Despite the fact that they had been defeated, Sidorenko was content. They had considerably weakened the German forces yet one more time. The Heeresgruppe Süd could not take many more strikes like this one. Still the Kursk Front was not yet by far. At first Sidorenko had underestimated his forces and clearly overestimated the forces of his foe. Putting his binoculars down, the Russian colonel general grinned with satisfaction, thinking about the fascists and their constant attempts to encircle their enemy. How predictable they had become! And that was exactly what played into the Russian officer's hands so well. He knew that the Germans wouldn't stop at the Kursk salient. The Nazis wanted to regain ground after the past year had been such an unsatisfying one for them. So their generals would keep pushing the troops to advance deep into the area, no matter how exhausted they were. One day the fascists would pay dearly for their arrogance! Despite the fact that the German Army was no longer capable of carrying out such attacks, they would keep their soldiers marching on to Kastornoye and even farther. By then the Germans would be so weakened that they would barely be able to do without any more forces in order to cover their flanks and back. They would believe that the encircled Russian armies were doomed anyhow and would just surrender. Oh, how wrong the Nazis were to think that! The thought cheered Sidorenko up because he had another ace up his sleeve that he intended to play against their meager flank cover soon – when the Germans thought the victory was theirs! The fascists had even taught him something they called *tank wedge*.

Sidorenko took one last look at the battle scene down there in the open field. These hundreds of burning tanks would never help another fascist to tear down the homes and farms of honest laborers. Satisfied, Sidorenko nodded. Then he slowly crawled backwards to return to his vehicle. He couldn't help reflecting that a defeat could sometimes turn into a victory.

Near Olchovatka, Soviet Union, May 6th, 1943
Heeresgruppe Mitte – 53 kilometers north of Kursk

Staff Sergeant Pappendorf had restructured the platoon into two squads. 1st Squad would be led by the only remaining NCO, Sergeant Berning, while 2nd Squad would be under the command of Senior Lance Corporal Weiss, a seasoned soldier with seven years of experience, a fact one could tell from the silver star over the white, angle-shaped rank insignia on his left sleeve.

Berning had the feeling that the senior lance corporal knew better what to do than he did himself– and the sergeant would have preferred to let someone else do his job as a squad leader. But that was out of the question.

So now he led his squad across wide open flat country. The whole space was only interrupted by a few thin fruit trees and sunflower fields, but up ahead, a steep incline limited the plain – the hills of Olchovatka, the German forces had conquered in a hard battle over several days. The Russians had withdrawn in a southern direction but they were already preparing to start a counter attack.

Therefore the hill had to be reinforced with infantry from the back, while the armored forces of Heeresgruppe Mitte advanced to Kursk on the right and the left, passing through Fatesh and Schtschigry.

The hill near Olchovatka was the decisive position for controlling the area between Oka and the Seym River, and from the hills in the east one could see already Kursk. That was what Staff Sergeant Pappendorf had told his platoon, and he had made sure that everybody was listening. The two squads had marched across the plains close to each other, laterally off-center to the rest of the company, and now they reached the bottom of the hill. To their right some carriages, loaded with ammunition and rations and driven by Russian Hiwis, rumbled off.

Pappendorf had run around his platoon like a satellite the whole way – more than twenty kilometers, barking orders and loudly admonishing soldiers who took their eyes off their sector even for just a second or who held their weapons the wrong way. Sweat spilled out of every pore of his body, soaking his tidy uniform, but he showed no signs of fatigue. All Berning could do was shake his head. He didn't know if he should admire his platoon leader or think he was crazy. In the meantime, he kept his eyes on the ground and the shrubs. The Russians had planted anti-personnel mines – wooden "cigar boxes" – throughout the salient. He couldn't believe how Pappendorf was jumping around here like a rabid dog.

*

It was already late in the afternoon when the platoon was assigned its trenches.

The soldiers had sincerely hoped that Pappendorf would collapse after his marathon run and crash until noon the next day but the staff sergeant seemed to have inexhaustible energy reserves. Now he was jumping around from one foxhole occupied by privates to the next, criticizing anything that wasn't according to the rules or harassing the men with questions and orders.

"Why did you take off your Stahlhelm? Put it on right now!"

"Button up your left chest pocket!"

"Put your field blouse back on, dammit! This is not a day at the lake!"

"Berning, tell me the caliber and combat distance of the Karabiner 98! Come on, Sergeant!"

Again and again, Berning had been the target of Pappendorf's temper, and of course he had kept giving Pappendorf plenty of opportunity. The staff sergeant just wouldn't leave him alone. Now Berning was glad that Pappendorf had turned to the 2nd Squad.

Relieved, he slumped back into his foxhole while his heart kept hammering. He stroked his weapon with trembling hands. He had never shot another human being before, but the Russians were going to attack this sector. That was certain because the enemy also knew that Olchovatka was the key to Kursk. Berning sighed. He didn't want to shoot at anyone.

When the sergeant realized that his thoughts and fears were about to overwhelm him again, he quickly climbed out of his hole to take a closer look at his squad's trenches.

The company's foxholes were spread 300 meters across the width of the hill, where several groups of trees provided cover as well. Other infantry companies were to the left and right, and the anti-tank gun crews of the anti-tank battalion of the division had put up their cannons everywhere among the infantry troops.

The 7.5-centimeter Pak 40 with their shaped charge rounds even posed a danger to medium-sized Soviet tanks; they were also equipped with explosives to combat so-called soft targets – i.e. human beings – a euphemism that made shooting HE shells at people sound less nasty.

Open fields providing nearly no cover at all spread across several thousand yards up ahead before they turned into a large forest that was several miles wide and deep, reaching up to the horizon.

That was where the Russians were.

Yet the traces of the enemy didn't even stop at the foot of the range of hills the Soviets had defended with an iron will almost until last man standing. Thousands of shell-holes lined the trenches while here and there Berning could make out dried blood on the ground and the leaves on the bushes. It made him sick to have to spend his time in such a cemetery. Under the cover of the back of the hill, the sergeant walked from trench to trench, crawling on his stomach the last few yards to the foxholes to avoid the attention of any Russian observer. Finally he reached the MG nest of the squad on the left flank that was slightly farther ahead and could therefore flank their own positions in close combat. Berning crawled on his hands and knees up to the dugout and let himself drop into it. He found his first assistant machine gunner, lance corporal Bongartz, with a cigarette in his mouth. His machine gun was resting on the edge of the trench.

Bongartz' eyes grew wide. "Is Pappe around or what?"

"No, no."

"Thank God!" Bongartz threw the glowing butt on the ground of the hole that was already covered with cigarette butts and cartridge cases from Russian machine pistols. They stared at each other for a moment.

"Where's Hege?" Berning asked finally.

"Taking a shit." Bongartz lit another cigarette and thoughtfully blew the smoke into the air.

They fell silent again for another minute.

"And – everything okay with you?" Berning asked.

Nodding, Bongartz answered with a grin, "Everything's Bochum." He had taken so many draws on his cigarette and taken them so quickly that half of it had already burned away.

"Aren't you scared of the Ivans at all?" Berning asked suddenly, peering over the edge of the trench into the distant forest.

Grimacing, Bongartz shook his head.

"Oh, it'll be okay," he thought aloud. "By the way, I'm Rudi." He offered Berning his hand but the sergeant just stared at him without knowing what to do. In Sigmaringen they had taught him not to get too close to the *Landsers* – the enlisted men. They would be killed too quickly and replaced by others. Plus it wasn't proper for a non-commissioned officer to make friends with his subordinates. Yet there was this longing to finally have something like a friend here.

"I know it's not really right for me to..." Bongartz began, trying to interpret Berning's hesitation, but then the sergeant reached out and shook his hand with determination.

"Franz," he said, beaming. "Franz Berning." His Austrian Burgenland dialect gave a special ring to his name.

For a few moments they fell silent again but Berning didn't want to end their conversation yet. "What team is Bochum playing against next?"

"Against Bielefeld. On Sunday."

"And?"

"Yeah. They're good. But we're better."

"So it's gonna be better than against Schalke, won't it?"

"Whoa, don't say that! We lost ten to one in March. But then they've got this guy Klodt now. He's supposed to be a top player."

"Mhh ..."

After that exchange they fell silent again, and Berning felt how much he missed his home and Gretel.

"Man, I can't wait to get back home. Then I'll watch the games every week," Bongartz said thoughtfully.

Berning just nodded. Silence.

"Oh well, I guess I'll get going," the sergeant said finally. "Check out the other trenches."

"Well, good luck then."

"Yeah, thanks."

"And watch out for Pappe, the old Nazi is out to rap your knuckles."

"You know me, Bongartz," Berning joked, grinning widely, "I don't give a shit about his crap. I'll be fine – after all, I'm not a nobody!" He didn't stop grinning until he noticed that Bongartz's grin had disappeared and that he was looking past Berning with fear in his eyes.

Turning around, Berning stared right at Pappendorf's face, whose eyes were narrow slits and whose every pore was about to explode with rage. The bastard had sneaked up on them without making a sound.

"BERNING!" he yelled.

Belp, Switzerland, May 7th, 1943

Thomas Taylor sat in a small café in the quaint small town of Belp right outside of Bern. Though he was here on business, he enjoyed the tranquility, he was able to indulge in for the moment. He really could use some peace and quiet after the turbulent past few days. After rushing from Remigen to Bern the same night he had received his next order. Taylor had reached Bern sometime in the afternoon of the next day. The first thing he had done was to drop down on the bed in the apartment military intelligence had provided for him in the center of Bern and sleep like a log until sun rose again. As of the next morning, Taylor had been busy preparing for his new job; he had studied documents the guys from the military intelligence had deposited in his apartment in Bern, and he had already followed her – the name of his job was Luise Roth – to get a feel for her. Through another agent who had already shadowed the target for some time, they knew her daily and weekly routines and were generally well-informed about her. These preparations made it possible for Thomas to start the approach soon.

So now here he was, sitting in this small Swiss café – run by a family of Italian origins offering as specialty Italian coffee and ice cream – and waiting for Luise Roth to quit her work early as she did every Friday to meet five other women of the Jewish community of Belp to plan their joint activities.

It was a pleasant early summer day. The birds were chirping, and the sun presented herself in all her glory, while the café was filled with Swiss state officials who were eating breakfast, reading the newspapers or talking about politics – of course they were also talking about the incident in Lucerne as well as the dangers the German Reich posed, which naturally was one of the major topics discussed in Switzerland these days.

Thomas always had to grin to himself whenever he overheard such debates; usually they were very naive and only superficially informed. He often wondered how horrified many Swiss would be if German soldiers ever stormed across the Swiss border.

Habits, Taylor thought while observing the Jewish community hall that actually was only a regular townhouse on the other side of the street, *habits are the things that'll kill you.*

He was enjoying a cup of coffee – his third– and an expensive cigar – a Montechristo – pleasures that had already cost military intelligence quite a tidy sum. But Thomas was prepared to make them pay for a good smoke, and that was exactly the way he smoked this cigar – as fast as a cigarette. A cigar connoisseur would surely have slapped him in the face for that.

It was still early in the morning; the little hand on his watch would reach the eight any moment now.

Why does this slut have to get up so early for her coffee party? He put out the cigar in an ash tray on the table without taking his eyes off of the car on the other side of the street – an old, yellow Maximag with an open driver's cab and strikingly narrow tires with spokes. Taylor was lucky that it looked like it was going to be a beautiful day today because otherwise Luise would have taken the train. Then he could have kissed his trick goodbye – but he wanted and had to get to her as fast as possible. The Reich was in a war, and therefore it might pay dearly for every day wasted without collecting adequate information.

While Taylor emptied his cup, the door across the street opened. An old woman said goodbye to a young lady in her early twenties. Luise Roth really *was* breath-takingly beautiful. Long blonde hair she usually wore pinned up, and light blue eyes – these were the high-lights in a lovely face with soft features, a cute little nose and narrow lips. The few sunny days of the year had already given her skin a healthy, light tan. She was dressed in a black skirt and a white blouse that showed a pleasant amount of skin.

Some time or other while doing his research on Luise, Taylor realized that he had never before had anything to do with a Jew – much less with a Jewess. He didn't really like the Nazis, and being a German with foreign roots himself, he might quickly have become a target of the Germans' racial fanaticism. Yet he had never under-stood their hatred of the Jews. Before the Nazis ap-peared on the German horizon, Thomas had never even once given a thought to the Jews, nor had he had any contact with them. This section of the population had simply never been an issue in his life. And all of a sud-den they were supposed to be the cause of all the world's problems? They had been dragged out of their homes, had been banned from their professions, and fi-nally they had disappeared somewhere in the East ... Taylor just never understood it. The Jewesses in the small community of Belp didn't have long noses or dirty fingernails – on the contrary: All of the women were a pleasure to look at and seemed to be of a friendly dispo-sition, too. On such occasions Taylor realized once again that it was a good thing the Nazis were no longer in power. The new government had finally stopped that madness of deporting Jews and restricting their civil rights.

So now he had had to do quick research on the Jewish culture, had studied the documentation collected by the military intelligence and familiarized himself with his new biography. But if he wanted to remain convincing for a longer period of time, he definitely needed to study the subject even more intensely and become acquainted with all of the trivia a Jewish life consisted of.

Luise Roth walked to her car, while the old woman disappeared in the house again, closing the front door behind her. Yes, Taylor's target was truly a feast for the eyes.

He grinned; in the meantime the engine of the automobile across the street kicked in. Luise put on sunglasses that concealed not only her eyes but also part of her face. Then the exhaust spat out black smoke, and the lady with British and Swiss roots sped off.

That was Taylor's cue.

He got up and left a generous tip on the table – after all, the military intelligence had enough funds. Then he swung himself on his bicycle and rode off.

*

Taylor had memorized Luise's route to work in detail and had found it to be perfect for making contact. For the most part it mainly consisted of a country road which, while passing a few small villages along the way, otherwise twisted through the middle of nowhere. Forests, brooks, hills, river meadows and fields that were starting to sprout agricultural crops dominated the area. In Taylor's opinion even Bern, which bordered on Belp, was surprisingly rural for a capital city – and Belp itself was a real one-horse town. In any case, the road Luise took to her workplace in Bern every day was completely cut off from the rest of the world – and therefore perfect for Taylor's job. Out here no one would disturb him.

Taylor pedaled down the road at a high speed. His bicycle vibrated on the bumpy road. A hundred yards up ahead, a small forest appeared and swallowed up the road after a right turn.

Pushing the pedals down even faster, he reached the forest. Riding under tall tree tops, he smelled pine cones and musty soil.

Suddenly he heard a gentle woman's voice.

He stopped, jumped off his bike and leaned it up against a tree. With silent steps, he sneaked away from the road into the underbrush so he could take a shortcut around the bend in the road. Then he saw the yellow steel flash between the bramble bushes that provided a dense cover at eye level.

There she is! He approached Luise slowly while her vocal complaints filled the air.

"No, that can't be true!" she moaned in a soft voice that sounded very pleasant. Her Swiss dialect had an exotic yet appealing ring to Taylor. "I don't believe it!"

He approached her. In the military, he had learned how to move through the woods as silently as possible. Cautiously he shoved pushed small twigs and rocks aside with his foot before taking each step.

Gradually he came closer to his target. He felt the hard metal of his Luger that he had put into the back waistband of his pants; it was invisible from the outside. His whole body was tense and his mind was totally focused.

Now he was only five yards away from his target.

Now he would strike.

*

Luise stood beside her Swiss vehicle that was already almost a vintage car and stared at the yellow metal hood, the dark radiator grille and the protruding round headlights. She had no idea what to do now. It couldn't be happening, her car breaking down right here in the middle of nowhere!

And she was late for work as it was, having had such a lovely talk with the girls of the community. So Luise cursed again in the way properly educated girls cursed. "It can't be happening," she moaned without realizing that someone was right behind her.

"Grüessech," a voice behind her said.

Startled, Luise squealed loudly and spun around. She looked straight at a man with a friendly smile and big freckles on his nose and cheeks.

He's cute, was her first thought. His red hair and strong features reminded her of a Scotsman. Immediately she felt embarrassed about having screamed. So she started to laugh nervously while putting her right hand over her heart.

"Dear God," she groaned. "You gave me quite a start."

"I'm so sorry," the man answered in a very friendly voice. He spoke excellent High German rather than the Swiss dialect but with a slight British accent, a fact that immediately made Luise curious.

"Oh no, that's quite all right." Again she had to giggle nervously. *Oh God, what must he think of me? I'm squeaking like a mouse!*

"I just noticed that you were standing by your car in the forest and thought you might need some assistance?" the man explained politely.

"Oh, that's too kind of you, thank you." Luise curtsied slightly and realized at once how stupid she must look to him. Embarrassed, she smiled again.

He really is cute, she couldn't help but think. She tried to shake off these thoughts.

"But where are my manners?" She offered him her hand. "Luise Roth."

"Aaron Stern." He shook her hand.

Firm handshake, she noticed, and smiled again bashfully. *But Stern? Aaron Stern? What a coincidence! And why does this nice man have to run into me right here in this situation? The way I look! Wearing only my stupid work clothes. What must he think of me? He probably thinks I'm a silly goose!*

She sighed silently yet things just were the way they were. She didn't really like to be perceived as a helpless little woman but right now that's exactly what she was.

It was only then that she noticed that Herr Stern wasn't wearing a yarmulke. Well, that meant that he was not an orthodox Jew, thank God! He might even be a liberal one...

"So can I help you in any way?" he asked, smiling pleasantly.

She sighed. There were no two ways about it – she had to get to work. So she said, "I was on my way to work when my car suddenly started to sputter and to rumble. And then it just died on me. And now I'm here and don't know how I can get away."

"Mhm." He frowned.

Could it really be that this handsome man even knows something about cars? Luise cheered up considerably. His name, his looks, this bright and sunny day … maybe this encounter was destiny.

"Maybe you ran out of gasoline?" he suggested.

"I filled this old wreck just yesterday."

"Or a leak in your tank? Anyway, it really sounds like you've run out of fuel. But then I'm no expert when it comes to cars, either."

"That's a pity." She sighed.

"But I might be able to help you in another way."

"You could?" Her eyes grew wide.

"I rode down from Bern on my bicycle this morning to take a walk in the forest. If you want, I could lend it to you."

"Oh no, I can't accept that! How would you get back then?"

"Oh, Miss. It's only six miles from here to the city, and I'm a good hiker. But you need to hurry if you have to get to work."

Luise didn't really want to accept this very generous offer. Her good manners wouldn't let her.

But then again she had no choice.

"That's very kind of you. I … I don't know what to say." Now she felt really embarrassed.

"Oh, that's quite all right. You can just return the bike to me tonight or tomorrow. There's no hurry. My address is Nägeligasse 6 in Bern."

"That's … that's incredibly kind of you. Thank you. Thank you so much!"

Of course she would return the bike to him. Luise immediately decided to ask her colleague at work later today if she could borrow some fresh clothes from her and get some help with her make-up. Because tonight she wanted her second impression to undo the first impression Herr Stern had of her.

Oh yes, she would most definitely return the bike to him. Luise Roth beamed happily.

Near Olchovatka, Soviet Union, May 8th, 1943
Heeresgruppe Mitte – 53 kilometers north of Kursk

Throughout the night the Russians made sure that Berning and his men could not get a wink of sleep. Even though there hadn't been any combat action, the Ivans knew how to keep their friends on the other side of the hills happy.

Apparently they had installed powerful speakers in their trenches, because the Russians' suggestions they should defect kept echoing loudly in Berning's foxhole, repeating the same recording all night without a break:

"German soldiers! Don't serve this criminal regime that makes you fight a hopeless battle many thousand kilometers away from your families any longer. Don't believe the lies of your Chancellor von Witzleben, who continues the crimes and atrocities of Hitler's Nazi Reich under the pretense of moderate politics. German Soldiers! Decide for yourselves: Do you want to go on being used to attack and abuse peace-loving human beings? Do you want to go on suffering for an unjust cause? Or will you put a stop to it today and forsake criminal behavior? Then drop your weapons and come over to the trenches of your Russian brothers! There's nothing to fear! We have warm food and cigarettes. The Union of the Soviet Socialist Republics will treat you well and send you home as soon as this war is over … German soldiers! Don't serve…"

The words were still drilling on Berning's ears when the speakers were finally switched off as the first sunlight touched the Russian plain after fourteen hours of permanent noise.

Even the commander of the battalion had recognized the effect the Russian propaganda had on his soldiers and therefore had ordered artillery fire here and there throughout the night to put a stop to it. But the effort had been in vain. Despite dozens of hits in the woods on the other side, the metallic voice continued to to spread its message over the land. Sleep was out of the question. The MG nests had shot some harassing fire, too, but that had not brought them relief either.

Berning didn't even notice the break of dawn. With bloodshot eyes he stared at the dirt wall of his hole and held onto his weapon as hard as he could. The words that had poured out of the Russian speakers kept running through his head. Maybe he, too, would have to decide for himself soon because he had started to wonder how much longer he would be willing to go along with this shit.

While pondering this question, he didn't notice that things were getting loud and hectic all around him. Then he heard suddenly the distant firing of flare guns. Berning looked up at the sky. Through the tops of the trees that were growing throughout the ridge he saw tails of purple comets flashing. They curled in the sky, indicating an enemy tank attack.

Oh no! Berning thought. He cautiously peered over the rim of his foxhole. In the early daylight he could barely make out the forest at the far end of the field, where T-34 tanks now started to break out from behind the underbrush, ready to storm across the open space. Soldiers with rifles and submachine guns had mounted the tanks and tried to present as little of a target as they could behind the turrets. More Russian infantry companies came out of their trenches and formed long columns of riflemen on the open field. They moved fast while the tanks also drove at full speed, quickly getting ahead of the foot soldiers.

Without a warning, the German anti-tank guns started to bang to Berning's left and right; then the first rounds hammered between the attackers. Explosive shells tore the infantry formations apart, while armor-piercing projectiles were fired to take care of the T-34s.

The first tank already exploded, and its turret flew high up into the air. But there were still so many other tanks coming at them. Berning counted alone eight T-34s in his company's section. Tanks to his right and left as far as he could see! And the infantry! Too many of them to count them all.

Oh no! Berning moaned in desperation.

After the Russians had passed the first third of the open space, the German handguns and mortars joined the ado of the unfolding battle. Pappendorf ordered both squads to fire, and Berning passed the order on to his men, but himself, he could only stare mesmerized on the enemy moving in closer by the minute.

The T-34s shot HE shells between the German trenches, destroying some of the anti-tank guns. Dirt and brush were hurled up to the tree tops from where they rained down on the soldiers' foxholes. Berning ducked all the way down when fat chunks of soil dropped down over his head. He shut his eyes tightly and prayed that his comrades would stop the storm before the Russians reached the ridge of the elevation.

The tips of the enemy forces had left the second third of the plains behind them. The flood of brown uniforms rolled ahead while the German arms spit fire here and there into their rows.

Hundreds of Red Army soldiers died in the hail of bullets and shrapnel, but even more continued to storm forward. One tank broke down after it had been hit by an anti-tank shell; its crew jumped out through the black cloud of smoke and just started running. Despite massive casualties – some companies turned into platoons and some platoons turned into squads within mere seconds – the Russians just stubbornly continued.

After long moments of fear, Berning got a hold on himself again and raised to have a peek out of his foxhole. The roaring of thousands of weapons around him filled the air. Somewhere out there Pappendorf barked orders at 2nd Squad. Berning tightened the grip around his rifle. He had to fire!

Then he froze. The enemy forces had reached the bottom of the ridge. Russian soldiers were already crawling up the hill in several places. Berning could hear Hege's MG firing away. The enemy soldiers dropped flies on the slope.

But more Russians followed, and then more and more and more. The German anti-tank canons and their crews died one by one in the firestorm of tank rounds. Thick tree trunks were chopped off like matches, toppling over and crushing soldiers underneath them.

"Berning!" Pappendorf's voice rang out through the chaos but Berning couldn't take his eyes off the scenes he was facing.

Right in front of his trench – no more than one hundred and fifty yards away – a Russian tank came to a halt. The infantry soldiers it had carried to this spot jumped off and stormed towards the hill. Hege saw them and turned his weapon around.

Two long bursts of fire later the Russians lay in the grass, writhing in pain and whimpering in the face of death. Then something heavy jumped into Berning's cover hole and landed behind him.

Berning was startled; he let out a shrill scream and turned around. He almost hit Pappendorf in the face with his rifle, but the staff sergeant already grabbed him by the shoulder and held him with his shovel-like hands.

"Berning, go farther left to your MG. I'm taking over here. Your second assistant machine gunner got hit. Send one of your men to get extra ammunition! And you stay there and make sure that the enemy bites the dust!"

Gaping, Berning stared at Pappendorf.

"Get your ass moving, boy!" Pappendorf bellowed, lifted his submachine gun and sent a fire burst into the area ahead. Then he grabbed the sergeant and pushed him roughly out of the hole.

And suddenly Berning stood right on the ridge without any cover while the Russian explosive rounds tore up the terrain.

Leaves and branches sailed down from the trees, and bark popped off the trunks. Tiny columns of dirt sprayed into the air. Berning ran off. He slid down part of the northern side of the hill in order to get to the level where the MG was positioned under the cover of the ridge.

He could hear guns fire and people scream. The Russians had already broken through in several places and stood in the German trenches. Heavy close combat flared up – with guns, with spades, with fists.

Berning dropped to the ground when he saw the brown uniforms that threw themselves into the foxholes of the company next to his and started to attack the men wearing field gray. The soldiers stuffed together in the narrow space of the holes. The wave of combat rolled across the ridge and down the northern hill, leaving still shapes behind them.

And Hege was still firing away! His MG never stopped rat-a-tatting into the assailing Russians. Biting his lower lip, Berning tensed his body and jogged towards his comrade's foxhole. Right in front of it he dropped to the ground, slid down the last yard, and finally his sorry rear hit the ground between what had to be hundreds of spent cartridges.

Though he had stuffed cotton balls into his ears, the loud blasts from the machine gun still seemed to saw into his head. Hege was already bleeding from his right ear. His face was filthy; only a few drops of sweat formed white tracks through the black layers of soot. He sent off long bursts of fire at the approaching infantry while the Soviet tanks already chomped down on the German anti-tank gun positions. Bongartz kept reloading. The sector of effective range of Hege's weapon was already covered with Russian soldiers, who were either dead or dying. The remaining Red Army soldiers were pinned down to the ground by the merciless suppressive fire form the German machine guns. They only advanced yard by yard, and with every jump, fewer men than before got up from the ground. But there were still too many of them – way too many! The Soviet attack came with overwhelming manpower.

"Where's the ammo?" Hege shouted and fired a whole belt, tearing up a Russian shock troop ahead of them.

"Rupp's dead!" Berning yelled back.

Bongartz forced a distorted grin. "I'll go get some ammo!" He patted Hege on his shoulder.

Then suddenly an explosive projectile tore a deep crater into the terrain right behind the position of the MG nest. Hege and Bongartz dropped into the hole while a wall of dirt swept over them. Berning pressed his helmet firmly to his head with both hands. The next boom already sounded close to the MG position, and again a brown column rose up. Bongartz risked a short glance.

"Scheisse!" he gasped. "A T-34 just shot at us! Two hundred meters on the terrain in front of our position! And the infantry's coming closer!"

"No shit," Berning cried but Hege jumped up without any facial expression. He grabbed the MG and pulled the trigger until the belt had been emptied. Then he dropped back into the hole with his weapon. Another shell tore up the ground; this time it was a very close call.

"There are too many of them!" Hege snorted, fumbling his third from last belt into the weapon. "And I need ammunition!" With these words he got up and went on firing. Less than a hundred yards ahead of him, the Russian soldiers dispersed and searched for cover behind trees while dozens of rounds cut through soft tissue, slaying some of the attackers. Berning also risked a glance.

At the same instant the T-34 fired but the projectile missed them, flying up too high, way too high. The shell didn't even detonate on the hill behind them. Yet Berning had felt the air draft of the projectile and heard the hissing sound cutting through the air. His hands shook uncontrollably while sweat ran into his eyes. His heart beat so hard that he felt it in his throat and nearly suffocated.

Hege kept firing while, to their left, German soldiers reconquered their positions. They ended dozens of lives with knives, potato mashers and pistols.

Berning saw clearly that the T-34 was lowering its barrel and taking aim again. It wouldn't miss them a second time! Berning wanted to flee but Hege just kept on shooting. Support on their right coming from the squad's trenches helped to suppress the Soviet soldiers ahead.

Bongartz already dashed from behind Berning to the rim of the hole and started to run to the platoon command post to fetch more ammunition.

"Shit!" Hege gasped after having emptied his MG again. He immediately dropped back down into the trench to reload.

Now he also switched barrels and pressed the used one that was glowing red from heat into the ground to cool it off – as if that would do any good.

"These damn barrels are already all bent from that bullshit here!" he complained and loaded his weapon.

In the meantime Berning was paralyzed by fear. Out of the corner of his eye he could see the Russian soldiers that tried to regroup in order to finally take the hill by storm. He noticed how Hege, who was next to him, emerged from the hole and raised his MG. He also saw how Russian soldiers again attacked the trenches to their left. The enemy fire on their right, however, was becoming too much. Berning could see that explosive shells were plowing the whole length of the ridge and that two of his comrades collapsed under the heavy fire. At that very moment the last soldier of the anti-tank gun crew behind Berning's squad, who had operated the tank gun up until the last second despite the fact that his buddies were already dead, was hit as well.

But all that didn't count right now because Berning was looking straight into the barrel of the T-34. *This is it!*

A small device on wheels – it looked something like a miniature tank without a turret – suddenly drove up to the Russian tank and stopped. Berning had never seen anything like it but he didn't think that a human being could fit into it. One moment later the strange object vanished in a huge explosion that tore the T-34 to pieces and silenced the tank gun forever.

While columns of dirt were spraying up around their MG position and Hege was cussing and firing, Berning dropped back in the hole like a piece of veggie and froze for a second, his eyes glassy, his fingers around his weapon. His body was soaked with sweat.

"Breakthrough!" he could hear Pappendorf yell in the distance. "Finish them off, men!"

Several submachine guns started to rattle in a relentless fire while Hege emptied his second to the last belt.

"Motherfuckers!" he boomed and let himself drop into the foxhole where he immediately opened the top cover of his MG and put in the last belt.

"Sarge, you gotta do something!" he groaned. "The Ivans are swarming all over our trenches, and I'm running out of bullets!"

Berning just stared at Hege. What was he supposed to do?

"Come on!", Hege urged him. "Get the guys and start a counter-attack. We have to beat them off before they penetrate our trenches!"

Hege stared at the sergeant emphatically. Reluctantly, Berning climbed out of the hole without really knowing yet what to do. Again he could hear Hege's machine gun fire behind his back.

Berning looked at the area ahead of him.

The open field was lined with smoking wrecks of dozens of T-34s; tall clover hugged the tanks in a green embrace. In the meantime more Russian armored fighting vehicles had been turned into junk than those that could still be used for combat. And the number of Russian infantry men had shrunk considerably as well. Some Red Army forces were already withdrawing back to their starting positions, followed by the detonations of German mortars.

But the fire on the ridge had not ceased yet. Berning noticed that suddenly the position of his squad was covered with motionless Russian soldiers lying on the ground. And then he discovered half an enemy platoon close by under siege of Hege's fire.

Berning threw himself behind a tree for cover and risked another glance. The projectiles from Hege's weapon shot up into the trees and into the ground around the Russians; yet the enemy lay low, waiting. Then Hege took a longer break. A Russian raiding party immediately stormed ahead on their way to the next cover. Hege pulled the trigger and mowed the men down without mercy. For one short moment nothing moved in the area ahead of them; then a German soldier scurried back and forth between two trees. Hege fired at him right away, and the German also collapsed, moaning while a fountain of blood sprayed from his neck.

"No!" Hege, who just now had realized what he had done, cried. "Shit! Bloody fool!" Without thinking, he moved his gun down to the Russians' cover and started to fire, but after a few seconds his MG fell silent.

"I'm out!" he yelled and disappeared into his foxhole.

Not a good idea, Berning thought. At least one of the Russians seemed to understand German, too. Under the cover of submachine guns, they all stormed up the hill at the same time.

Only now did Berning notice that Bongartz was pinned down behind a tree just forty yards ahead of him. Due to the submachine gun fire he couldn't even think of returning it with his repeating rifle. By now the

Russians had moved up to only a few yards away from them and threw hand grenades. Detonations rocked the position and created high walls of soil that reached up to the treetops.

When the dust had settled and Berning could see again, the Russians were already everywhere. Soviet submachine guns punched holes in German soldiers at almost point-blank range while Pappendorf's weapon took Russian lives in return. Apparently the staff sergeant had regrouped part of the platoon for a counter attack to outflank the Russians and throw them out of the trenches again.

Then Berning's eyes found Bongartz. The lance corporal stood facing a Russian soldier; both were armed with rifles which they used to fence with each other like musketeers. The Russian smashed the shaft of his weapon into Bongartz's hand, bruising it. The lance corporal howled and dropped his weapon; then he immediately grabbed his opponent's gun with his fingers. The Russian pushed himself up against Bongartz; both screamed and fell backwards down the hill into a hollow.

"No, please don't," Berning groaned. He could no longer see the two combatants from his position but he was also unable to move. He just stood there, trembled and tried as hard as he could to swallow his tears.

Suddenly some power took over his body, and he started to run – right to the hollow where Bongartz and the Russian were struggling. He could hear the moaning and groaning of the soldiers who were fighting for their lives. Berning stopped next to the hollow and froze again.

Bongartz lay on the ground, turning blue. The Russian's hands – he had huge paws – were wrapped tightly around the lance corporal's neck and continued to press down. Sitting on Bongartz, the Russian pushed his whole weight down on the lance corporal. Apparently he didn't even notice Berning and groaned bitterly while he pushed down his weight on Bongartz even harder. The lance corporal's arms and legs flailed around but he was trapped helpless under his enemy. Berning was paralyzed. He wanted to help his comrade but he couldn't move his hands. They gripped the wood of his weapon so hard that his fingers cramped up and hurt. So Berning just kept looking at the two: Bongartz's flailing and kicking became wilder and more desperate. The lance corporal's eyes rolled back into his head and he spat at the Russian but his opponent didn't let go of him. Then the lance corporal's movements gradually grew weaker. He was still swinging his arms wildly in the air, but a few seconds later he stopped moving and his body started to jerk. The Russian kept up his strangling hold. Bongartz's arms were the first to totally stop moving. His legs were still kicking. Then the kicks turned into jerks, and finally the jerks gave way to complete immobility. Bongartz's eyes rolled back even farther in his head but suddenly his gaze became clear and focused again. His eyes stared at Berning – for just one second that seemed like two eternities to the sergeant. Then the light of life left the lance corporal's face forever.

Several moments passed without the Russian soldier loosening his grip. Finally he let go. He reached for the rifle that was next to Bongartz's dead body in the hollow and repeatedly smashed the shaft into the lance corporal's face. Bongartz's features turned to a bloody mush.

The Russian got up, turned around and saw Berning. The distance between the two men was only a few yards.

The Russian was a tall and sturdy fellow. His face was covered with dirt and splattered blood, somewhat concealing his blue eyes and blond hair.

Berning was unable to move even though he realized that his adversary was tensing the muscles in his arms and grabbing the gun more tightly. Suddenly the Soviet soldier dropped his gun and raised his hands. Berning's body shook with rage. This guy had murdered Rudi!

Murderer! The sergeant thought. *Murderer! Goddamn murderer!*

Berning's whole body trembled. His hands grabbed his rifle again with determination, his grip tightened around the wood. He narrowed his eyes and focused on the Russian. The man looked back with an empty glance and an exhausted look on his face. Berning's arms tensed while he slowly raised his firearm – almost automatically.

The word *murderer* echoed in the sergeant's head.

Pappendorf suddenly appeared behind Berning and the Russian, trailing five soldiers behind him. "Berning!"

The Russian turned around and nodded his head to point at his hands, which he had raised. Meanwhile the fire and combat racket had died down almost completely while the remaining Soviet soldiers escaped into the woods. Their attack had been warded off.

"Well done, Sergeant!" Pappendorf said, surprised. "You've taken a prisoner of war."

Berning was still trembling.

Belp, Switzerland, May 8th, 1943

Everything had actually gone according to plan – which Taylor had not expected beforehand because women were unpredictable, and in general one could control the affection or dislike of others only to a certain degree. Yet it seemed to work.

As promised, yesterday evening Luise had returned the bicycle to the military intelligence apartment Taylor used in Bern. All dressed up and made up with cosmetics and lipstick – and her curvy body wrapped in a red dress – she had shown up on his doorstep, and that despite the fact that she had worked in Bern all day while her apartment and therefore her closet, too, were in Belp. Unsure of herself and with a flustered smile on her lips she had said hello and thanked him profusely yet again. And then she had hesitantly asked him with a stutter – Thomas liked her shy demeanor – if they could meet for a coffee and a walk in beautiful Belp the next day. Though she knew it wasn't proper for a lady, she said, she would like to treat him to a cup of coffee as an expression of her gratitude.

Taylor had just smiled and naturally accepted the invitation.

He also had further adapted Aaron Stern's biography that had been prepared by military intelligence because the master spies of the Abwehr had forgotten one important detail: Thomas wasn't circumcised. So that there wouldn't be any unpleasant questions later, Stern's new story was: Mom died during his birth, Dad was killed in the Great War. Therefore he grew up in an orphanage; so no circumcision, no bar mitzvah, and so on. Simple enough.

*

The afternoon sun had to struggle through the thick clouds, and so it was very humid without being hot. The soil and the vegetation cracked under the weather that had denied them any raindrop for weeks now.

In many spots the grass had already turned yellow and was burned by the sun, while ponds were slowly drying up, turning into swamps.

Thomas and Luise had finished their coffee and were now taking a walk on the outskirts of Belp, along a country lane running along an evergreen forest.

In the background, the land rose up above the flat plains on which the town was located, while a few farms were scattered here and there, looking as if they had long since been overrun by nature. In the distance Belp was nothing more than a larger collection of cozy brick houses. Thomas and Luise had chatted about all kinds of things without getting much beyond trivialities. She had told him that even though she lived in Switzerland, she also had British roots.

Her father was a high-ranking officer in Her Majesty's Armed Forces who was currently stationed somewhere in Africa. Her mother, who was Swiss, had passed away

212

while giving birth to Luise's sister, Stella. Luise worked as a secretary at the British Consulate in Bern.

Taylor had already known, but of course, he didn't let show. Instead he told her about his alleged home, a small village near Inverness in Scotland. He told her that he worked for a British trade company, and that four weeks ago his employer had sent him to Switzerland where he intended to spend a few years.

This biography smartly evaded the fact that small Jewish communities were usually well connected, which might cause a problem if no one in Bern had ever heard of Aaron Stern.

Furthermore he had presented himself as a liberal Jew who didn't take his religion all that seriously, because first of all, Thomas could never have learned all the rites and traditions of such an extensive culture in such a short time, and second, Luise's family supposedly didn't practice the Jewish faith that zealously, either. His story about being an orphan helped, too, because it gave credibility to the fact that he had not been raised as a Jew.

As the day went on, Luise had lost a bit of her shyness, but she was still cautious and approached him as hesitantly as a wild animal.

Thomas genuinely liked her. She was pleasant, polite, well-mannered as well as breathtakingly beautiful, and she also excited him physically.

Now they were walking side by side in silence and smoking freshly lit cigarettes, while a dense forest opened up in front of them. Unexpectedly the expression on Luise's face had turned serious, and she looked down with narrowed eyes.

"Aaron?" she finally interrupted the silence. They had agreed to keep conversing in German even though both could speak English, too, but Luise felt more comfortable conversing in her first mother tongue.

"Yes?"

"Doesn't the current situation in Europe scare you, too?"

"No, why should it?" As soon as Thomas had uttered these words, he winced. He needed to finally start thinking like a Jew, too! And how could the Jews *not* be frightened by the anti-Semitic atmosphere in Germany and Italy – yes, even in the Soviet Union and in parts of France? He definitely had to be more careful!

"I mean the situation in the German Reich and in Italy." She looked at him wide-eyed.

"I see," he responded sheepishly. "But Hitler's gone, and a lot has changed since then."

"No, I don't believe it. That's just German propaganda! If this Witzleben and his generals really were as righteous as they claim to be, they'd have ended this miserable war a long time ago. After all, the Germans also started it! They marched into their neighbors' countries, and now they suddenly claim that they no longer want to have anything to do with the Nazis? Then why don't they pull their forces out of Russia and France, where they occupy foreign territory that's not theirs?"

"I can't tell you why."

"But I can tell *you*: Because the same Nazis are in the new government – they just have different names now."

Thomas was silent. What could he say? After all, he couldn't really start defending his country now.

"But at least the Jews are supposed to be better off now, I heard," he finally interjected.

Apparently – and obviously understandably as well – this issue was a sore point for Luise, who was now getting into a mixture of rage and fear.

"What utter nonsense!" she cried. "My Dad has a few connections in occupied Europe. He's heard of Jewish families in mortal danger who had to be hidden from the Germans by courageous Dutch and French people because the Germans wanted to deport them to labor camps. Didn't you ever wonder where they're taking the Jews?"

Thomas shrugged and said thoughtfully, "I guess they have been exiled and taken to Jewish settlements in the East where they can live in peace."

He wasn't sure if a Jew these days, who, after all, had been affected by the European anti-Semitism and the events in Hitler's Germany, would really respond like that, but Luise didn't seem to become suspicious.

She was much too busy keeping her emotions in check while she continued, "Yes, that's what they're saying. But I don't believe it. Where are all these settlements supposed to be, huh? Where in the East? All there is, is the front line and occupied Russia ahead of that, where nobody wants to take in any Jews. And I don't think that the Germans would clear whole sections of Russia to let us settle down there. They're much too busy with their war!"

Luise's words actually did make Taylor reflect. Only now did he realize that he had always taken the claim at face value that the Jews would be resettled in the East without questioning the issue. Yet Luise was basically right.

"My Dad knows even more, I could tell by his face, but he doesn't want to tell me any more." Luise was literally trembling. "Since the beginning of this year, some Jews have allegedly returned to Germany. But all of their belongings are gone, and suddenly there are strangers living in their homes. They get a few reichsmarks handed to them and are then left on their own! And that's not all there is, because many of them *didn't* come back and many of those who did are extremely upset and confused."

"Well, I had no idea. That's … that's really frightening."

"Yes, when I think about it, I could cry. Why would anyone do something like that to other people? Why?" She fell silent for a moment to let her words sink in. Then she continued, "But then I haven't told you about the biggest audacity and dirty trick so far that the Germans have been playing."

"What's that?" Taylor would have preferred to stop this conversation right then and there but he had to prompt her to keep playing his part.

"The Jewish men who return from these so-called labor camps are immediately drafted by the German Wehrmacht to fight their war for them! First everything is taken from them and they're deported from their homelands, and now they're supposed to go to war for those who did that to them? That's the kind of crude disrespect only Germans are capable of. I find that truly disgusting!"

All of a sudden she broke down while tears ran down her cheeks. Thomas went over to her right away and held her tight.

"Oh, Aaron," she cried. "Why does the world have to be so cruel?"

He didn't know why – he honestly didn't, and so he just shook his head while his warm hands stroked her head and Luise slowly calmed down.

"Everything is going to be all right," he said finally.

"Will it really?" There was sarcasm in her voice when she lifted her head and looked at Thomas with wide, deep-blue eyes.

"Of course it will."

"I wish I had your optimism."

"Well, I mean what could happen?"

"Switzerland is surrounded by fascists! I'm just frightened, Aaron. I'm so scared." She pressed her body against his and started to cry again.

Thomas felt her grip tightening. She shifted her weight, leaning against him and trusting that he would hold her tight. He liked that.

Yet inside he was torn apart by doubts. For the first time ever there was something – more a hunch than real certainty – that was gnawing on his trust that the German Reich really was on the side of the good guys.

South of Kursk, Soviet Union, May 10th, 1943
Heeresgruppe Süd – Two kilometers south of Kursk

Kursk had been taken and was now in German hands once again. Army Group South had already taken the city the day before, after the Russian troops had withdrawn to the West almost without putting up a fight and therefore into the encirclement that was closing in on them. But Engelmann couldn't really taste victory yet.

Why on Earth did the Russians flee into the pocket instead to the East? He wondered without finding an answer while peering out of the commander's hatch at the southern suburbs of the city. A narrow stream – the Seym River – cut through the terrain while primitive roads led to the center of Kursk. On the horizon one could already see the houses of the outermost southern district peeking through numerous treetops. The buildings Engelmann could make out had been battered by the previous battle. A lot of them were ruins with blown-out windows, and many of the houses were partially or completely collapsed. Just this morning Engelmann had been in the city for a briefing at the regimental command post. Actually, civilians were still living everywhere throughout the ruins, most of them old men, women and children. Filthy and smelly, they were always looking for food and useful objects in the rubble. These people were scarred by the war. Their eyes were filled with fear in the face of their old, new occupying forces because the last time the Germans had come, they had been followed by the Einsatzgruppen, SS death squads that had to pick up deserters, partisans and other wanted persons. Little did the people of Kursk know that these Einsatzgruppen no longer existed, and even if they had known, their previous experiences were enough to make them terrified of the field gray uniforms for the rest of their lives.

The battle of Prokhorovka, the occupation of Oboyan and securing control of the important bridge over the Psel River there had broken the Russian resistance, so that the further advance had been more like mopping up the remains.

That was the reason why Engelmann's platoon had reached its new operational area south of Kursk while the reunion with Heeresgruppe Mitte was expected for that night. Then several Russian armies would be encircled and face their imminent destruction.

In the distance three shots suddenly rang out in the city, and their echoes reverberated for a long time. Then there was silence again, only accompanied by a concert of songbirds. There were still a few nests of resistance in Kursk, but these last defenders stood no chance at all.

Engelmann looked at the area ahead expectantly while the rest of his crew sat near the tank or ate or slept. By noon his platoon had already tightened the tracks of their panzers, refueled them and replenished the ammunition supplies as well as camouflaged them sufficiently to conceal them from enemy pilots. Now there was nothing else to do but wait for new orders – and precisely these possible new orders were what Engelmann was worried about.

Engelmann enjoyed the pleasant warmth while his tank was protected from the sun by the shade of tall birch trees. He reflected over the current situation. As of that morning he had been convinced – with sad certainty – that Field Marshal von Manstein, the Commander-in-Chief East, had decided to go through with Phase II of Operation Citadel despite the fact that the German attack forces were worn-out and exhausted: the advance into the depths of the country, with Voronezh as their goal.

Engelmann thought that was a big mistake because the forces were just too depleted for that. The 16th Panzer Division only had fifty-five percent of its panzers left, and the heavy tank battalion that had accompanied Engelmann's platoon to Kursk only had fifteen Tigers left that were fit for service. This situation was typical for many forces assigned to the salient.

Sure, Engelmann could relate to the opposite argument that his battalion commander had again explained to him: In the East the Russians were on the run. Their commanders had to organize them laboriously all over again to set up proper defense positions. In addition, up until Kastornoye, there would be no more deeply staggered systems of trenches, mine belts and foxholes like the ones the German attackers had had to fight it out with in the North and south of Kursk last week. Another attack certainly wouldn't result in the same high numbers of casualties.

Therefore von Manstein, Colonel General Paulus and Field Marshal von Kluge argued that if the Wehrmacht didn't use the attack momentum right now, that they would give the Russians enough time to organize reserve forces and dig themselves in again. Then a year from now the Wehrmacht would have to plow through twenty miles of defense systems again. But Engelmann didn't budge: The available forces were too ground down. In his opinion, it would be better if the generals focused on reality rather than on wishful thinking because at the present time the German Army was obviously not able to do more than storm the Kursk salient.

Several Russian armies were still encircled – and though they were surrounded, they were not defeated yet. However, the front line had been straightened out, saving the Germans enormous numbers in men and material in the long run. A successful attack leading up to Kastornoye would only produce a salient again in the other direction, thus eating up those savings again.

Yet this attack would take place.

For that precise purpose, right now the strongest forces were removed from the weak cover and mobilized around Kursk; several reserve corps were joining them in order to start the attack the next day at dawn. Panzer Regiment 2 and all the other companies that were more or less clinically dead would provide the cover in the direction of the pocket. That was a lousy life insurance for the attack forces.

Engelmann sighed. Who would listen to a mere lieutenant anyway these days?

He climbed out of his cupola and jumped off the hull onto the soft ground. The sun set slowly, birds sang and insects hummed. At least the animals didn't participate in the war and kept on doing what they had always been doing. The fight for survival, that eternal struggle to eat or be eaten, was won or lost out here in the woods and the fields every day but no one objected to it.

Maybe, Engelmann thought, *maybe human beings have to understand that war is not a horrible atrocity but just human nature. Maybe this is just the natural way for human beings to participate in the game of eat or be eaten?*

But he quickly rejected such thoughts. Whether it was natural or not, Engelmann wanted this war to finally end and another war never to start again. At least he wished that his daughter would be able to grow up in a world without any wars. He could hear children's voices in the distance and looked up to see Russian boys roughhousing and splashing each other on the bank of the Seym River.

No, Engelmann didn't just want a life without any wars for his own daughter. He wanted it for all children. Again he had to sigh; then he turned away. It hurt him to see these children playing by the river because they reminded him of all the things in his daughter's life that he was missing out on.

Was she crawling already? Actually he didn't know anything about Gudrun, except the things his wife wrote to him. That really hurt.

While the lieutenant was lost in his thoughts, taking in the calm setting, Born scrambled out from under the tank with his book and shook himself like a dog. He walked over to an old pine tree close by and sat down in its shade. He was already engrossed in his book again.

Engelmann approached him and glanced at the cover. Born was still reading *The World Set Free*.

"And – is it any good?"

Born nodded. "Yes, Sir."

"Is it about Martians again?"

Born shook his head and put the book down. "It's about new bombs with incredible destructive powers that are used during the war."

"Something like a two-ton bomb?"

"No, these ones are a lot worse. In this book you can eliminate a whole city with just one bomb. They're called atomic bombs."

Engelmann smiled warmly. "Well, in that case we can be glad that things like that just exist in books, can't we?"

North of Kursk, Soviet Union, May 11th, 1943
Heeresgruppe Mitte – One kilometer north of Kursk

All that commotion for this hick town? Sergeant Berning thought when his unit reached the rather rural northern outskirts of Kursk. With over 100 000 inhabitants – at least before the war – the city was anything but a hick town and also had a sizeable industrial park, but 1st Reconnaissance Squadron of Schnelle Abteilung 253 had only reached the peripheries of the city and started to move slowly towards the center, following the road in long rows. One could see a few separate buildings – most of them homes with black roofs – to the left and right of the street. Between the houses there were fields, trees and paddocks for farm animals. From here one could not see the downtown area of the city yet. A few holes in the walls of the buildings and cartridge cases littering the sides of the road hinted at the moderate combat activities that had taken place around Kursk in the last few days. In one spot, a large pool of blood had even trickled into the pavement.

Yet Berning barely noticed his surroundings because he couldn't shake off what had happened while defending the hill ridge near Olchovatka. At night he dreamed of Bongartz standing on the side of a soccer field, watching one of his team's games, or he was haunted by cruel accusations that even led to a court martial. He could see

Pappendorf, Bongartz, who had turned blue in the face, and Hege, all of whom were summoned to court to testify in detail about Sergeant Berning's ineptitude and incompetence. In that dream, Field Marshal von Manstein personally proclaimed the sentence. The high-ranking officer rendered a guilty verdict, accusing Berning of not being a good comrade, of failure to render assistance, of cowardice in the face of the enemy and the inability to lead his soldiers, while in the courtroom his father— the proud postal official from Austria — his ailing mother and Gretel lowered their heads in shame. After the trial Berning's shoulder boards had been torn off, he had been forced to wear a Soviet uniform, and he was put in a Russian POW camp, where he had to dig anti-tank ditches until the end of the war. Berning felt that he didn't fit in. Everyone here had shown him more than once that he didn't belong in this army – or even in this world.

Pappenorf circled around his platoon like a satellite once again. By now it had shrunk to an eerily small number. No more than nine men plus the sergeant had survived Operation Citadel. The same held true for the Schnelle Abteilung 253 as it did for any other unit: Companies had turned into platoons, platoons had shrunk to squads, and most of the original squads had completely fallen apart. At least the battalion wouldn't have to move on for the time being. For the next few days, maybe even weeks, they would be able to take a rest in the area of Kursk.

"Unteroffizier Berning!", Pappendorf yelled. 2nd Platoon would probably never rest as long as that staff sergeant was still breathing. Berning ran over to his platoon leader, stopped and pushed the helmet back up that had slid down into his face.

"Here, Herr Unterfeldwebel."

"We'll be reaching our designation in five hundred yards. Go to the HQ platoon leader, inquire about our operation zone, take up position there and gather the platoon."

"Yes, Herr Unterfeldwebel. Five hundred ahead, inquire about operation zone, gather platoon."

"Move it, Sergeant!"

Berning started to move, passing first the tip of the platoon and then the men of 1st Platoon. Again and again, his Stahlhelm slid down into his face, and again and again he had to push it back up. Each time it happened, his rage grew.

Why me again? He kept thinking. *Dammit, any grunt can do this for a change! Why's he always picking on me?*

Obsessing about these thoughts, he passed more comrades with sooty faces who were trudging up the street.

Sergeant Berning had enough. More than enough.

Plakhino, Soviet Union, May 12th, 1943
Kursk Front "inside the pocket" – 30 kilometers west of Kursk

The day had gradually turned into evening when Colonel General Sidorenko finished giving orders to his army commanders. The highest-ranking Russian officers in the pocket west of Kursk, all with stern expressions on their faces, had gathered around him, but now they nodded in agreement, murmuring "Da". They had a tough job ahead of them, but the commanders actually had to admit that Sidorenko – despite all doubts, they had had about him in the beginning – had not only developed an outstanding combat plan but also managed to organize and carry out major retreat movements of whole formations in the middle of the battles of Olchovatka and Prokhorovka without the Germans noticing it. Now the fascists were about to concentrate the pitiful remains of their military forces in order to chase the fleeing Red Army into the hinterlands. What they left behind to protect Kursk and the eastern front line of the pocket was a ridiculous bunch of exhausted soldiers with damaged equipment. To believe that hostile troops inside a pocket were beaten the moment the encirclement was closed truly fit into the theory of German arrogance.

"Pah! Woobrashayuc 'hii sbrod!" Sidorenko spit it out loudly after having sent the commanders back to their companies. *Conceited pack of trash!* He would teach the Nazis a lesson! There was only one goal left for him in this war: to kill Germans – as many as possible – and then to break through the German defense lines. Sidorenko was already looking forward to the moment when he would finally fight on German soil. Then he would repay the German people for what the fascists had done to his country. An eye for an eye.

If that self-appointed superior race really believed it had the right to occupy his country, well, then he would teach them differently! At the same time he would teach the Stavka not to write off its loyal servant Nikolay Sidorenko so fast.

A German reconnaissance aircraft roared with a steady sound in the sky, but there was a dense roof of leaves between the plane and Sidorenko's command post. In addition, farmers with their cows were moving in the fields that surrounded him, which made for a perfect camouflage, just as the Russians had spent a great deal of time concealing their attack forces from curious eyes in the past few days.

Turning around again, Sidorenko's glance fell on the sandbox he had built on the ground – a training principle he had learned from German officers back in Kama. He had to smile. In the sandbox Sidorenko had shown something else, something he had learned by the Germans, too – although recently: the tank wedge. Yes, he still had a few aces up his sleeve, and like any good poker player, he had kept them concealed from his opponents so far.

Birsfelden, Switzerland, May 14th, 1943

To Taylor's delight, which wasn't only due to professional reasons, he had spent more time in the past few days with the charming Luise. Since the heartfelt embrace in Belp and her tears about the situation of the Jews in Europe, he had sensed a deeper connection to her that kept him awake at night. Every time he thought of her, especially right before their next date, he felt sharp but wonderful stinging sensations in his stomach. When he was around her, he was filled with a kind of excitement he had never felt before – something totally different from the adrenaline rush in combat. When he was with Luise, he was nervous in a pleasant way to which he was glad to surrender. Yet in those times when he was by himself, he could no longer stop thinking of her.

Then he imagined what their first kiss would feel like, and the first time they would make love, and he hoped that these images wouldn't just remain wishful thinking. Indeed Luise's affection for Thomas also seemed to grow steadily; at least he had no other explanation for her even canceling a date with her beloved sister, Stella, on Sunday just to be with him. And every evening of the week, except Wednesday, she had appeared on his doorstep after work. And yes, he had wondered if those were really signs of her affection or if he was simply misinterpreting them. When he was by himself, he mentally played through every scenario possible, and though the result was always satisfactory – namely that he and she would become lovers – there was always this nagging doubt eating away at him. Could it be love? If he was in love, he couldn't allow himself to acknowledge these feelings but had to focus on his duty; that much was certain. A life together with Luise wouldn't work anyway because she didn't even know his real name. He had been thinking a lot about things like that lately but on the days he was with Luise, there was only one thing: her.

Today Luise didn't have to work, and so they had started out early to explore the city of Basel. After all, Aaron Stern had just recently come to Switzerland and hadn't seen much of the country yet, while Luise, just like a tour guide, had something to say about every city, every location and every building. Thomas was impressed.

All morning Luise had dragged Taylor through Basel to show him all the attractions of the city: the synagogue of Basel, the Spalen Gate and of course the famous landmark of the city, the cathedral. Yet Taylor also noticed that the Swiss Armed Forces were swarming around in this border town.

For lunch they went to a Swiss restaurant, dipped chunks of bread and potatoes into melted cheese and had beer and wine with their meal. After lunch they drove on to Birsfelden, a sleepy, little village on the Birs River that bordered on Basel, to get away from the hectic rush of the city and end the day on a quieter note.

Taylor had to grin because the wine obviously made Luise a little tipsy even though lunch with wine had been quite a while ago. She kept giggling and snorting with laughter at trivialities and teased Thomas at every opportunity. Yet maybe she was just happy?

Now they were getting away from Birsfelden; they strolled across a stone bridge over the river and followed the road into a sprawling forest where they both enjoyed a cigarette and laughed hilariously over and over again.

"I can't go on," Luise finally moaned and broke out in laughter. "My feet are killing me." She dropped into the grass that lined the road and grinned widely. Thomas sat down next to her, and they gazed at each other.

"You should at least make it back to the car," he said. Their eyes locked while their bodies were already touching. Thomas put his hand around her waist and stroked her gently.

"I bet you'd carry me if I asked you to," she replied, chewing her lower lip while her gaze sent out an invitation. Their faces came closer together.

"I would carry you anywhere you want me to," he breathed more than he spoke. Then their lips met. They kissed, passionately and long. Luise moved towards Taylor and wrapped her arms around him. Their bodies kept moving closer together. He could feel the heat of her chest that radiated pleasantly onto his while she pulled him closer. Then their tongues met. Luise closed her eyes and enjoyed the moment. Thomas's hand kept caressing her waist, then her belly. She moaned with pleasure and didn't let go of his lips. His hand slowly moved up until it finally touched a soft curve. Luise immediately pushed him away and jumped up.

"What do you think you're doing, Aaron?" she shrieked.

"I ..." Taylor's eyes grew wide. He didn't know what to say.

"I'm not that kind of girl!" she screamed shrilly. She turned around and stalked off.

"Luise!" he called after her but she didn't react, and one minute later she disappeared behind the bend.

"Damn," Thomas groaned as he dropped down on the grass. Had he ruined the whole thing?

West of Kursk, Soviet Union, May 16th, 1943
Heeresgruppe Süd – Two kilometers west of Kursk

The attack into the depths of the Kursk Oblast and towards Voronezh dragged on. Despite little resistance from the enemy, the Wehrmacht only advanced slowly. The 6th Army didn't participate in the attack but had been ordered to cover the pocket's front line in the rear. The formations that were still strong enough, such as the Panzergrenadier Regiments 64 and 79, had been detached from the 6th and assigned to the 2nd Panzer Army, while those formations that were particularly battle-weary, such as Major General Becker's 253rd Infantry Division, had in return been attached to the 6th Army.

Lieutenant Engelmann hid with his tanks in a small forest section west of the city. The area the regiment was responsible for was located considerably far behind the main combat line intended to serve as "fire fighters" for the whole sector, meaning they had to stay combat ready in order to engage once the enemy would be on the verge of a breakthrough somewhere. The first sunbeams just touched the ground but gunfire already thundered to the west of them. The men of Schützen-Brigade 16 had been battling massive Russian forces for the past twenty minutes. Engelmann had already put his platoon on alert.

Squinting, he peered out of the commander's hatch of Elfriede at the area ahead, where lightning-like bolts were sweeping across the sky. The first radio messages didn't sound good at all; the enemy was obviously getting ready to break out of the pocket. Lieutenant Engelmann prepared himself mentally for the moment when he would receive the command for the counter attack. Again he felt the uncomfortable excitement that always overtook him when a battle was imminent. He dug a red can out of his chest pocket and put a piece of chocolate in his mouth without moving his eyes from the terrain ahead.

*

The drums of battle merged to an almost homogenous deep constant threatening thunder filling the air over the small farm settlement west of Kursk, preparing the stage for the inevitable slaughter to come. The sounds came closer as the combat activities did, but Berning paid no attention to them. Since the pitiful remains of his reconnaissance squadron had moved into one of the farms and taken up their defense positions there, the men of 2nd Platoon also got for a change to enjoy a roof over their heads again. The group of farms, which consisted of a tight cluster of seven farmhouses that formed a kolkhoz, was located on a wide, open field that sloped down on all four sides. Dense woods rose to the left and right, while in the West the open plains stretched out in form of a lane through the groves all the way to the horizon. If the Russians were to attack here, they would be seen for miles while the Germans could hide in the buildings and the surrounding woods.

But Sergeant Berning didn't care. He sat on a chair in a bedroom on the second floor of one of the farmhouses. The door to the adjacent room, where Hege had established his MG perch, was closed, and Berning had asked the other men not to disturb him for a moment. Most of the soldiers of the platoon were downstairs, sleeping or playing skat, while Pappendorf was scurrying around the company's command post.

Berning's entire body trembled. His hands shook. His eyes were closed. His lips throbbed and had turned gray.

The muzzle of the K98k felt cold and strange on his mouth. The weapon was loaded and the safety catch was off. The index finger of his right hand lay unsteady on the trigger. Berning was just tall enough to kill himself with the gun. He sat there like that for several minutes.

Everybody had shown him often enough that he didn't belong here – that they didn't want him here. So this was his solution. This way he wouldn't be a burden for anyone anymore. His finger was still on the trigger but he just couldn't bring himself to pull it. No matter how much power he thought he was applying to his finger – the trigger refused to move. Berning tensed up his whole body.

So count down! He ordered himself, *ten … nine … eight … seven … six … five … four … three … two … one … and … fire!*

Nothing. His finger didn't move. Berning groaned. He was angry. Angry at the war. Angry at everything. Angry at himself. He wasn't even good enough for this! But then again no! After all, the muzzle was still in his mouth!

Again! Count down! Berning closed his eyes so tightly that they hurt. *Ten … nine … eight … seven … six … five … four … three … two … one … fire!*

It just didn't work. Berning opened his eyes and the tension left his body.

Come on! Come on! He urged himself on. But he couldn't do it.

He took the weapon out of his mouth and hurled it against the far wall. *To hell with the point of aim!* He cursed silently. Then he collapsed on the ground.

He made a fist and slugged it into the wooden planks with all the force he could muster. One time – two times – three times. He felt a sharp pain in his wrist.

Minutes that felt like an eternity passed while the booming noise in the background became louder and the noise of propellers filled the sky. Berning looked up slowly. His eyes were bloodshot and tracks of dried tears marked his face.

Straightening up, Berning rubbed his eyes. Through the window he could see purple signal strips drawing lines into the sky.

Then a detonation very close by tore Berning out of his own little world and carried him mercilessly back into the here and now. The whole building shook under the power of the impact. Berning ran to the window and froze. The terrain in front of the positions of the formation had become invisible because it had been completely swallowed up by attacking Russian forces. Infantry, tanks, even cavalry. An olive-brownish mass moved towards the positions of the Germans. Heavy assault guns – nothing Berning had ever seen before – formed the tip. Twelve of these beasts with low silhouettes and fully enclosed casemates carrying monstrous gun barrels – larger and longer than those of the Tigers – moved directly towards the farmhouses. The sergeant estimated these monsters to be longer than twenty-five feet. They shot and drove in turns. Their high explosive rounds tore up the dirt around the collective farm while half of a smaller shed collapsed after being hit. The steel leviathans were immediately followed by T-34s and other medium-sized combat tanks that fanned out widely, forming a wedge with the assault guns on its tip. And behind them more infantry forces stormed ahead; there were even soldiers on horses, holding sabers and guns in their hands. It was one gigantic wedge, and its tip was pointing directly at the positions of Schnelle Abteilung 253.

Gunfire lit up everywhere, and tracer rounds raced into the rows of Russian soldiers while they already flooded the forward operating positions of the division at the left and right edge of the woods, just swallowing up the bullets in the pure mass of bodies. Artillery fire cracked between the attacking forces of the Red Army, killing many soldiers, but even more just kept on running. The Russian Ratsch Bumms piped up, too, blowing German positions to hell.

Petrified, Berning still stood at the window unable to move. He could already hear Hege's MG comencing its murderous hail of bullets. Then the door to his room was kicked open and Pappendorf stepped in, a radio in one hand, his MP 40 in the other.

"Dammit, Sergeant! Grab your gun and run over to the MG! You'll lead its fire! I'm going down to the platoon!"

"Jawohl, Herr Unterfeldwebel!"

"Go, go, go!"

"Herr Unterfeldwebel?"

"Yes?"

"Wouldn't it be better to retreat?"

Now Pappendorf did something he rarely ever did: He grinned. "Becker's just received confirmation of tank support. The Slavs will soon discover that they've made a big mistake."

*

Now the tanks of the regiment set into motion. Panzer IIs, Panzer IIIs and – thank God – also several Panzer IVs shot across an open field that slightly sloped uphill, along the edge of the forest. Massive enemy tank forces appeared at the positions of the 253rd, and the regiment was going to intercept the Russians exactly there.

Engelmann looked out of his cupola with a grave expression on his face; then he disappeared into the turret to study the map. The thunder of gunfire and the noise of airplanes even drowned out the roar of the tank engines.

"Hans, follow the edge along the woods. At approximately four thousand meters ahead we'll come to a lane in the woods. It is near a farm compound to the east. That's exactly where the enemy is bound to break through. Full speed ahead, man!" Once again the 1st Platoon was the leading platoon, and the 9th Company was the leading unit. Engelmann hated always having to be right at the front. But then that was the fate of those who were competent.

"Roger," Münster yelled as he pushed Elfriede to the limit. Though the tank groaned and creaked, she gained a few more mph in speed.

Just at that moment Nitz received a radio transmission. Leafing through his radio logbook, he listened carefully and jotted down a few key words that, due to the rumbling of the tank, looked like the scribblings of a six-year old.

"The 253rd reports twelve assault guns." Nitz paused; then he continued, "and a whole shitload of tanks! T-34s and the likes." His eyes widened. "Two to three hundred, all in all."

"Ebbe, the platoon should stay close together."

Nitz sent the message. Then they received an order originally from Colonel Sieckenius, but the CO of the 9th had it already itemized down for his units. Nitz translated the jumble of numbers into words they could understand: "Regiment takes up position behind the hill at level 254.2. Decoy provided by 9th Company. Guess whom the old man has chosen."

"First platoon to the front!" Born yelled with rather dubious motivation.

"That's what it looks like. We'll play the bait, attract the Russian tin cans, and then the trap springs." Nitz's voice sounded concerned, and Engelmann was anything but enthusiastic, either, but there was a chance that they might get a hold on the overpowering enemy tank forces this way.

"Remember the Dnieper salient in '41? This is gonna be the same thing," Engelmann declared ironically.

"I didn't like the Dnieper salient," Ludwig retorted.

Their own regiment had been melted down to barely more than one hundred tanks. Lieutenant Engelmann frowned. It would be a tough ride but the situation wasn't hopeless. After all, the enemy's wedged-shaped line of attack had to battle dozens of German anti-tank guns, and the infantry was likely to thin out the rows of Russian forces.

*

Berning held onto his rifle and narrowed his eyes to a slit while the building was shaken by the fire of the explosive shells that made the windows burst. Hege fired one ammunition belt after another at the advancing infantry soldiers, who for their part were busy to drive the German soldiers into the woods like cattle when they tried to flee from their trenches. The Russian tank wedge had slowed down and stopped in places. Now the tank guns tore apart the German anti-tank gun positions in the forest and on the collective farm.

The Germans didn't stand a chance. Only one T-34 burned somewhere in the sea of advancing enemy forces while nearly all German anti-tank guns had been blown to pieces. The defense lines crumbled away everywhere while Russian infantry soldiers stormed the woods from both sides. Some soldiers tried to reach the life-saving farm buildings, which were groaning under the fire of the huge assault guns, but most of them were just slaughtered by Russian fire.

"When will the goddamn tin cans get here?" Hege yelled while one comrade wearing a protective glove pulled the glowing barrel out of the weapon and pushed barrel number two into it.

"I don't know," Berning yelled back, ducking even farther. He could hear the enemy bullets from handguns smash into the outer walls of the building. Right now the fleeing Germans still kept the Russians busy, but all too soon they would focus their attention on the collective farm, which then would stand in the way of the red flood like a breakwater barrier.

"We have to get away from here!" Berning gasped and tightened his grip around the gun while Hege let the cocking handle of his weapon shoot forward again and pulled the trigger. The MG immediately spit steel and death into the horde. At the same time, Pappendorf came running up the stairs, rushed over to the MG position and threw himself on the ground next to Hege.

"The tanks'll be here in two minutes", he shouted at the top of his voice, drowning out the noise of the machine gun. It was only now that Pappendorf noticed that Berning was rolled up like a hedgehog, pressing himself against the wall in a defensive attitude.

"Berning! Dammit! What are you waiting for – an order to attack? Shoot, man!"

Looking up, Berning opened his mouth. "I ..."

An explosion tore a huge hole into the wall next to the window from which Hege was shooting with his MG. Fragments and parts of the wall flew throughout the room and pulled the soldiers to the ground. They cursed, groaned and covered their helmets with their hands to protect their heads. Pappendorf and Hege immediately struggled to get up while Berning coughed and writhed. The first assistant machine gunner stayed on the ground – forever. Hege was already back at his machine gun again and engaged in combat. He shot long bursts of fire into the masses of enemy forces that were pushing through the lane between the two wooded areas in the distance.

Pappendorf peered at the area ahead. His eyes grew wide. To their left, a huge throng of Cossacks on horses – more than one hundred and twenty of them – broke out of the Russian formation. Armed with sabers, guns and submachine guns, they drove their horses into a wild gallop as they raced past the tanks and assault guns and headed straight for the collective farm. Meanwhile, the enemy tanks continued to move again; yet they stopped firing. They would just break through now and leave the rest up to the infantry and cavalry.

"Private!" Pappendorf yelled and grabbed Hege by the shoulders, "over there, at eight o'clock, six hundred, the effing Knights of the Round Table. Blow 'em up!"

Hege swung his machine gun around, aimed and fired. The rounds smashed into the throng of horseback riders, threw horses and men onto the ground and mercilessly decimated the rows of Cossacks.

"My God, the horses...," Hege moaned and kept firing; yet the bullet storm did not impress the Cossacks. They just kept shooting back while galloping forward. Gunshots riddled the farmhouse walls. Berning, who had just gotten up again and shaken himself like a dog, threw himself back on the ground and pushed his Stahlhelm down hard on his head while he closed both eyes. Again he wished himself away from this living hell.

*

Engelmann looked at the terrain through his eye slit. In the distance he could see a compound of buildings under heavy fire. Tiny blocks whizzed around in this whirl of infantry and horsemen on the horizon. Engelmann counted an unbelievable number of tanks.

"Hans, keep the pedal to the floor."

They quickly shrank quickly. Now the lieutenant could recognize the enemy assault guns. *They're as huge as Sperm whales!*

"Armor-piercing round!" he gasped, and Born rammed a shell in the breech.

"We'll close in on them, hit them and run! Get ready!"

"Yep, Sepp," Münster confirmed.

They were only one and a half miles away now, and when Engelmann saw the extent of the Russian attack, tiny beads of sweat formed on his forehead. His infantry comrades were either fleeing or hiding on the collective farm, which was now being blown to pieces and surrounded by hostile infantry forces. Then Engelmann refocused his attention on these huge assault guns that were moving between all of the T-34s.

What the hell are they? He wondered. *Could they be these new SU-122s? No, they're much too big for that!*

One of the steel beasts now turned so that its front armor – as well as the giant barrel – faced Engelmann's platoon. Despite the distance the lieutenant could tell that the weaponry of this self-propelled artillery vehicle was oversized.

"Theo, can you see through the sight what these big things are?"

"I can't see anything – with all this shaking going on."

"Hans, slow down. Half speed."

"Jawohl, half speed." Hans gently stepped on the brake to slow Elfriede down.

"The platoon is to do the same and stay behind me."

"Jawohl, slow down and stay behind us," Nitz repeated and got behind the radio.

"I want to approach the situation slowly and check it out while we're still at a safe distance," Engelmann whispered and leaned forward as far as he could so as to get a good look through the narrow glass of his turret. They were more than a mile away.

"Cautiously approach to one point five; then we start to enter the danger zone..."

But without a warning Laschke's tank exploded. The turret was torn off, and the hull was enveloped in flames and smoke.

"What the...?" Engelmann said without being able to finish the sentence.

"Laschke's been hit!" Nitz screamed. At the same time more anti-tank projectiles rained down on the platoon and tore up the ground. A spray of dirt and grass and rocks created walls around the German panzers, blocking their view.

"Who's shooting?" Engelmann yelled, moving to the left and the right. But it didn't help; the view his eye slit provided didn't get any bigger.

Marseille's tank got the next hit. With the driver killed, its sides torn open, the tank rolled on while inside all life had been extinguished by the impact.

"Stop, Hans!" Engelmann roared. Elfriede came to an abrupt halt. A second jerk went through the tank when, one second later, it was rammed by Marseille's ghost tank. Engelmann was thrown to the front and hit his head badly. He held his forehead with his right hand while he saw flashes of light dancing in front of his eyes.

"Is that coming from the woods?" the lieutenant gasped. "Hans, pull back right now; they're killing us!"

"Jawohl!" Münster literally attacked the transmission to push the engine to the max. With a violent jerking movement Elfriede rolled backwards, shoved Marseille's dead tin can aside and revved in reverse. More shells exploded between the platoon's two remaining tanks.

"Who the hell's firing?" Engelmann cursed.

"It's coming from over there!" Münster cried into his throat microphone while he hung in the levers. He could see clearly through his window that the monstrous assault guns were lining up a good mile ahead, focusing all of their attention on the platoon.

At this distance? The lieutenant wondered. *No way!*

Engelmann's and Meinert's tanks drove in reverse at full speed while the Russians smothered them with shells.

"Step on the gas! Two point nine left to get to the ambush. Pedal to the metal, Hans!"

"I am! I am!"

A projectile hit Meinert's track with a loud bang and smashed it. Howling, the tank stopped.

"Fire!" Engelmann yelled frantically.

"...but..."

"I don't care! Fire!"

Ludwig fired and actually hit one of the assault guns in the center. But the monstrosity just ate the shell for breakfast and didn't even belch!

"AP round!"

"Meinert has stopped. Has thrown off his track!" Nitz gasped while the next messages were already rushing over the airwaves.

"No! Hans, stop the tank!"

243

"Do *what*?"

"Stop and drive up to Marseille's wreck. We'll use it as cover! We won't abandon the guys!"

Elfriede came to a halt. Something knocked against her steel skin. The chinking and humming of projectiles that ricocheted off the tank hurt Engelmann's eardrums.

"Where's that coming from?" the lieutenant asked. "Theo, move the turret to the left!"

The loader turned the turret. The shells from the Russian assault guns kept coming. The beasts fired three to four times per minute, pronging many square feet of land with every shot. But now the T-34s also threw themselves into the fray. They pushed forward out of the gaps between the gargantuan self-propelled cannons and raced towards Elfriede, eager to make it into combat distance. Sparks peppered Elfriede's armor as well as Meinert's immobile tank. AP rounds scorched the armor.

"Infantry with anti-tank gun from the left of the woods," Nitz, who had just received the information from Meinert's radio operator, reported, gasping for breath. Streams of sweat ran down the staff sergeant's face; the rest of the crew was sweating just as badly.

No breeze moved the heat inside the tank, and it smelled of stress, gasoline and fire. The air was filled with soot that settled on the oily faces and in the lungs of the men, making them burn and itch. But in the presence of the enemy, these were minor matters.

"From the left?" Engelmann repeated incredulously. "But that's where ours were supposed to be!"

Before he could give another order, Meinert's tank burst into flames. A hit! Who knew where it came from!

244

Then an enormous blast went through Elfriede, making her steel glow with heat. At the very next moment, Born's shrill scream echoed through the interior, drowning out the din of battle. Engelmann looked down from his seat and saw that Born's arms and torso were soaked in blood while the young man was screaming his head off. Born fell sideways and suddenly lay twitching across Nitz. The radio operator could barely reach his instruments any more. Elfriede stopped while more anti-tank rounds tried in vain to penetrate the armor of the Panzer IV. Again sparks rained on Elfriede's armor.

Everyone was quiet for a moment. Engelmann, Münster, Nitz and Ludwig held their breath while Born bubbled blood and foam. The lieutenant froze at the sight of his loader. He had never seen a hit like this one. The sight shook him to the core. For a split second the situation paralyzed him, and the sickly-sweet smell of burned flesh filled his nostrils. He almost threw up.

"Ebbe," Engelmann whispered as if there was the risk of being overheard by the enemy, "tell the old man that we won't make it. They must come ASAP. After that no more radio communication! As for the rest: Put on your gas masks! We'll try our old trick."

They all knew the drill and put on the gas masks they had stored near their seats. Then Münster and Ludwig pushed the twitching Born back onto his seat and put his mask over his face as well.

Engelmann grabbed the first of four smoke grenades he had been carrying with him in his tank since the beginning of 1941; they looked almost like common stick grenades. He pulled the fuse and dropped it. It fell on the floor of the tank with a metallic clink.

Carefully and very slowly Nitz opened his hatch. Then they waited while the grenade hissed and suddenly started to spit dense white smoke. Though it immediately billowed outside through the open covers, the inside of Elfriede was completely filled with the dense fumes.

They waited. They didn't move and hardly dared to breathe. All they could do was hope that this would fool the enemy even though the artificial smoke was white, not black. But the trick had worked before, close to Kiev. They kept waiting. Engelmann stared at the ceiling of the tank without blinking and made a fist. The enemy fire had actually subsided. Then the radio crackled. Carefully – oh so carefully – Nitz bent down to the receiver unit and pressed it to his ear. Finally he looked up, directly at the lieutenant.

"The regiment's coming," he said.

*

"Goddammit, boy, if you don't start shooting soon, I'll beat you to a pulp!" Pappendorf blared and pulled Berning up to his feet. Bullets flew through the windows and the hole in the wall, hitting the far side of the room. Hege continued to shoot like a madman, but he run of ammo fast, and his gun jammed now that all three change barrels were glowing red from too much use.

Pappendorf pulled Berning to a window and forced him to take his place right next to Hege.

"SHOOT, WILL YA?" he yelled at the top of his lungs, the loudness of his voice even topped the noise of the MG.

Berning stared out the window at the chaos outside; his eyes became wider with every heartbeat. The red flood had poured over the whole sector. Russian and German soldiers ran around on the ground and fought bloody close combat. Here, a private rammed his dagger into a Russian's loins; there, several Red Army soldiers kicked a German lying on the ground until he stopped moving. The adversaries fired at each other at close range, and when the cartridge chambers were empty, they used their firearms as clubs. They grabbed at anything that could kill. They bashed each other's heads in with pitchforks, helmets, shovels and crowbars. Screaming men rolled across the ground that was already littered with corpses. Dead men in brown and field gray uniforms covered the battlefield. And right in the middle of this chaos were the Russian tanks. They were everywhere, and their tracks smashed the ground and the grass, buildings and bodies alike.

Berning quivered. His whole body trembled like during an earthquake. His hands gripped his rifle and soaked it in sweat. Obviously the Russians were slowly gaining the upper hand down there.

Now Pappendorf himself fired two short salvos with his submachine gun and killed a Russian. Then he grabbed Berning by the neck of his uniform, pulled him so close that their helmets collided and yelled in his face, "DAMMIT, START SHOOTING!" He grabbed Bernings weapon and pulled on it until Berning was roughly in a shooting position.

The sergeant looked over the iron sights of his gun at the mass of Red Army soldiers down on the ground. His index finger rested on the trigger. Straight in front of him, a hundred and sixty yards away, a throng of Russians moved across the open space. Berning focused on one of the enemy soldiers. He could see a man with a strained expression on his face. He might have been a farmer or a bank teller who wanted to get away from this war as much as Berning did. Maybe he had a wife and kids, and if he didn't, then at least he had a mother and a father. Berning's finger shuddered. He couldn't muster the strength to pull the trigger.

Pappendorf stood directly next to him and screeched into his ear, his face distorted with rage and looking as if it might explode at any moment, while Hege reported that he was down to the reserve rounds, which meant that he only had five hundred cartridges left.

"If you don't shoot now, Sergeant," Pappendorf sputtered with rage, "if you don't stop them right here, then these barbarians will step on German soil next year! Is that what you want? They'll come; they'll march into your hometown, too! They'll make your father their slave! They'll make your mother and your sisters their whores if you don't stop them right HERE! Is THAT what you want? Is that what you want, you MISERABLE BASTARD, you?"

Berning's ears rang while the words echoed in his head. He looked down at the battlefield. This one Russian out of that crowd of enemies was still in his sights. He didn't really look dangerous, and he didn't look like a rapist, either. In fact, he looked pretty much like a German. Berning's finger trembled over the trigger.

"DAMMIT, I'VE HAD ENOUGH OF YOU. SHOOT ALREADY!" Pappendorf's fist hit Berning on his Stahlhelm. The blow made Berning's head pulsate while his finger pulled the trigger, and the primer at the rear edge of the cartridge ignited with a loud bang. The projectile of the 7.92-millimeter round left the barrel of the gun and made its way down into the combat zone. It zoomed over the heads of Germans and Russians fighting for their lives. It hissed over a soldier who was sitting on another soldier, smashing his face to a bloody pulp with his helmet. It zoomed over an anti-tank fire team that eliminated the crew of a panzer with firebombs and sticky charges. Then the projectile hit the soldier Berning had made his target. It hit him in his abdomen, shredding his uniform, scorching his flesh, tearing his liver apart, and made the tissue behind it burst so that the blood flooded the surrounding organs. The man's face contorted. He started to run but then he stumbled, crashing on the ground face down. Screaming and twisting like an earthworm, he suffered through his death throes while life bleed out of the wound in his belly.

Time seemed to have stopped. Berning's heart started to pound and pushed up against his throat. He had clearly seen the Russian down there fall over and lie there, twisting and turning in pain. But the sergeant's fingers didn't stop.

His left hand held the rifle tightly, and his right hand grabbed the bent bolt handle, pressed it up and pulled it. This way it pulled the firing pin and spring back, and the cartridge case was ejected from the weapon. Berning pushed the bent bolt handle back into its anterior position. Thus the spring pressed the next cartridge up where it was grasped by the firing pin and fed into the bolt lugs of the cartridge chamber. Automatically, just as he had been trained, just as he had been drilled to do without any emotion or pity, he went through the motions. Berning's Karabiner 98k was ready to fire. Before the sergeant had comprehended it, before he could comprehend anything since his mind was still occupied with the Russian he had shot, his weapon seemed to raise itself again.

His eyes found the next target through the iron sights, his finger pulled the trigger, and another Russian fell over down there and stayed on the ground forever. This procedure was repeated three more times without Berning really being in control of his body.

Five shots, five hits. After the last cartridge case had been ejected from his weapon, the sergeant squatted near the window and loaded the next five rounds. Pappendorf nodded, satisfied, and turned back to the enemy forces. He emptied his submachine gun into the crowd. Hege cursed and groaned because his gun was malfunctioning at every second burst of fire by now. Still the ammunition was used up more quickly than was good in this situation.

"Two hundred fifty left," he yelled and kept firing. All of a sudden something hissed through the window, tore up the wooden frame and made Hege scream. The private first class fell on his side and held his bleeding hand, but he immediately struggled to get up again.

"It's nothing!" he grunted, grabbed his MG and started to shoot again.

Berning squatted in his cover, breathing through his mouth. He narrowed his eyes to slits; then he jumped up and fired the next five rounds into the crowd. He could see that in the south, where earlier four smoking German tanks had littered the plain, now dozens of gray panzers with Balkenkreuzes rolled into battle - but half of them were already burning while the oversized Russian assault guns still fired, underwhelmed by everything, the Germans threw at them.

*

The hope that the regiment would bring salvation dissipated as quickly as these huge assault guns could shoot. Almost half of the German panzers were burning or already torn apart, while wounded crew members abandoned their tanks and perished in the fire of the Russian infantry.

Holding the last smoke grenade in his hand, Engelmann looked at his three remaining crew members – Born had stopped breathing three minutes ago.

"We have to get out of here," the lieutenant whispered.

Nitz pulled out his pistol. "My suggestion, Sepp: I'll be the first one to leave and sprint over to Meinert's tank. I'll draw the fire on me while you guys run for our tanks."

"No way. We run together, it's all or none of us."

Nitz nodded with a serious expression on his face.

"Then let's go," the lieutenant began to order. "I'll go first, then Theo, Hans, Ebbe. Stay close behind me. We'll try to reach the nearest panzer at six o'clock and hitch a hike."

"Roger," Münster whispered.

Regimental commander Sieckenius just announced the troops' withdrawal over the radio.

"It's high time! Let's go!" Engelmann pulled the fuse of the last grenade and let it drop in Elfriede's belly. The German tankers quickly opened all hatches. The fog of the last smoke grenade still enclosed the panzer, and now fresh smoke was added. Engelmann climbed out of his cupola, jumped on the hull and then down on the grass. He was surrounded by dense fog; a moment later the silhouettes of three figures came through the white wall and stumbled towards him. *Well then, off we go!*

The lieutenant started to run, and his men immediately followed him. They pushed through the wall of white smoke onto the open field. Burning tank wrecks were everywhere while the remaining panzers of the regiment went into reverse and began to withdraw. Russian armor-piercing shells landed on the grass and tore craters into the ground. Chunks of dirt and rocks flew around. The sound of Russian voices and the fire of hand weapons emerged from the forest. But Engelmann and his crew just kept on running. They ran farther and farther. Engelmann discovered his company commander's tank, which was hit at that same moment and exploded. Within the blink of an eye, a Panzer III that was right next to it was blown into the air.

The regiment had shrunk to about sixty vehicles but suddenly things started to happen. In the midst of heavy enemy fire, the German panzers halted, started up again and accelerated. Gunfire threw tiny spurts of dirt at Engelmann's feet up into the air. The officer headed for a wrecked tank and threw himself behind it, using it as cover from the fire that came out of the woods. His crew followed his example.

"We have to keep going," Nitz urged him.

"No," the lieutenant replied, pointing at the remaining forces of the regiment driving towards them, advancing again at the cost of even more casualties. Then he turned his head and glanced in the direction of the collective farm where the large assault guns suddenly started to turn around.

*

Berning had already fired one third of his ammunition when he heard a loud bang and one of the enormous Russian assault guns burst apart.

"What on Earth was that?" the sergeant gasped and loaded the next strip into his gun.

Pappendorf took cover under the window and proclaimed, "Now, comrades, the Slavs are in for a big surprise!"

Unexpected by friend and foe equally, a massive formation broke out of the sparse woods to the east. Dozens of main battle tanks, Panzer IVs mostly, rolled on the battlefield, but the téte of the formation was formed by a group of new Panthers around four tank destroyers that in size nearly matched the Russian gargantuan assault guns. Admittedly, neither the Panthers nor the Ferdinands, as those German tank destroyers were called, had overcome their teething problems yet. They had a certain propensity for engine fires when the motors were started - but if they were running without going up in flames they were a match for even the Russian assault guns and those rolling now on the bloody grounds had already survived Operation Citadel till this day. The Panthers, which were obviously based on the T-34 model, and the sixty-five-ton Ferdinands destroyed half of the Russian assault guns before they could even turn. In between, the German tanks ate up medium-sized Russian tanks and spat them out in the form of blazing clumps of metal.

Immediately the Russians started to panic when their tanks dropped like flies. Part of the infantry started to withdraw while several other groups doggedly defended the few yards of farmland they had gained during combat. German Panzergrenadiers charged ahead under cover of their half-tracks and started to target positions in the woods.

One of the Ferdinands suddenly broke out of formation and drove straight between the farm buildings – a serious mistake. Russian soldiers immediately crept towards it. The crew of the Ferdinand realized too late that they were trapped. The massive tank destroyer did not come with a machine gun on board yet many crews carried one inside it so they could fire it through the main barrel in an emergency situation. But since it could be moved only slightly, the steel colossus was just what the Russian infantry was waiting for. Soviet soldiers destroyed the tracks of the Ferdinand by aiming hand grenades at it. Then they climbed onto the steel monster.

But that didn't change the overall situation. The strong tank formation from the east and Panzer Regiment 2 from the south mercilessly shot the Russian tanks to pieces.

"Berning, come with me! We'll drive the Slavs back!" Pappendorf ordered, and Berning followed him down the stairs. The remains of the platoon and the squadron lay there – many wounded, some dead. The floor was flooded with spent cartridges and on the window sill, hand grenades were lined up, ready to be used. Some of them were already tied together into the bigger explosive packages, the German soldiers called *geballte Ladung*, a pack able to damage a tank but equally prone to blow its user up. Pappendorf grabbed the four remaining soldiers of his platoon who were still able to fight and stormed outside.

"Take the hand grenades with you!" he barked before he left.

Ahead of them, the Ferdinand was in flames. Whole groups of Russian soldiers were climbing all over it. Pappendorf and his men opened fire. The enemy soldiers scattered into all directions; some of them were hit and fell off the tank destroyer.

"Sergeant, take it from the right! I'll take two Landsers and come from the left side!" Pappendorf illustrated his orders by giving hand signals. Berning confirmed and charged ahead, two privates behind him. He ran around the tank from the right side and saw the Russians run away. He shot two of them and took cover. His privates, who were still behind him, as well as Pappendorf's assault detachment on the other side of the tank took care of the rest.

Everywhere, Russian soldiers ran away while the last tank forces of the Red Army started to drive around aimlessly, more and more getting decimated by the merciless crossfire.

"You two – take up position in front of the Ferdinand!" Berning ordered the two privates who immediately ran to the front and dropped on the ground besides the tank destroyer. Berning turned around, hoping to find a position at the building wall behind him where a narrow alley between two buildings opened up so he could roughly cover the southeast direction. The tank battle still raged while the soldiers of the Red Army fled. Berning entered the alley when suddenly a door was pushed open and a Russian soldier stumbled out. The sergeant froze; their eyes met. The Russian raised his gun but Berning was faster. He shot the Russian, hurried on without even getting out of step and found himself a suitable position.

Bern, Switzerland, May 16th, 1943

Thomas had suffered from a profound sense of emptiness and a bad feeling in the pit of his stomach after Luise's rejection last Friday. Because she had taken off in her car without him, he had had to wait for the next train and spent the whole night at the Basel main train station, where he had enough time to ponder the situation and become consumed with his thoughts. He had been too fast, too forceful! He had had her where he wanted her but then he had put his foot on his mouth!

Why the hell do I always have to grab the women by the tits? Taylor could have kicked himself in the ass. Of course he could write off his job now; he had to notify his supervisor. But he could still do that tomorrow. Then he would return to the cottage near Remigen and probably not get a new assignment but would have to somehow sneak into the Reich on his own. What was worse than the failed mission, though – at least for the moment – was what Luise's rejection had done to him. Thomas was sure that his lovesickness – as silly young ladies called his condition – would pass, but until then he would just have to put up with it. The night from Friday to Saturday that he had spent at the train station had been unpleasant, and even though he had been dead tired, he hadn't really been able to sleep on the train and in the apartment. In his mind, he kept replaying the situation in Birsfelden, watching his own stupidity, over and over again. He had acted like a real jerk. *Oh man!*

Saturday night, after several hours of tossing and turning in bed, he had tried to distract himself with the help of alcohol and Swiss hookers – after all, military intelligence provided the means. Yet the whores had only managed to satisfy him for a short period of time. At least the alcohol had helped him through the night to Sunday morning though of course he didn't drink enough to lose control of himself – that would be too dangerous in this hostile territory. Even though he was drunk enough to get into a fight with some Swiss guy – an adolescent – he was still sober enough to be able to escape the guy's friends. At least the alcohol made him sleep through the second night.

Now it was Sunday afternoon, and Thomas already felt considerably better. He no longer thought about Luise and seemed to be ready for a new mission.

Maybe Russia again for a change? Taylor reflected while he stuffed several personal items into his bag, where he also hid his pistol beneath a false bottom he had crafted himself.

Later he sat on his bed, a cigarette between his lips, and examined the two abrasions on the back of his right hand. Last night's fight had left its marks. Shaking his head, Taylor had to laugh.

How could that stupid bitch put me in her pocket like that? He wondered. It bothered him, that someone, anyone, could confuse him and throw him off the track like this despite he had perceived himself always as a mentally stable young soldier. His conduct had been highly unprofessional. Therefore he was glad that he had obviously gotten over her so fast.

It wouldn't have worked out anyway, he told himself. When emotions were involved, he might have had a problem focusing on what mattered. *It's better this way!* He kept thinking.

Someone knocked on his door. At first Thomas was startled and looked for his bag. But then he figured that the police or enemy spies would hardly sneak into the building just to knock on his apartment door. So he opened it. It was Luise. Her lips were a luscious red, and today she wore her hair down, which was unusual for Luise. Thomas's heart beat all the way up to his throat but she didn't give him any time to think about it. She walked up to him so that their lips were almost touching.

"Éxgüsee last Friday," she whispered, looking at him wide-eyed. Then she took the cigarette out of his mouth and put her tongue inside. Kissing and touching him, she shut the door with one of her high heels and pulled him into the center of the room.

Kursk, Soviet Union, May 18th, 1943

After the Russians' attempted breakout, the remaining forces of the 253rd Infantry Division were removed from the pocket front line and transferred to the center of Kursk as a reserve formation. Since the division had suffered a sixty-four percent casualties, killed in action, wounded or sick, it was no longer capable of participating in any significant combat action.

While other units looked still okay, the 253rd had paid in lives and limbs the highest price of Citadel. Currently the remaining officers were busy with the total reorganization of the division. They would probably gather all remaining soldiers under two reinforced regiments until the division could be replenished with fresh forces from the reserve troops.

Meanwhile the Landsers, NCOs and officers enjoyed the time in rear echelon waiting for the marching orders that would take them out of the mud zone for the time being so they could regain their strength and reorganize themselves. In the meantime, fresh units were brought in to stabilize the new front lines.

Pappendorf, who, due to the lack of officers, had been promoted to commissarial company commander and was responsible for thirty-six men, had set up his office in the backroom of a hardware store. He was not only a slave driver but he also didn't care about the local people; he deliberately just ignored the regulation that pillages of civilian property were strictly prohibited and even helped to cover up such offenses within his company.

"They're just Slavs," was his shady motto. So the men of his company had plenty of food these days while the civilians became more and more reserved towards the Wehrmacht soldiers.

Pappendorf sat behind a narrow desk in a room decorated with wood paneling and brooded over documents prepared by the Quartermaster's office that had to be signed. It was raining outside; black clouds passed over the city, though in the darkness of the night one couldn't see them with the naked eye. It had cooled down considerably, and Pappendorf had lit a fire in the clay oven that heated up the room to a pleasant temperature. He had also decorated the space with some of his "personal items"; next to his desk, a portrait of Adolf Hitler hung on the wall, and next to that, his confirmation of acceptance in the NSDAP as Member No. 6.547. These days it wasn't always smart to show off one's Nazi membership but it depended on one's superior. When it came to this subject, the Wehrmacht was still torn apart.

Of course a lot of soldiers clung to that ideology but there were just as many who were happy about last year's change in the government.

There was a knock on the door but Pappendorf didn't move at first. He stoically finished reading the document in his hands, jotted down something on a piece of paper and finally said – after more than a minute – in a loud voice, "Herein!"

He had no idea that the person who had knocked on his door had already been standing in front of his office for three minutes because it had taken him that long to gather all his courage. The door opened and Sergeant Berning walked in.

He immediately stood at attention, saluting. "Herr Unterfeldwebel – Unteroffizier Berning reporting in a personal matter," he said.

"At ease!"

Berning immediately stood at ease.

"I'm listening."

Pappendorf's attitude indicated that he didn't want to invest a lot of time in this conversation. Stuttering a little, Berning came out with his request. "I heard that you'll be in a meeting with the division commander tomorrow morning, Herr Unterfeldwebel?"

Pappendorf nodded curtly.

"I want to ask you for a favor, Herr Unterfeldwebel?" Berning obviously had to muster all his courage to come to his new company chief with such a request. The latter narrowed his eyes and leaned forward.

"Would you ask the commander about the results of today's soccer game between Bochum and Bielefeld, Herr Unterfeldwebel? I am sure he has ways to find out."

"And why do you think the commander would waste his time on such civilian nonentities, Herr Unteroffizier?" Pappendorf responded in a sharp voice.

Berning pressed his lips together; he suddenly felt hot. Had he gotten himself in trouble again without meaning to?

"Well, I just thought," he stammered, "I thought – because Staff Sergeant Claassen always managed to find out the results, too."

Pappendorf bent forward even farther and focused on the sergeant like a hawk who was watching its prey. He considered the request for a few seconds. Then he nodded.

"I'll see what I can do," he said. "And now get out! Dismissed!"

"Jawohl, Herr Unterfeldwebel."

Berning couldn't suppress a smile. He turned around, reached for the door knob – but before he could leave, Pappendorf added, "Oh, Herr Unteroffizier?"

"Sir?" When Berning turned around again, he was startled. There they were again, these merciless eyes of a hawk.

Pappendorf got up but this time his voice was calm, which made his words even more menacing. "If you think that it'll wash away your guilt if you follow the soccer results for that good lance corporal who was killed in action, then you're barking up the wrong tree."

Berning started to sweat all over. What was Pappendorf saying?

"Don't think for a minute that I didn't see what happened!" Pappendorf's voice was getting sharper with every syllable. "Don't think I didn't see that you just stood there and did nothing while that Slav killed the lance corporal! You just stood there! You didn't do anything about it! You even watched! Even though it was not only your duty to interfere but it would also have been so damned easy. All you had to do was raise your gun and blow the enemy away! You let your comrade die!"

Berning shook his head apathetically but Pappendorf repeated his last sentence even more insistently: "You *let* him die."

Berning stared at Pappendorf. His face was frozen while his eyes twitched and his mouth gaped. Everything collapsed inside of him again.

Now Pappendorf came from behind his desk and slowly went up to the sergeant while he continued to speak. "Don't you dare consider yourself a big war hero just because you finally figured out how to fire your gun!" He now stood directly in front of Berning.

Berning's heart raced.

"I should have reported you, and then you would've been shot for that. They call it cowardice in the face of the enemy. My sealed lips are my gift to you though you don't deserve one. But if you don't start to dig in your heels and act like a German NCO, I'll light a fire under your ass, you military moppet, you. Dismissed!"

Berning left the room with a stomach ache.

East of Lgov, Soviet Union, May 19th, 1943
Kursk Front "In the pocket" – 65 kilometers west of Kursk

The biplane of the Red Army the fascists called "sewing machine" because of the sound of its engine glided gently across the territory that was still in the hands of the Soviets. Yet Sidorenko was aware of the fact that the fate of the 720 000 comrades locked in the pocket west of Kursk was sealed. The attempt to break out had failed; the supply situation in the pocket was desolate.

"Sogeodnya nam ne povislo," Sidorenko thought aloud, but due to the hum of the engine and the airflow around the plane his female pilot couldn't hear him. *Today we didn't have any luck!*

The Germans had sealed the encirclement completely; a Soviet relief attack attempt across the front line of Bryansk had been beaten back yesterday, and the supply from the air wasn't working because of the enormous loss of airplanes during the battle of Kursk.

So the Red Army had to write off hundreds of thousands of good soldiers once again. After all, they had enough replacements!

Sidorenko was boiling with rage. Not only had he been forced to fight a hopeless battle because of what the Stavka had failed to do, but now they would even blame him for the defeat!

"Oni menya sa eto strogo nakashyut," he mumbled to himself. *They'll tear my head off!* He would have to listen to a lot of crap in Moscow but if this old klunker actually stayed in the air until he was past the German lines, he would at least stay alive and not be taken a POW, as was the fate of his divisions in the pocket. That meant that he could continue the war against the fascists from another place – and yes, he would continue this war as long as he had to! Now Sidorenko had to grin despite his situation. He wouldn't be put on ice by the Stavka because he still had an open account with the Nazis, and they had to pay!

"Ostoroshjno tovaritsch, mi salitayem w nemtzkii protivo vossdushnii obstrel," the pilot informed him in a loud voice; then things became bumpy. *German anti-aircraft guns ahead!* Black detonations powdered the sky but the plane got through safely.

South of Kursk, Soviet Union, May 26th, 1943

Lieutenant Engelmann had been promoted to the commissarial company commander of the 9th, but under the circumstances he would have gladly done without this career boost. He still had a total of twenty-nine subordinates who, however, had to share the only four tanks that were more or less in working condition. Together with the remains of the regiments, they had been relocated to almost the same sector they had moved to shortly after having taken the city of Kursk. Again he looked at the Seym River, on the bank of which a group of elderly women were sitting together, chatting and washing their laundry. Engelmann still had to be careful. The Russians hadn't forgotten the conduct of the Germans during their first occupation of the city and showed great willingness to hurt their occupying forces wherever they could. Yet right now everything seemed quiet. Leaning against a tree and enjoying the shade – the sun was burning down relentlessly – Engelmann stared at a blood-smeared book. By now the blood had dried; some of the pages stuck together and would have to be separated carefully with a knife. But he could still make out the black letters on the red background.

All in all the lieutenant recalled Operation Citadel with mixed feelings. Though they had managed to take Kursk, he didn't want to overrate that victory.

What's a salient of a hundred and fifty kilometers width on a front line of 2 500 kilometers? His pessimism clung to his mind like a leech. It troubled him deeply that since yesterday the Russians had been pressing against Oryol and Kharkov with incredible masses of human and material resources. Well, at least the eastern front line was holding up – still. And everything was quiet around Kursk, which they had accomplished by dealing the Russians a violent blow. At the same time, Panzer Regiment 2 was too battered to engage in any combat, which was why Engelmann guessed that they would soon be transferred to the far rear echelon in order to recover. And he felt uneasy when he thought about the fact that Field Marshal von Kluge and his generals had been really sly foxes to lure the Russians in: There had been reconnaissance just in time which had shown that a large concentration of enemy troops had gathered in the then pocket to come in order to penetrate the allegedly weak German lines near Kursk so as to subsequently cut off the German attack that were driven towards Voronezh and then encircle them themselves. Intercepted radio messages had revealed that Soviet intent to attack. They actually owed the idea for this battle to Paulus – and it had worked: Simulate an attack directed at the Voronezh area in order to let the Russian forces run up against alleged weak German formations that had been left behind for securing the pocket's front line; yet in truth it had been possible to fight off the attack with the aid of the armored forces the Russians thought were on their way to the East. The whole ploy had been backed by enormous logistics. Formations had had to be moved; needle-like attacks with massive forces in the Voronezh area had served to convince the enemy of the pending danger of a German attack. Von Kluge had pulled out all the stops: Imaginary radio messages had been sent, orders for attack had been "leaked to the enemy", and an armada of trucks had driven behind the lines so as to provide the Russians with aerial photos of huge troop movements. Even the German defense forces in and around Kursk had been left in the dark until the end so that no real information would leak through to the enemy. These tactics were as risky as they were brilliant, but in the end the Germans had had to pay a price for them – as they always did. That became obvious when Engelmann compared the actual numbers of the divisions with those of the time they had still been in their area of deployment.

A figure holding something in one hand approached the lieutenant. Since Engelmann was facing the late afternoon sun, he couldn't immediately recognize Staff Sergeant Nitz, who was holding a small package.

"Evening, Herr Leutnant," he said to his company commander.

"Herr Feldwebel." Engelmann nodded at Nitz warmly.

"Field post," the latter informed him curtly, handing him the package.

"Danke." Engelmann reached for the small box. He was delighted when he saw the name of the sender: Else Engelmann.

"And – how's your back?" the lieutenant inquired politely though he could hardly wait to open the package.

"Bearable, Herr Leutnant, bearable." They both nodded. Then the staff sergeant walked away again.

Engelmann immediately tore the package open. At first he was overwhelmed by piles of red cans of chocolate.

Wonderful! Elly had also sent him a new shaving kit, a current photo of her and Gudrun – *man, how much my little girl has grown!* – as well as candy and hard tacks. *Thank you, Elly, thank you, thank you*, the lieutenant thought happily. *This package is really something!*

Then he discovered her letter – scented stationery with her beautiful handwriting in ink that Else's bad spelling made even more endearing to him. Josef unfolded the sheet and started to read. Then he nearly started to cry.

Lieutenant Josef Engelmann,
May 16th, 1943
F.P. 34444

My dear Sepp!
I want to wish you a belated happy wedding anniversary because it most likely will be over before you get this package. Don't worry; I didn't forget your beloved chocolate!
And a few other things that you can probably use. We were very happy about your last letter and hope you're healthy and will come back unharmed. I don't laugh at you for praying to God again. That's okay. You know that I'm not much of a believer but I would never judge you. It must be so hard to be in the war and in combat and to fear for your life every single day! It hurts me so much that you're so far away and we can't be together!
Unfortunately the war has become apparent more often here, too. The city frequently gets bombed, even in the daytime, and then we have to run to the basements. Many people have fled to their relatives in the country but unfortunately we're not that lucky! Because your family and my family both live in the city! But still we're getting by. Please don't worry about us.

Gudrun is fine. She's already taking her first steps and babbles all day long. I enclosed a picture of her. Oh, how much she misses her daddy! And I miss you even more! Every time there is a blast somewhere, she starts to scream. But what can I do? Oh Sepp, when will all of this finally be over? Please come home soon and take good care of yourself! There are two people here in Bremen who need you!
Love,
Elly

Southwest of Poltava, Soviet Union, May 26th, 1943

The Knight's Cross with Oak Leaves dangled from Field Marshal Erich von Manstein's collar; the Iron Cross 1st Class adorned his right chest next to the highest-ranking Rumanian military badge Order of Michael the Brave. Von Manstein, an old veteran of the Great War with broad face and short hair that he had combed from the right to left, pulled his spectacles out of their case and put them on his nose to study the situation map, which was spread out on his table. He was in his mobile command post, a train car on the outskirts of Kharkov. It was parked in a narrow forest strip, camouflaged by German soldiers who, dressed like farmers, drove cattle in the fields that surrounded the forest.

Reich Chancellor von Witzleben and Field Marshal Hermann Hoth, whom von Manstein had appointed his chief of staff even though he would rather have kept a command, were also there. But von Manstein wanted to be around someone who thought like him and didn't have a high regard of humanists like Beck and his followers. Both – von Manstein as well as Hoth – were convinced that the war against the Soviet Union was a total war and had to be led like one. Both were also convinced that this war wasn't just a war of soldiers against soldiers but rather a war of nations against nations. Therefore, in their opinion, the civilian population shouldn't be spared either. Both officers had carried out the Commissar Order under Hitler, which had been highly controversial among the officer corps, and neither of them had stopped the harsh actions against partisans, Jews and other ethnic groups the Nazis thought unwelcome in the territory they had conquered – not because they had been afraid of Hitler, as many other officers had been, but out of conviction.

Yet now von Manstein faced the "new" Reichskanzler, that man with the narrow face and the balding head who appeared weak. In the presence of the Chancellor, whom von Manstein couldn't size up, he was careful and kept his distance. At least von Witzleben went along with the whole of the Beck Doctrines – instructions on how to handle the civilian population in occupied areas and the so-called war criminals – that in von Manstein's opinion didn't really show much understanding for this conflict the German Reich was involved in. A lot had changed last year in the way how POWs were treated, too. Von Manstein wasn't sure yet where all these changes were leading to, but he realized with relief that so far they hadn't restricted his military options.

"A shame," von Witzleben mumbled. He looked at the enemy attack movements marked on the map and sighed.

"This is my first visit to the troops in the East– and our enemy start his offensive right now."

"Next time I'll let the people in Moscow know about your schedule ahead of time," von Manstein retorted dryly, which evoked a tired smile from the Reichskanzler. Then he nodded and again focused on the map that made him sigh.

Von Manstein frowned. At least von Witzleben wasn't a dreamer like Hitler had been. The chancellor clearly realized the difficult situation of the Wehrmacht despite its success at Kursk. Everything was still in the balance, and von Manstein was sure that the greatest possible success in this war could only be a tie. Back then – in 1941 – they had clearly underestimated the Russian capacities. They thought they would be able to hit and destroy the Red Army in its moment of weakness and destroy it right away. Yes, they had hit it in a moment of weakness, and for more than two years the Red Army had taken a beating. But now – in mid-1943 – it was still standing on both feet, suffering one blow after another, and it still wasn't about to collapse. On the contrary: The enemy kept delivering more and more massive counter-attacks, and all high-ranking officers of the Wehrmacht were aware of one thing: The German Armed Forces were much worse at taking a beating than the Red Army was. While problems with supply had become a daily matter on the German side and they had to improvise in every area, the Russians kept spitting out tanks, soldiers, guns and lately even airplanes in increasingly huge masses. It was appalling. Von Manstein exhaled.

During Operation Citadel they had sent over one thousand nine hundred Russian tanks to hell while suffering a loss of three hundred and ten of their own. And while the German Army was licking its wounds now and was likely to need several more months for that, the Russians were again attacking it fearlessly.

In two concentrated attacks, they sent their forces up against Oryol and Kharkov and outnumbered the Germans five to one on both sections of the front line while further holding attacks worked on other German front line sections.

"Herr Feldmarschall," von Witzleben began, "as you know, I've always given you free reign."

He took a pause to think, which made von Manstein jumpy. *What's he up to?*

But von Witzleben reassured the Commander-in-Chief East right away. "And I don't intend to tell you what to do in the future, either. So you can see that I'm more agreeable than the Führer was." He smiled gently. Von Manstein nodded. "Plus I have enough political issues that demand my full attention." The chancellor seemed to be lost in thought for a moment.

"Sometimes I ask myself how Hitler did it all. All I'm doing is taking care of the political level – and that already takes up all my time," he moaned.

"With amateurishness, Herr Reichskanzler," von Manstein interjected.

Von Witzleben looked at him quizzically. Then he nodded, and finally he said, "Please inform me about how you'll proceed and what your intentions are. And now I already have to say my goodbyes. I have other appointments lined up." The chancellor glanced briefly at the clock over the door that led to the adjacent wagon.

"Certainly. Would you please take a look at the map?"

Then von Manstein started to outline his plan while Hoth stepped up, too, and bent over the map without taking an active part in the conversation.

"Two enemy army groups are pushing against our lines north and south of Izium." While he explained the situation, von Manstein pointed at each spot on the map he was talking about. Now he tapped his finger on the medium-sized city of Izium in eastern Ukraine that was situated directly by the Donets south of Kursk and Kharkov.

"At the same time five red armies are trying to break through the Belgorod – Kharkov line."

Von Manstein's index finger traced the map – following the Donets – up north, first to Kharkov and then to Belgorod. "I hope you can see what masses the Russians step up with again. It can drive you crazy. We think we have dealt them a serious blow, and one minute later they come around the corner with even greater force.

Farther up north, six armies are moving against the area around Oryol. That's an incredible contingent of manpower and material the Red Army's lining up here."

Von Manstein didn't say that without a certain admiration. What wouldn't he give to have options like these just once!

In the meantime the chancellor whistled through his teeth. He had known that the Russians had responded with a counter-attack but he had obviously not been aware of the intensity of these combat actions. He frowned with concern.

"And finally the Russians are attempting to break through to Stalino in the south." Von Manstein's index finger pointed at the region between Izium and the Sea of Azov. "Here the enemy is applying the same tactics I already described. I think I don't need to mention that I wasn't thrilled with the plans for Operation Citadel from the start. It was obvious to me that – with the options currently available to us – an offensive may have meant biting off more than we could chew."

Von Witzleben just shook his head while his eyes lingered on the map.

"Well, whatever. The enemy let us come, and now he's hitting us with his backhand." Again his admiration was obvious in von Manstein's voice. Clearing his throat, he added, "As you know, our forces are limited, and what's more, some of them are spent and exhausted by Operation Citadel. But nevertheless we're not a toothless tiger! There are still heavily armored reserve formations near Kursk that I will use."

"What about the Russian troops encircled in the Kursk pocket?" von Witzleben exclaimed.

"Oh, they're done for. It's just a matter of time before they'll surrender, which is why weak defense forces on our side should suffice."

The chancellor nodded with a serious expression on his face while von Manstein continued. "As a result of the operation, we now have several worn-out divisions that are hardly capable of the job of securing the front line. I don't want numerous split-up formations and regiments defending only narrow sections of the front line. That's bound to lead to coordination issues we can't afford. Therefore I intend to do the following: First, I'll use the reserves to guarantee the encirclement of the Russian armies in the Kursk salient and to secure all lines not exposed to any attacks by the enemy. Second, I'll form two kampfgruppen out of the severely exhausted units near Kursk. Up north that'll be Kampfgruppe Becker, led by Major General Becker. Outstanding man."

Von Witzleben nodded and repeated, "Major General Becker."

The chancellor seemed lost in thought again. Hoth nodded, too, and stared at the map with a serious expression on his face. Everyone in the room knew that it was a challenging situation.

"I'll throw Becker's combat formation against the enemy attackers in the Oryol area. I assume the Russians won't expect an attack coming from Kursk. Hit them with your backhand, Herr Reichskanzler. *That* must be the order of the day!"

"I'm completely with you."

"Kampfgruppe Sieckenius will tackle the South near Kharkov. We must prevent the enemy from advancing to the Dnieper River as all costs. In all other sectors we'll just let the enemy come and react in the form of counterattacks."

"Sounds good. Where, do you think, is the situation most critical?"

Von Manstein didn't have to think twice. "In Oryol," he exclaimed. "Oryol is our last foot in the door to Moscow. If Oryol falls, the enemy's capital is out of danger – probably forever."

"Well, then I'll pull out the 15th Panzer Division from Italy and have it moved to the Oryol area."

"Mhm," said von Manstein, who wasn't good in expressing delight. "The boys from Africa, eh?" Now he had to grin despite himself. "They're always welcome here."

Von Witzleben, on the other hand, stretched his back. The chancellor looked exhausted and seemed to be distracted by a thousand other thoughts. Yet Field Marshal von Manstein was satisfied. These briefings always showed von Witzleben's qualities as the official commander-in-chief of the Wehrmacht – qualities, Hitler had surely lacked. The chancellor was a professional who didn't have any ludicrous ideas about warfare but instead listened to his officers' down-to-earth advice. He also wasn't like a little kid whose decisions about the same facts were one thing today and the opposite tomorrow and who was seized by temper tantrums. No, von Witzleben was, with all due respect to Beck, a good – at least a better – leader than his predecessor.

He had, of course, pushed Operation Citadel through against the opposition of several officers, including von Manstein, but there had also been numerous supporters of the offensive. The success had proved the supporters right. Still, Kursk had cost the Wehrmacht many resources.

Hoth suddenly broke the silence. "How do things look in the West?"

"Don't worry, Gentlemen. We can sit back and concentrate on the East. We've got nothing to worry about from the Western Allies," von Witzleben replied confidently. "The Brits are hiding on their island, and, except for the bombers, we have nothing to worry about from the Americans."

"There are rumors that an invasion on the European mainland is imminent. Italy, Greece or even the Balkans. Maybe even Norway. Or France?"

Hoth sounded concerned – and von Manstein knew that his old comrade was worried indeed, as he was himself. He was always saying that an attack from the West would finish off the war. And he was right.

Von Witzleben chuckled. "My dear Herr Generalfeldmarschall, surely you don't believe the grapevine, do you? Oh please! There won't be an invasion on the mainland; it would be a suicide mission in every conceivable constellation. Believe me – the Allies haven't forgotten Dieppe."

Aftermath

The sunbeams of the still young morning shone through the small window in Taylor's bedroom. The air was dense with cigarette smoke. It smelled of tobacco and sweat. Luise leaned against the bed frame; she was completely nude and only partly covered by the blanket. She enjoyed her cigarette and closed her eyes while smoke filled her lungs. Though the act of making love was already over, her nipples were still erect in pleasant excitement. Thomas's hand gently stroked her belly and started to move downwards.

"You're in such a good mood today, Luise."

"Yep." Grinning, she bit her lower lip. "That's because you rocked my world."

"No, that's not it. You were already so ... well, so cheerful this morning."

"Sorry, but I can't talk about it. It's because of work, you know?"

His hand touched her vagina and she started to giggle.

"So you have your secrets, you mystery woman! You make it sound like you're a spy." Thomas laughed and penetrated her vagina with his finger.

Again Luise closed her eyes and uttered a long sigh.

"We're ... mhhm ... obligated to ... mhhhm ... keep our mouths shut." She moaned when Thomas found the right spot. "Oh my God, Aaron, again?" Of course that was a rhetorical question.

"Actually my boss ... mhhm ... wasn't allowed to ... ohhhhhhh ... tell me anything, you know?"

"I see."

"But he thought ... oh Aaron, ohhhh ... I already knew anyway, because of my dad." Her body trembled.

"Come on, tell me, will you?"

"No!" She laughed and shoved Thomas on his side but then she paused and froze while her lips trembled and her body shuddered. Thomas was good.

"You're so mean!" he complained. "You just wanted to tease me!"

"May ... yyy ...be." She grinned while his finger explored the insides of her vagina, penetrating deeper.

"Oh well!" she suddenly moaned. "I can't keep it to myself anyway!"

Raising his head, Thomas looked at her expectantly. Of course that didn't mean that his finger stopped bringing her to climax.

"You see, the Nazi threat will soon be over ... ahhh ... It's finally starting."

Pleasant vibrations tore through her body.

"I see. Well, that sounds good."

"Yeah, the Allies will ... ahhh ... land in Italy next summer."

Acknowledgement

EK-2 Publishing takes the chance to thank some people, without whom this translation never would have come into existence. First we would like to thank Johanna Ellsworth and Mary Jo Rabe for the great deal of effort they spend on this project – far more than could have been expected from a translation team, since this text is not a normal one, but a book that is full of difficult vocabulary even an average German without deep military understanding struggles with.

Then we also thank Peter Brendt for proofreading the novel paying special attention to military language and America English.

Thank you, guys, you are great!!

Note from Tom Zola

Dear readers,

while the book itself was translated by a team of true English experts, I wrote this small note myself. Since English is not my mother tongue, this note contains some weird Germanized grammar and sentences for sure. I suggest you read it in a strong German accent ☺

I would like to take the chance to thank you for buying our book. The EK-2 Publishing Team put a lot of effort into the first entry in the PANZERS series, especially was the translation one hell of a job. As said, we are glad to have real English experts on board (at this point I would like to gratefully thank Johanna Ellsworth, Mary Jo Rabe and Peter Brendt once more for their marvelous efforts and commitment!!!) Even for professional translators it is one heck of a task to transcript a text that is full of technical terms and detailed military descriptions.

On the one hand you have ranks, German trivia and other national or regional specialties. Should we translate German nicknames like *Stuka* for the Junkers Ju 87 or should we leave it in its German form in the text? Almost from line to line we struggled with this very question and had to find a new answer to it each time.

When it comes to ranks, we did translate them to obtain a better reading experience, although in direct speech we sometimes kept original German or Russian ranks – that depends on the overall paragraph and how it would influence readability. Take a look at the glossary of characters below to find out about the actual ranks they possess.

On the other hand, in the original text there are a lot of references to typical German trivia, which gave all of us a hard time translating them. Things like the military function of a "Kompanietruppführer" only exists in the German Army. There is no translation, no comparable function in other armed forces, and it even is very difficult to explain its meaning without a deep understanding of the functioning of the German military. So, what should we do with such things? How should we translate the text in a way that its originality does not get lost, but that it is at the same time fully understandable in English? Believe me, finding that balance is no easy task! I hope we have gotten most things right!

Our overall goal was to provide a very unique reading experience for English readers. This text is written by a former German soldier (me), it focuses on a German perspective and is very technical in its details. I often find posts and articles on the Internet that are about Germany or the German Army, written by foreigners in English, and that hilariously mistake our very special little German idiosyncrasies (no accusation meant, I would struggle similarly trying to understand a culture I am a total stranger to). Thus, I hope it is interesting for you to read something from Germany that really tries to translate these idiosyncrasies correctly into English. Nevertheless we tried everything to preserve a special German touch. That is why we sometimes left a German word or phrase in the text. At the same time, we tried to ensure that English readers can understand everything without using a dictionary or Wehrmacht textbook from time to time and that the whole thing stays readable.

Another thing we did in order to manage this balancing act is that we separated German words for better readability and understanding although they are not separated originally. We Germans are infamous for our very long words like Bundeswehrstrukturanpassungsgesetz or Donau-Dampfschifffahrtsgesellschaft. In English words are separated way more often to keep them short. Germans say Armeekorps, English folks say army group. So for example we made Panzer Korps out of Panzerkorps in the text hoping that this will help you to read the book without stumbling too often.

The PANZERS series consists of 12 books, and I promise in book 12 I provide a satisfying ending. No cliffhangers! In book 2 I introduce my major American protagonist to the story: Private First Class Tom Roebuck. Fighting continues and catapults the reader into the battlefields of the Pacific, China, the polar region and so on in the books to come. Besides a strong focus on German soldiers, there are chapters about British, Japanese, Russian characters and even more from other nations.

Additionally, EK-2 Publishing holds a bunch of other German military literature licenses that we really would love to introduce to English readers. So, stay tuned for more to come! And please give us feedback on what you think about this book, our project and the EK-2 Publishing idea of bringing military literature from the motherland of military to English readers. Also let us know how we can improve the reading experience for you and how we managed the thin red line between readability and originality of the text.

We love to hear from you!!

info@ek2-publishing.com

(I am connected to this email address and will personally read and answer your mails!)

In the following I provide some additional information: a glossary of all words and specialist terms you may have stumbled upon while reading, an overview of Wehrmacht ranks, German military formation sizes and abbreviations, a glossary of all characters as well as a sketch of the Kursk salient. Since I wrote those glossaries myself, too, I recommend you keep the German accent …

Glossary

76 millimeters divisional gun M1942: Soviet field gun that produced a unique sound while firing, which consisted of some kind of hissing, followed by the detonation boom. Therefore the Germans Wehrmacht soldiers called it "Ratsch Bumm".

Abwehr: German Military Intelligence Service

Afrika Korps: German expeditionary force in North Africa; it was sent to Libya to support the Italian Armed Forces in 1941, since the Italians were not able to defend what they had conquered from the British and desperately needed some backing. Hitler's favorite general Rommel was the Afrika Korps' commander. Over the years he gained some remarkable victories over the British, but after two years of fierce fighting ... two years, in which the Axis' capabilities to move supplies and reinforcements over the Mediterranean Sea constantly decreased due to an allied air superiority that grew stronger by the day, Rommel no longer stood a chance against his opponents. Finally the U.S.A. entered the war and invaded North Africa in November 1942. Hitler prohibited the Afrika Korps to retreat back to Europe or even to shorten the front line by conducting tactical retreats. Because of that nearly 300 000 Axis' soldiers became POWs, with thousands of tons of important war supplies and weapons getting lost as well when the Afrika Korps surrendered in May 1943, just months after the 6th Army had surrendered in Stalingrad.

In the PANZERS series von Witzleben allows the Afrika Korps to retreat just in time. Axis' forces abandon North Africa by the end of 1942, saving hundreds of thousands of soldiers and important war material.

Arabic numerals vs. Roman numerals in German military formation names: I decided to keep Arabic as well as Roman numerals in the translation, therefore you will find a 1st Squad, but an II Abteilung. Normally all battalions and corpses have Roman numerals, the rest Arabic ones.

Armee Abteilung: More or less equivalent to an army. The Germans of WW2 really had confusing manners to organize and name their military formations.

Assault Gun: Fighting Vehicle intended to accompany and support infantry formations. Assault guns were equipped with a tank-like main gun in order to combat enemy strongholds or fortified positions to clear the way for the infantry. An assault gun had no rotatable turret, but a casemate. This made them very interesting especially for Germany, because they could be produced faster and at lower material costs than proper combat tanks.

Assistant machine gunner: In the Wehrmacht you usually had three soldiers to handle one MG: a gunner and two assistants. The first assistant carried the spare barrel as well as some small tools for cleaning and maintaining the weapon plus extra belted ammunition in boxes. The second assistant carried even more ammunition around.

In German the three guys are called: MG-1, MG-2 and MG-3.

Ausführung: German word for variant. Panzer IV Ausführung F means that it is the F variant of that very tank. The Wehrmacht improved their tanks continuously, and gave each major improvement a new letter.

Babushka: Russian word for "grandmother" or "elderly woman"

Balkenkreuz: Well-known black cross on white background that has been used by every all-German armed force ever since and also before the first German unification by the Prussian military.

Battle of Stalingrad: The battle of Stalingrad is often seen as the crucial turning point of the war between the Third Reich and the Soviet Union. For the first time the Wehrmacht suffered an overwhelming defeat, when the 6th Army was encircled in the city of Stalingrad and had to surrender after it had withstood numerous Soviet attacks, a bitterly cold Russian winter and a lack of supplies and food due to the encirclement. Hitler was obsessed with the desire to conquer the city with the name of his opponent on it – Stalin – and thus didn't listen to his generals, who thought of Stalingrad as a place without great strategic use.

In reality the battle took place between August 1942 and February 1943. The encirclement of the Axis' forces was completed by the end of November 1942. The Axis' powers lost around 300 000 men. After surrendering 108

000 members of the 6th Army became POWs, of which only 6 000 survivors returned to Germany after the war. In the PANZERS series von Witzleben listens to his generals and withdraws all troops from the city of Stalingrad in time. Thus the encirclement never happens.

Beck Doctrines: A set of orders issued by President of the Reich Ludwig Beck that demands a human treatment of POWs and civilians in occupied territories. The doctrines are an invention of me, neither did they exist in reality, nor was Beck ever President of the Reich (but the main protagonists of the 20 July plot, of whom Beck was one, wanted him for that very position).

Bohemian Private: In German it is "Böhmischer Gefreiter", a mocking nickname for Hitler, which was used by German officers to highlight that Hitler never got promoted beyond the rank of private in World War I. Besides basic training Hitler never attended any kind of military education. It is said that president Hindenburg first came up with this nickname. He did not like Hitler and wrongfully believed he was from the Braunau district in Bohemia, not Braunau am Inn in Austria.

Brandenburgers: German military special force (first assigned to Abwehr, on 1st April 1943 alleged to the Wehrmacht) that consists of many foreign soldiers in order to conduct covert operations behind enemy lines. The name "Brandenburgers" refers to their garrison in Brandenburg an der Havel (near Berlin).

Büchsenlicht: Büchse = tin can (also archaic for a rifle); Licht = light; having Büchsenlicht means that there is enough daylight for aiming and shooting.

Churchill tank: Heavy British infantry tank, with about 40 tons it was one of the heaviest allied tanks of the war. Through the Lend-Lease policy it saw action on the Russian side, too. Its full name is Tank, Infantry, Mk IV (A22) Churchill.

Clubfoot: Refers to Joseph Goebbels, a high-ranking Nazi politician, one of Hitler's most important companions and Reich Minister of Propaganda (Secretary of Propaganda). He coined names like "Vergeltungswaffe" (= weapon of revenge) for the A4 ballistic missile and glorified a total war, meaning all Germans – men, women, elderly and children alike – had to contribute to "final victory". He is one of the reasons why German children, wounded and old men had to fight at the front lines during the last years of the Third Reich. "Clubfoot" refers to the fact that Goebbels suffered from a deformed right foot.

Commissar Order: An order issued by the Wehrmacht's high command before the start of the invasion of the USSR that demanded to shoot any Soviet political commissar, who had been captured. In May 1942 the order was canceled after multiple complaints from officers, many of them pointing out that it made the enemy fight until last man standing instead of surrendering to German troops. In the Nuremberg Trials the Commissar Order was used as evidence for the barbaric nature of the German war campaign.

Comrade: This was a hard one for us. In the German military the term "Kamerad" is commonly used to address fellow soldiers, at the same time communists and social democrats call themselves "Genosse" in German. In English there only is this one word "comrade", and it often has a communistic touch. I guess an US-soldier would not call his fellow soldiers "comrade"? Since the word "Kamerad" is very, very common in the German military we decided to translate it with "comrade", but do not intend a communistic meaning in a German military context.

Danke: Thank you in German

Eastern Front Medal: Awarded to all axis soldiers who served in the winter campaign of 1941/1942.

Edi: Eduard Born's nickname

Eiserner Gustav: German nickname for Iljushin Il-2 "Shturmovik" (= iron Gustav). Gustav is a German male first name.

Elfriede: Nickname, Engelmann gave his Panzer IV. Elfriede was a common German female given name during that time.

Endsieg: Refers to the final victory over all enemies.

Éxgüsee: Swiss German for "sorry". By the way German dialects can be very peculiar. Bavarian, Austrian, Low German or other variations of German are hard to understand even for Germans, who are not from that particular region. Especially Swiss German is one not easy to understand variation of German, so often when a Swiss is interviewed on German TV subtitles are added. For interregional communication matters most Germans stick to High German, which is understood in all German-speaking areas.

Fat Pig: Refers to Hermann Göring, one of Nazi Germany's most influential party members. As the commander of the Luftwaffe he was responsible for a series of failures. He also was infamous for being drug-addicted and generally out of touch with reality. Moreover he coveted military decorations and therefore made sure that he was awarded with every medal available despite the fact that he did not do anything to earn it. Göring was the highest-ranking Nazi leader living long enough to testify in the Nuremberg Trials. He committed suicide to avoid being executed by the Allies.

Ferdinand: Massive German tank destroyer that later was improved and renamed to "Elefant" (= Elephant, while Ferdinand is a German given name – to be precise, it is Ferdinand Porsches given name, founder of Porsche and one of the design engineers of this steely monster). Today the Porsche AG is known for building sports cars. Like many other very progressive German weaponry developed during the war, the Ferdinand suffered from

Hitler personally intervening to alter design and production details. Hitler always thought to be cleverer than his engineers and experts. E.g. he forced the Aircraft constructor Messerschmitt to equip its jet-powered fighter aircraft Me 262 as a dive bomber, while it was constructed to be a fighter and while the Luftwaffe already had lost air superiority at all theaters of war (so you need fighters to regain air superiority before you can even think about bombers). Same story with the Ferdinand: Hitler desperately wanted the Ferdinand to take part in the battle of Kursk, so he demanded its mass production on the basis of prototypes that hadn't been tested at all. German soldiers had to catch up on those tests during live action! Despite its enormous fire power, the Ferdinand proofed to be full of mechanical flaws, which led to lots of total losses. Due to a lack of any secondary weapon and its nearly non-movable main gun the Ferdinand was a death trap for its crew in close combat. Another problem was the Ferdinand's weight of around 65 tons. A lot of bridges and streets were to weak or narrow to survive one of these monsters passing by, let alone a whole battalion if them.

Nevertheless the heavy tank destroyer proofed to be a proper defense weapon that could kill a T-34 frontally at a distance of more than two miles.

Its full name is Panzerjäger Tiger (P) "Ferdinand" (or "Elefant") Sd.Kfz. 184. Sd.Kfz stands for "Sonderkraftfahrzeug" meaning "special purpose vehicle".

Frau: Mrs.

Front: May refer to a Soviet military formation equal to an army group

Führer: Do I really have to lose any word about the most infamous German Austrian? (By the way, it is "Führer", not "Fuhrer". If you cannot find the "ü" on your keyboard, you can use "ue" as replacement).

Gestapo: Acronym for "Geheime Staatspolizei" (= Secret State Police), a police force that mainly pursued political enemies of the state.

Gröfaz: Mocking nickname for Adolf Hitler. It is an acronym for "greatest commander of all times" (= größter Feldherr aller Zeiten) and was involuntarily coined by Field Marshal Keitel. During the battle of France Keitel, who was known for being servile towards Hitler, hailed him by saying: "My Führer, you are the greatest commander of all times!" It quickly became a winged word among German soldiers – and finally the acronym was born.

Grüessech: Swiss salute

Heeresgruppe: Army group. The Wehrmacht wasn't very consistent in naming their army groups. Sometime letters were used, sometimes names of locations or cardinal directions. To continue the madness high command frequently renamed their army groups. In this book "Heeresgruppe Mitte" refers to the center of the Eastern Front (= Army Group Center), "Heeresgruppe

Süd" refers to the southern section (= Army Group South).

Heimat: A less patriotic, more dreamy word than Vaterland (= fatherland) to address one's home country.

Heinkel He 177 Greif: German long-range heavy bomber. "Greif" means griffin. The Germans soon coined the nickname "Fliegendes Reichsfeuerzeug" (= flying Reich lighter) due to the fact that the He 177's engines tended to catch fire while the bomber was in the air.

Henschel Hs 127: German ground-attack aircraft designed and produced mainly by Henschel. Due to its capabilities to destroy tanks German soldiers coined the nickname "can opener".

Herein: German word for "come in". Hey, by the end of this book you will be a real German expert!

Herr: Mister (German soldiers address sex AND rank, meaning they would say "Mister sergeant" instead of "sergeant")

Herr General: In the German military, it does not matter which of the general ranks a general inhabits, he is always addressed by "Herr General". It is the same in the US military I guess.

Hiwi: Abbreviation of the German word "Hilfswilliger", which literally means "someone who is willing to help". The term describes (mostly) Russian volunteers who served as auxiliary forces for the Third Reich. As many military terms from the two world wars also "Hiwi" has deeply embedded itself into the German language. A lot of Germans use this word today to describe unskilled workers without even knowing anything about its origin.

HQ platoon leader: In German "Kompanietruppführer" refers to a special NCO, who exists in every company. The HQ platoon leader is best described as being the company commander's right hand.

IIs, IIIs, IVs: In German you sometimes would say "Zweier" (= a twoer), when talking about a Panzer II for example. We tried our best to transfer this mannerism into English.

Iljushin Il-2 "Shturmovik": Very effective Russian dive bomber, high in numbers on the Eastern Front and a very dangerous tank hunter. There are reports of groups of Shturmoviks having destroyed numerous panzers within minutes. Stalin loved this very aircraft and personally supervised its production. The German nickname is "Eiserner Gustav" (= iron Gustav). Gustav is a German male given name.

Iron Cross: German war decoration restored by Hitler in 1939. It had been issued by Prussia during earlier military conflicts but in WW2 it was available to all German soldiers. There were three different tiers: Iron Cross (= Eisernes Kreuz) – 2nd class and 1st class –, Knight's Cross of the Iron Cross (= Ritterkreuz des Eisernen Kreuzes) – Knight's Cross without any features, Knight's Cross with Oak Leaves, Knight's Cross with Oak Leaves and Swords, Knight's Cross with Oak Leaves, Swords and Diamond and Knight's Cross with Golden Oak Leaves, Swords and Diamond –, and Grand Cross of the Iron Cross (= Großkreuz des Eisernen Kreuzes) – one without additional features and one called Star of the Grand Cross. By the way the German abbreviation for the Iron Cross 2nd class is EK2, alright?

Island monkeys: German slur for the British (= Inselaffen)

Ivan: As English people give us Germans nicknames like "Fritz", "Kraut" or "Jerry", we also come up with nicknames for most nationalities. Ivan (actually it is "Iwan" in German) was a commonly used nickname for Russians during both World Wars.

Jawohl: A submissive substitute for "yes" (= "ja"), which is widely used in the German military, but also in daily life

K98k: Also Mauser 98k or Gewehr 98k (Gewehr = rifle). The K98k was the German standard infantry weapon during World War 2. The second k stands for "kurz", meaning it is a shorter version of the original rifle that already had been used in World War 1. Since it is a short version, it is correctly called carbine instead of rifle – the first k stands for "Karabiner", which is the German word for carbine.

Kama: Refers to the Kama tank school, a secret training facility for German tank crews in the Soviet Union. After World War 1 the German Armed Forces (then called "Reichswehr") were restricted to 100 000 men because of the treaty of Versailles. Also no tanks and other heavy weaponry was permitted. The Germans sought for other ways to build up an own tank force, so they came to an agreement with the Soviet Union over secretly training German tankers at Kama. The German-Soviet cooperation ended with the rise of the Nazis to power in Germany.

Kampfgruppe: Combat formation that often was set up temporarily. Kampfgruppen had no defined size, some were of the size of a company, others were as big as a corps.

Kaputt: German word for "broken"; at one Point in the story Pappendorf uses this word describing a dead soldier. This means that he reduces the dead man to an object, since "kaputt" is only used for objects.

Katyusha: Soviet multiple rocket launcher. The Katyushas were feared by all German soldiers for its highly destructive salvos. Because of the piercing firing sound, the Germans coined the nickname "Stalin's organ" (= Stalinorgel).

Knight's Cross: See Iron Cross

Kolkhoz: Also collective farm; alleged cooperatively organized farming firm. Kolkhozes were one important component of the Soviet farming sector. In the eyes of the Soviet ideology they were a counter-concept to private family farms as well as to feudal serfdom. In reality kolkhozes were pools of slavery and inequality.

KV-2: Specs: Armor plating of up to 110 millimeters thickness, a 152-millimeters howitzer as main gun; ate Tiger tanks for breakfast … if its crew managed to move that heavy son of a bitch into a firing position in the first place.

Lager: Short for "Konzentrationslager" = concentration camp

Landser: German slang for a grunt

Luftwaffe: German Air Force

MG 34: German machine gun that was used by the infantry as well as by tankers as a secondary armament. And have you ever noticed that some stormtroopers in the original Star Wars movie from 1977 carry nearly unmodified MG 34s around?

MG 42: German machine gun that features an incredible rate of fire of up to 1 500 rounds per minute (that's 25 per second!). It is also called "Hitler's buzzsaw", because a fire burst literally could cut someone in two halves. Its successor, the MG 3, is still in use in nowadays German Armed Forces (Bundeswehr).

Millimeter/centimeter/meter/kilometer: Since Germans make use of the metric system you will find some of those measuring units within direct speeches. Within the text we mostly transferred distance information into yards, miles or feet.

Moin: Means: good morning. "Moin" or "Moin, Moin" are part of several dialects found in Northern Germany. Pay this region a visit and you will hear these greetings very often and actually at EVERY time of the day.

MP 40: German submachine gun, in service from 1938 to 1945

NCO corps: This was a hard one to translate, since we did not find any similar concept in any English armed force. The NCO corps (= Unteroffizierskorps) refers to the entity of German noncommissioned officers. It is nor organized not powerful by any means, but more of an abstract concept of thought.

Officer corps: Same thing as in NCO corps. The officer corps (= Offizierkorps) refers to the entity of German officers. It is nor organized not powerful by any means, but more of an abstract concept of thought.

Pak: German word for anti-tank gun (= abbreviation for "Panzerabwehrkanone")

Panther: Many experts consider the Panther to be the best German WW2 tank. Why, you may ask, when the

Wehrmacht also had steel beasts like the Tiger II or the Ferdinand at hand? Well, firepower is not everything. One also should consider mobility, production costs and how difficult it is to operate the tank as well as maintain and repair it on the battlefield. While the hugest German tanks like the Tiger II suffered from technical shortcomings, the Panther was a well-balanced mix of many important variables. Also it featured a sloped armor shape that could withstand direct hits very well. Since the Panther tank development was rushed and Hitler personally demanded some nonsensical changes the tank finally also suffered from some minor shortcomings, nevertheless it proofed to be an effective combat vehicle after all.

Panzer 38(t): Or Panzerkampfwagen 38(t) was a small Czechoslovak tank adopted by the Wehrmacht after it occupied Czechoslovakia. The 38(t) was no match for Russian medium tanks like the T-34 and was only adopted, because the German Armed Forces desperately needed anything with an engine in order to increase the degree of motorization of their troops.

Whenever you find a letter in brackets within the name of a German tank, it is a hint at its foreign origin. For example, French tanks were given an (f), Czechoslovak tanks an (t). Since the 38(t) was riveted instead of welded, each hit endangered the crew, even if the round did not penetrate the armor. Often the rivets sprung out because of the energy set free by the hit. They then became lethal projectiles to the tankers.

Panzer II: Although being a small and by the end of the 1930s outdated tank, the Panzer II was the backbone of the German Army during the first years of the war due to a lack of heavier tanks in sufficient numbers. With its two-Centimeter canon it only could knock at Russian tanks like the T-34, but never penetrate their armor. The full name is Panzerkampfwagen II (= tank combat vehicle II).

Panzer III: Medium German tank. Actually the correct name is Panzerkampfwagen III (= tank combat vehicle III). Production was stopped in 1943 due to the fact that the Panzer III then was totally outdated. Even in 1941, when the invasion of Russia started, this panzer wasn't a real match for most medium Soviet tanks anymore.

Panzer IV: Very common German medium tank. Actually the correct name is Panzerkampfwagen IV (= tank combat vehicle IV). I know, I know … in video games and movies it is all about the Tiger tank, but in reality an Allied or Russian soldier rather saw a Panzer IV than a Tiger. Just compare the numbers: Germany produced around 8 500 Panzer IVs of all variants, but only 1350 Tiger tanks.

Panzergrenadier: Motorized/mechanized infantry (don't mess with these guys!)

Papa: Daddy

Penalty area: Soccer term for that rectangular area directly in front of each soccer goal. When a rival striker enters your team's penalty area, he or she impends to score a goal against you. By the way, soccer is an enhanced, more civilized version of that weird game called "American Football" – just in case you wondered ;)

Plan Wahlen: A plan that was developed by Swiss Federal Council Wahlen in order to ensure food supplies for the Swiss population in case of an embargo or even an attack of the Axis powers. Since Hitler had started to occupy all neighboring nations he considered to be German anyway, a German attack on Switzerland felt very real for the Swiss. Because of the war they suffered supply shortages and mobilized their army. They even suffered casualties from dogfights with misled German and Allied bombers, because Swiss fighter planes attacked each and every military aircraft that entered their airspace (later they often "overlooked" airspace violations by allied planes though). Switzerland also captured and imprisoned a good number of German and Allied pilots, who crash-landed on their soil.

Since the war raging in most parts of Europe influenced the Swiss, too, they finally came up with the Plan Wahlen in 1940 in order to increase Swiss sustenance. Therefore every piece of land was used as farmland, e.g. crops were cultivated on football fields and in public parks.

I think, the situation of Switzerland during the war is a very interesting and yet quiet unknown aspect of the war. I therefore used the Taylor episode to explore it.

Order of Michael the Brave: Highest Rumanian military decoration that was rewarded to some German soldiers, since Rumania was one of Germany's allies until August 1944.

Reichsbahn: German national railway (Deutsche Reichsbahn)

Reichsheini: Mocking nickname for Heinrich Himmler (refers to his function as "Reichsführer SS" (= Reich Leader SS) in combination with an alteration of his first name. At the same time "Heini" is a German offensive term used for stupid people.

Reichskanzler: Chancellor of the German Reich

SA: Short form for "Sturmabteilung" (literally: storm detachment); it had been the Nazi Party's original paramilitary organization until it was disempowered by the SS in 1934.

Scheisse: German for "Crap". Actually it is spelled "Scheiße" with an "ß", but since this letter is unknown in the English language and since it is pronounced very much like "ss", we altered it this way so that you do not mistake it for a "b".
Same thing holds true for the characters Claasen and Weiss. In the original German text both are written with an "ß".

Scho-Ka-Kola: Bitter-sweet chocolate with a lot of caffeine in it

Sepp: Short form of Josef, nickname for Engelmann

Sherman Tank (M4): Medium US-tank that was produced in very large numbers (nearly 50 000 were built between 1942 and 1945) and was used by most allied forces. Through the Lend-Lease program the tank also saw action on the Eastern Front. Its big advantage over all German panzers was its main gun stabilizer, which allowed for precise shooting while driving. German tankers were not allowed to shoot while driving due to Wehrmacht regulations. Because of the missing stabilizers it would have been a waste of ammunition anyway. The name of this US-tank refers to American Civil War general William Tecumseh Sherman.
Let's compare the dimensions: The Third Reich's overall tank production added up to around 50 000 between the pre-war phase and 1945 (all models and their variants like the 38 (t) Hetzer together, so: Panzer Is, IIs, IIIs, IVs, Panthers, Tigers, 38(t)s, Tiger IIs and Ferdinands/Elefants combined)!

Sir: Obviously Germans do not say "Sir", but that was the closest thing we could do to substitute a polite form that exists in the German language. There is no match for that in the English language: In German parts of a sentence changes when using the polite form. If one asks for a light in German, one would say "Hast du Feuer?" to a friend, but "Haben Sie Feuer?" to a stranger or any person one have not agreed with to leave away the polite form yet. During the Second World War the German polite form was commonly spread, in very conservative families children had to use the polite form to address their parents and even some couples used it among themselves. Today the polite form slowly is vanishing. Some companies like Ikea even addresses customers informally in the first place – something that was an absolute no-go 50 years ago.

In this one scene where the Colonel argues with First Lieutenant Haus he gets upset, because Haus does not say "Sir" (once more: difficult to translate). In the Wehrmacht a superior was addressed with "Herr" plus his rank, in the Waffen SS the "Herr" was left out; a soldier was addressed only by his rank like it is common in armed forces of English-speaking countries. So the colonel is upset about Haus carrying on with his old Waffen SS habits by leaving out the "Herr".

Another scene that makes use of the German polite form is the one between Berning and Bongartz, when the private tells the sergeant his first name. Doing this in German means offering to drop the polite form. Normally the older or higher ranked person offers this to the younger one or subordinate (in the military as well as in civil life, e.g. in firms), not the other way round, which makes Bongartz attempt unusual.

SS: Abbreviation of "Schutzstaffel" (= Protection Squadron). The SS was a paramilitary Nazi-organization, led by Heinrich Himmler. Since the SS operated the death camps, had the Gestapo under their roof as well as had their own military force (Waffen SS) that competed with the Wehrmacht it is not easy to outline their primary task during the era of the Third Reich. Maybe the SS is best described as some sort of general Nazi instrument of terror against all inner and outer enemies.

Stavka: High command of the Red Army

Struwwelpeter: Infamous German bedtime kid's book that features ten very violent stories of people, who suffer under the disastrous consequences of their misbehavior. Need an Example? One story features a boy, who sucks his thumbs until a tailor appears cutting the boy's thumbs off with a huge scissor. The book definitely promises fun for the whole family!
(Nowadays it is not read out to kids anymore, but even I, who grew up in the 90s, had to listen to that crap). In the U.S.A. the book is also known under the title "Slovenly Peter".

Stahlhelm: German helmet with its distinctive coal scuttle shape, as Wikipedia puts it. The literal translation would be steel helmet.

Stuka: An acronym for a dive bomber in general (= "Sturzkampfbomber"), but often refers to that one German dive bomber you may know: the Junkers Ju 87.

Sturm: Among other things Sturm is an Austrian vocabulary for a Federweisser, which is a wine-like beverage made from grape must.

Tank destroyer: Tanks specifically designed to combat enemy tanks. Often tank destroyers rely on massive firepower and capable armor (the latter is achieved by a non-rotatable turret that allows for thicker frontal armor).

T-34: Medium Russian tank that really frightened German tankers when it first showed up in 1941. First the T-34 was superior to all existing German tanks (with the exception of Panzer IV variant F that was equipped with a longer canon and thicker armor). The T-34 was also available in huge numbers really quick. During the war the Soviet Union produced more than 35 000 T-34 plus more than 29 000 of the enhanced T-34/85 model! Remember the Sherman tank? So the production of only these two tanks outnumbered the overall German combat tank production by a factor of more than two!

T-70: Light Soviet tank that weighted less than 10 tons. Although it was a small tank that featured a 45-millimeters main gun, one should not underestimate the T-70. There are reports of them destroying Panthers and other medium or heavy German panzers.

Tiger tank: Heavy German combat tank, also known as Tiger I that featured a variant of the accurate and high-powered 88-millimeters anti-aircraft canon "Acht-Acht". The correct name is Panzerkampfwagen VI Tiger (= tank combat vehicle VI Tiger).

Tin can: During World War 2 some German soldiers called tanks tin can (= Büchse), so we thought it would be nice to keep that expression in the translation as well.

SU-122: Soviet assault gun that carried a 122-millimeters main gun, which was capable of destroying even heavy German tanks from a fair distance.

Vaterland: Fatherland

Waffen SS: Waffen = arms; it was the armed wing of the Nazi Party's SS organization, which was a paramilitary organization itself.

Waidmannsheil: German hunters use this call to wish good luck ("Waidmann" is an antique German word for hunter, "Heil" means well-being). As many hunting terms, Waidmannsheil made its way into German military language.

Wound badge: German decoration for wounded soldiers or those, who suffered frostbites. The wound badge was awarded in three stages: black for being wounded once or twice, silver for the third and fourth wound, gold thereafter. US equivalent: Purple Heart.

Zampolit: Political commissar; an officer responsible for political indoctrination in the Red Army

Wehrmacht ranks

Rank	US equivalent
Anwärter	Candidate (NCO or officer)
Soldat (or Schütze, Kanonier, Pionier, Funker, Reiter, Jäger, Grenadier ... depends on the branch of service)	Private
Obersoldat (Oberschütze, Oberkanonier ...)	Private First Class
Gefreiter	Lance Corporal
Obergefreiter	Senior Lance Corporal
Stabsgefreiter	Corporal
Unteroffizier	Sergeant
Fahnenjunker	Ensign
Unterfeldwebel/Unterwacht-meister (Wachtmeister only in cavalry and artillery)	Staff Sergeant
Feldwebel/Wachtmeister	Staff Sergeant
Oberfeldwebel/Oberwacht-meister	Master Sergeant
Oberfähnrich	Ensign First Class
Stabsfeldwebel/Stabswacht-meister	Sergeant Major
Hauptfeldwebel	This is not a rank, but an NCO function responsible for personnel and order within a company
Leutnant	2nd Lieutenant
Oberleutnant	1st Lieutenant
Hauptmann/Rittmeister	Captain

(Rittmeister only in cavalry and artillery)	
Major	Major
Oberstleutnant	Lieutenant Colonel
Oberst	Colonel
Generalmajor	Major General
Generalleutnant	Lieutenant General
General der … (depends on the branch of service: - Infanterie (Infantry) - Kavallerie (Cavalry) - Artillerie (Artillery) - Panzertruppe (Tank troops) - Pioniere (Engineers) - Gebirgstruppe (Mountain Troops) - Nachrichtentruppe (Signal Troops)	General (four-star)
Generaloberst	Colonel General
Generalfeldmarschall	Field Marshal

Overview of military units in the Wehrmacht
(size in brackets; data refers to the Army)

Fire team: Smallest military unit in the Wehrmacht
Squad: (Or section for our British readers) – consists of ten to twenty soldiers
Platoon: Three to five squads
Company: Varies greatly; usually three platoons plus support and HQ elements
Abteilung: Some Wehrmacht battalions were called Abteilung because of traditional matters, e.g. some panzer battalions due to there roots in the cavalry

Battalion: HQ plus two to five companies plus support elements
Regiment: Two to four battalions
Brigade: Varies greatly; a total of up to 5 000 soldiers
Division: Varies greatly; 5 000 to 30 000 soldiers
Corps: Two to five divisions
Army: Three to six corpses
Army Group: Consists of more than one army

Characters

Rank, unit and position concur with the situation **while the character makes his or her first appearance in the novel**. The sequence is: Name, surname, rank in its original language, function.

Bauer, Heinz Gerd, Obergrenadier, machine gunner of Squad Pappendorf

Baum, Herbert*, Jewish member of the German resistance against the Nazis; was tortured to death in 1942

Beck, Ludwig*, Generaloberst a.D., former chief o general staff of the German Armed Forces

Becker, Carl*, Generalmajor, commander of the 253rd Infantry Division

Berning, Franz, Unteroffizier, squad leader of 3rd Squad / 2nd Platoon / 1st Reconnaissance Squadron / Schnelle Abteilung 253 / 253rd Infantry Division / XXIII Army Corps / 9th Army / Army Group Center / Commander-in-Chief East

Bongartz, Rudi, Gefreiter, machine gunner of Squad Berning

Born, Eduard, Stabsgefreiter, loader of Engelmann's tank

Canaris, Wilhelm*, Admiral, chief of Military Intelligence Service "Abwehr"

Churchill, Winston*, Prime Minister of Great Britain

Claassen, Mauritius, Oberfeldwebel, platoon leader of 2nd Platoon / 1st Reconnaissance Squadron / Schnelle Abteilung 253 / 253rd Infantry Division / XXIII Army Corps / 9th Army / Army Group South / Commander-in-Chief East

Engelmann, Else, Lieutenant Josef Engelmann's wife

Engelmann, Gudrun, daughter of Josef and Else Engelmann

Engelmann, Josef "Sepp", Leutnant, platoon leader 1st Platoon / 9th Company / III Abteilung / Panzer Regiment 2 / 16th Panzer Division / XI Army Korps / 6th Army / Army Group South / Commander-in-Chief East

Feitenhansel, Udo, Obergrenadier, soldier of Squad Berning

Fellgiebel, Fritz*, Chief Signal Officer of High Command, therefore chief of Wehrmacht communication lines at the Führer's headquarters

Fromm, Friedrich*, Generaloberst, Commander of the Replacement Army

Göring, Herrman*, Generalfeldmarschall, mainly: commander-in chief of the Luftwaffe under Hitler

Haus, Theodor, Oberleutnant, company commander of the "black company" / Schnelle Abteilung 253 / 253rd Infantry Division / XXIII Army Corps / 9th Army / Army Group South / Commander-in-Chief East

Himmler, Heinrich*, Reichsführer SS and leading Nazi party member under Hitler

Hitler, Adolf*, "Führer" and Reichskanzler (Chancellor) of the German Reich

Hoth, Hermann*, Generalfeldmarschall, chief of staff of the Commander-in-Chief East

Junghans, Gretel, Franz Berning's girlfriend

Kelekian, Sesede, girl from Arthur Petrosjan's hometown

Klodt, Bernhard*, soccer player with Schalke 04

Kolter, Steffen, Obergefreiter, soldier of company Haus

Konev, Ivan Stepanowitsch*, General Polkovnik (Colonel General), commander-in-chief of the Steppe Front

Kreisel, Helmut*, Stabsfeldwebel, NCO of II Abteilung / Panzer Regiment 2 / 16th Panzer Division / XI Army Korps / 6th Army / Army Group South / Commander-in-Chief East

Laschke, Henning, Unteroffizier, tank commander in Engelmann's platoon

Ludwig, Theo, Obergefreiter, gunner in Engelmann's tank

Marseille, Fritz, Oberfeldwebel, tank commander in Engelmann's platoon

Meinert, Fridolin, Unterfeldwebel, gunner of Müller's tank

Meyer, Norbert, Oberfeldwebel, tank commander in Engelmann's platoon

Milch, Erhard*, Generalfeldmarschall, Chief of Aircraft Procurement and Suppy

Müller, Gottfried, Oberfeldwebel, tank commander in Engelmann's platoon

Münster, Hans, Unterfeldwebel, driver in Engelmann's tank

Nitz, Eberhardt, Feldwebel, radio operator in Engelmann's tank

Pappendorf, Adolf, Unterfeldwebel, squad leader of 2nd Squad / 2nd Platoon / 1st Reconnaissance Squadron / Schnelle Abteilung 253 / 253rd Infantry Division / XXIII Army Corps / 9th Army / Army Group Center / Commander-in-Chief East

Paulus, Friedrich*, General der Panzertruppe, commander-in-chief of Army Group South

Petrosjan, Arthur, Rjadovoi (soldier), Armenian soldier of the Red Army, 2nd Squad / 1st Platoon / 2nd Company / 1st Rifle Battalion / 1072nd Rifle Regiment / 102nd Rifle Division / 67th Rifle Corps / 70th Army / Central Front

Raumann, Jürgen, Feldwebel, platoon leader of 1st Platoon of company Haus

Rommel, Erwin*, Generalfeldmarschall, commander-in-chief of the Africa Korps

Roth, Luise, employee of the British Consulate in Bern

Roth, Stella, Luise's younger sister

Rößler, Rudolf*, publisher of Vita Nova publishing house

Rupp, Karl, Grenadier, soldier of Squad Schredinsky

Schredinsky, Marek, Unterfeldwebel, squad leader of 1st Squad / 2nd Platoon / 1st Reconnaissance Squadron / Schnelle Abteilung 253 / 253rd Infantry Division / XXIII Army Corps / 9th Army / Army Group Center / Commander-in-Chief East

Schröder, Günther, Obergrenadier, soldier of Squad Berning

Sieckenius, Rudolf*, Oberst, commander of Panzer Regiment 2 / 16th Panzer Division / XI Army Korps / 6th Army / Army Group South / Commander-in-Chief East

Sidorenko, Nikolay, General Polkovnik (Colonel General), commander of the 5th Guard Tank Army, Steppe Front

Stalin, Josef*, Soviet Chief of State and Party Leader, *Generalissimus* of the Red Army

Taylor, Thomas, Unteroffizier, soldier of Sonderverband Brandenburg

von Angern, Günther*, Generalmajor, commander of the 16th Panzer Division / XI Army Korps / 6th Army / Army Group South / Commander-in-Chief East

von Blomberg, Werner*, Generalfeldmarschall, former Reich Ministry of Defense

von Bock, Fedor*, Generalfeldmarschall, Leader's Reserve (that was a pool for all high-ranking officers, who got in conflict with Hitler – they were put in a backwater there)

von Brauchitsch, Walther*, Generalfeldmarschall, Leader's Reserve

von Kluge, Günther*, Generalfeldmarschall, commander-in-chief of Heeresgruppe Mitte

von Lahousen, Erwin*, Oberst i.G., commander of II Department of the Division Ausland (= foreign countries) / Abwehr

von Leeb, Wilhelm*, Generalfeldmarschall, Leader's Reserve

von Manstein, Erich*, Generalfeldmarschall, Commander-in-Chief East

von Witzleben, Erwin*, Generalfeldmarschall, Leader's Reserve

Werner, Rolf, Obergrenadier, radio operator of Squad Pappendorf

Weiß, Otto, Obergefreiter, soldier of Squad Schredinsky

*historical person

Map of the salient of Kursk
The dashed line indicates the front line as of May 3rd 1943

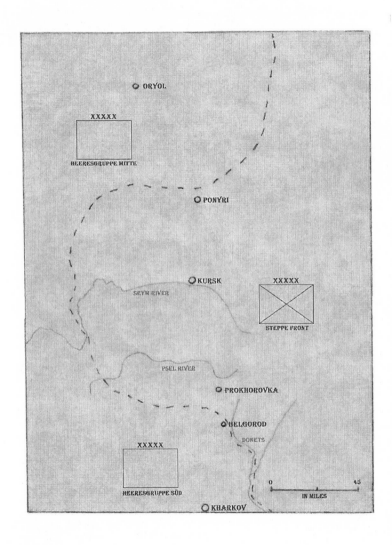

Stay tuned ... the PANZERS series will continue in 2019!

11906698R00197

Made in the USA
San Bernardino, CA
08 December 2018